THE SKELETON IN
THE ROSE BED

Also by Alys Clare from Severn House

The World's End Bureau Victorian Mysteries

THE WOMAN WHO SPOKE TO SPIRITS
THE OUTCAST GIRLS
THE MAN IN THE SHADOWS
THE STRANGER IN THE ASYLUM

The Gabriel Taverner Mysteries

A RUSTLE OF SILK
THE ANGEL IN THE GLASS
THE INDIGO GHOSTS
MAGIC IN THE WEAVE
THE CARGO FROM NEIRA
THE CHRYSANTHEMUM TIGER

The Aelf Fen Series

OUT OF THE DAWN LIGHT
MIST OVER THE WATER
MUSIC OF THE DISTANT STARS
THE WAY BETWEEN THE WORLDS
LAND OF THE SILVER DRAGON
BLOOD OF THE SOUTH
THE NIGHT WANDERER
THE RUFUS SPY
CITY OF PEARL
THE LAMMAS WILD

The Hawkenlye Series

THE PATHS OF THE AIR
THE JOYS OF MY LIFE
THE ROSE OF THE WORLD
THE SONG OF THE NIGHTINGALE
THE WINTER KING
A SHADOWED EVIL
THE DEVIL'S CUP

THE SKELETON IN THE ROSE BED

Alys Clare

SEVERN
HOUSE

First world edition published in Great Britain and the USA in 2025
by Severn House, an imprint of Canongate Books Ltd,
14 High Street, Edinburgh EH1 1TE.

severnhouse.com

Copyright © Alys Clare, 2025

Cover and jacket design by Nick May at bluegecko22.com

All rights reserved including the right of reproduction in whole or in part in any form. The right of Alys Clare to be identified as the author of this work has been asserted in accordance with the Copyright, Designs & Patents Act 1988.

British Library Cataloguing-in-Publication Data
A CIP catalogue record for this title is available from the British Library.

ISBN-13: 978-1-4483-1302-0 (cased)
ISBN-13: 978-1-4483-1303-7 (e-book)

This is a work of fiction. Names, characters, places and incidents are either the product of the author's imagination or are used fictitiously. Except where actual historical events and characters are being described for the storyline of this novel, all situations in this publication are fictitious and any resemblance to actual persons, living or dead, business establishments, events or locales is purely coincidental.

No part of this book may be used or reproduced in any manner for the purpose of training artificial intelligence technologies or systems. This work is reserved from text and data mining (Article 4(3) Directive (EU) 2019/790).

All Severn House titles are printed on acid-free paper.

Typeset by Palimpsest Book Production Ltd., Falkirk,
Stirlingshire, Scotland.
Printed and bound in Great Britain by TJ Books,
Padstow, Cornwall.

The manufacturer's authorised representative in the EU for product safety is Authorised Rep Compliance Ltd, 71 Lower Baggot Street, Dublin D02 P593 Ireland (arccompliance.com)

Praise for the World's End Bureau Victorian Mysteries

"A page-turning mystery with a well-hidden motive and a surprising number of twists"
Kirkus Reviews

"An engaging plot and two richly developed leads. Fine reading for fans of English historical mysteries"
Booklist

"Anne Perry fans will want to check this out"
Publishers Weekly

"Mystery and social commentary combine in a heartbreaking and sadly relevant tale"
Kirkus Reviews

"Impressive . . . the solid plotting, colorful Victorian settings, and fun detective duo bode well for future instalments"
Publishers Weekly

"Engaging, dark, atmospheric, and, at times, quite charming and humorous . . . A fine choice for all mystery collections"
Booklist

About the author

Alys Clare lives in the English countryside where her novels are set. She went to school in Tonbridge and later studied archaeology at the University of Kent. She is the author of the Aelf Fen, Hawkenlye, World's End Bureau and Gabriel Taverner historical mystery series.

*For my family,
with all my love.*

PROLOGUE

Autumn 1882

In the pre-dawn darkness of Tower Hill, a man sits leaning against an old wooden barrow. The gentle rise affords a good vantage point over the river. The Thames is almost still, its great surging power gathering itself, and he is waiting for slack water to give way to the ebb tide. He doesn't mind waiting. His body is resting, regaining strength after the night's violence. His mind, however, is as active as ever.

You might think, he muses, that the city was deserted. Around him the houses are shuttered fast against the night, with not a light showing. No footstep rings out; no dark, furtive figures flit between the shadows. London is never entirely asleep and now is as close as it gets. Not that it would bother him if there were others abroad besides himself, for he has learned to be invisible. Or, if not quite that, to blend so seamlessly into the background that nobody notices him, which is as close to invisible as a man can be.

There is something eerie about those who give the illusion of moving unobserved. It can turn them into figures out of old tales and myths. It can make them awesome. Magical.

He gazes down at the massive bulk of the Tower, rising up square over to his left and shining white in the moonlight. Above the north-west corner of its forbidding walls is the site of the scaffold, where hundreds lost their lives in the brutal and perpetual violence of the past.

Not, of course, that the past has a monopoly on violence.

He is still accustoming himself to urban life, for of late his has been a rural, nomadic existence, and at times the longing for London was intense. He has spent some time on the canals – the navigations, as the boatmen call them. He is familiar with the Grand Junction, the Kennet and Avon, the Regent's Canal and the Kensington, with Chelsea Creek at its southern end. He spent nearly two years among the misty and mysterious waterways of East Anglia, whose legend-rich past called to him strongly. Of late, although he has moved around, he has made sure always to be very close to the Thames.

The Thames obsesses him.

He wonders – when his mind is sufficiently calm to allow rational thought – if this is because of the river's ancient and enduring association with death. Accidental death, death by suicide, death at the hands of another. Death by the state – hangings, beheadings and the brutal, ever more drawn-out and elaborate methods of killing in the terrible dungeons under the Tower. His mind leaps to a legend of Queen Elizabeth: incandescent with rage on a level that might well have outdone even her father, she had demanded of the executioners working on those who had betrayed her that they come up with something more brutal and agonising than hanging, drawing and quartering. Not far downstream was the site of Execution Dock, where pirates were hanged and their tarred, cage-confined corpses left for the passage of three tides. As well as these judicial acts of murder, there has always been death by mischance; from the outpourings of filth and human detritus that pollute the majestic waters and kill almost as fast as drowning. Nearly seven hundred dead in the *Princess Alice* disaster alone, four years ago, and many of those who perished that September evening never identified. Given the state they were in – coated in the raw sewage into which they fell, and the corpses so foul and stinking that men accustomed to nauseating stenches turned away, ghost-white and faint – who would have had the stomach to look closely?

That cache of unknown, unclaimed corpses has served the man well in the past; how easy it is to disappear, if you can state with sufficient conviction that a person bearing your name is definitely dead.

Not that it had been his real name.

He smiles in the darkness.

It is so easy to discard a name and adopt a new one. People take you on trust, by and large, or so he has found. You tell a man you're called George Henderson, or Lawrence Styles – casually, in answer to a question – and you can bet a florin he'll believe you. Why not?

Names, so many names.

He has lost count of the names he has used since leaving behind the one he was born with.

He lives for history. He smiles at the mild irony of that: his own life pushing relentlessly into the future while his mind is wrapped in the past. Returning to London and its magnificent river – king of rivers – has been a homecoming, of sorts, and the heady days of reacquainting himself with the habits of the city and the water has promoted a fresh and dedicated delve into his studies. He is an autodidact. Thrown out of his last school too soon, he has been making up the deficit in his education ever since.

He pauses his soaring thoughts, his attention caught. He sits quite still, breathing deeply and calmly. There is a change in the air: the tide has turned. He makes a very slight movement, then stops.

Not yet, he thinks. Wait a little.

All is silent and still.

It is a good spot, this secluded hideaway he has found to the west of Tower Hill. It has the feel of a forgotten place. The surrounding area has been altered, developed and re-developed over the decades and the centuries, but, as is sometimes the way in a great city, small pockets have kept their heads down and been overlooked. A narrow, secluded court leads off a cobbled lane, bordered to the south by an ancient church, to the east and north by busy streets. Life in its preoccupied busyness goes on all around, but the old court lies quiet and serene. The houses have been enlarged and much altered over the years, but their ancient essence is unchanged. There are long, narrow gardens, running wild now; the rampant spread of once tended and tamed plants is stealthily being overcome by uninvited intruders: buddleia, rosebay willowherb, ragwort, birch and, most vigorous of all, brambles. A forgotten and overgrown little passage runs along the southern end of the gardens. On the other side of the high stone wall lies All Hallows graveyard.

Abandoned gardens may serve as graveyards too . . .

The air is full of iron and he breathes in slowly and deeply. His body relaxes. He leans back against the side of the barrow, moving minutely until he finds his familiar, comfortable position.

The barrow is ancient, made of thick planks of wood worn silvery and smooth with time, and the simple structure would not have challenged the ingenuity of whoever made it. The flat bed is capacious and slopes gently down towards the front, where a series of neat holes have been drilled to allow the egress of liquids.

The barrow has been his companion for some time. He tends it carefully, returning it to its hiding place when it is not in use. People are accustomed to seeing him pushing it. Since nobody knows his name, they refer to him, on the infrequent occasions that they need to, as the Barrow Man.

The barrow has been in use this night. He has cleaned it, but still he can detect the smell of blood. Or perhaps – given how much blood there was and how much he likes it – he is merely imagining he can smell it. He smiles again.

He returns to his silent meditation. But not for long; he is becoming restless. He sits up. He sniffs at the air again. He stares intently down at the river.

Slowly, gracefully, he gets to his feet. He rubs his hands together, braces himself – the barrow is weighty even when, as now, it is empty – and grasps the handles. Then, with a last affectionate look at his hiding place – it is a *good* place – he heads off towards the water.

ONE

Lily is at work in her Inner Sanctum. It is early autumn, and the year is 1882. Mrs Clapper has just put her mid-morning cup of tea on her desk, and Lily pauses to thank her – very briefly, for she is absorbed in finishing a report on a recent case. Mrs Clapper takes the hint and does not linger. Of late Lily has been perpetually busy, as has Felix. After they returned to London at the conclusion of the French affair in the spring, the World's End Bureau was suddenly deluged with cases. Quite a lot of these arrived at the Bureau from an anonymous source. Lily and Felix are uncomfortably aware that they bowed to pressure at the conclusion of the French business.[1] It sits ill on Lily's conscience, but as the pragmatic Felix observed, what choice does anyone have when a secretive government department is utterly determined that they should keep their mouths shut?

These mysterious commissions involved long spells of steady discreet observation. Lily became heartily sick of sitting in cafés and on station forecourts pretending to be concentrating on her newspaper while covertly she watched and noted what Subject X or Suspect Y was doing, and whether they muttered a few words to Unknown Z. Felix did his share of these jobs; disliking them as much as Lily did, they shared the assignments scrupulously. They were never told why these people had to be watched, or what they were suspected of doing. Lily and Felix have been dutifully handing in their well-written, conscientious reports, always precisely on time, but there has never been any response. Frustratingly, they have no idea now whether their diligent watchfulness and the careful reporting of it were of any value at all to their invisible, silent masters.

The remuneration, however, has been very generous. As Felix observed, 'We're entitled to wring as much out of them as we can, given how boring it is.'

1 See *The Stranger in the Asylum*

If it is some well-buried government department that has been employing them on this work – and they are all but certain it must be – the government has deep pockets and can afford to pay. They nudged up their customary fees by quite a generous percentage, and nobody has yet complained. They refer to the extra earnings as the Tedium Bonus.

Lily finishes what she hopes will be her final report; the number of cases has fallen off recently. She draws a neat line under the last sentence and blots the page. She taps the pages together and fastens them with a clip, then puts them in the bottom drawer of her desk and turns the key, putting it back in the little pocket in her waistcoat. Another annoying thing about the anonymous employer is the constant, oft-repeated insistence on utter secrecy. 'As if we don't keep *all* our clients' secrets!' she had muttered angrily to Felix when yet another reminder of the need for 'extra security measures' had arrived. Felix had agreed and suggested putting on another extra percentage, this one to be the Annoyance Bonus.

She sits up straight, rotating her shoulders. Felix should be back soon. She glances at her watch. It is a small gold half hunter that belonged to her Aunt Eliza and was left to Lily in Eliza's will. It is a masculine sort of watch, and originally Lily wore it on a chain around her neck. Recently, however, she has taken to keeping it in her other waistcoat pocket, attached to an Albert chain secured to a button. Instead of a fob, she has a small gold Indian elephant on the other end of the chain.

In a moment of stillness, Aunt Eliza emerges from memory and strides into Lily's mind. Lily's father, Andrew Raynor, died when she was twelve. She loved him very much, and it was thus all the harder for her when her mother remarried within six months of Andrew's death and bore her second husband's child five months later. Lily did not disguise her contempt for her mother, and it suited both of them when Lily went to live with her paternal grandparents – who ran an apothecary – and their daughter Eliza. Grandparents and aunt made her welcome from the moment she crept over the doorstep, and she grew to honour, respect and love them. She lost all three within four years. If there could be any consolation for the loss, it came in the form of the house in which she now lives and works.

She has closed her eyes, and now she sees her grandparents as well. Both of them turn to look lovingly at her, and her grandmother's softly full face creases in a smile.

'What would you think, Grandmama?' Lily whispers. 'An enquiry agency, run from the old family home.' In her mind, her grandmother makes a wry comment, and Lily smiles. 'Don't worry. Mrs Clapper is reconciled to the Bureau,' she says.

Mrs Clapper had worked for Lily's grandparents for as long as Lily can remember. There had been no option but to inherit her along with the house; both parties were, and remain, quite happy with the arrangement.

With reluctance, Lily pulls herself out of the past and tucks her watch back in its pocket.

She has half an hour or so before Felix is due back. She is reluctant to start on the next task; her shoulders are still sore. She leans back and listens to the sounds of the house. Apart from a faint clatter and splash from the scullery – Mrs Clapper's domain – all is quiet. The old house exudes elegance and serenity.

This sense of calm is new: there has been a change of inhabitants at Number 3, Hob's Court. Lily thanks the good Lord every day for removing the Little Ballerina from the suite on the middle floor and whirling her off to wherever she is now. Lily neither knows nor cares where her former tenant has gone, as long as she never comes back.

The new tenants are in their mid-forties. They are scholarly spinsters and professional women: one teaches in a girls' school off Eccleston Square, near Victoria station; the other is a librarian at the grandly named Pavie Archaeological Research Institute, off the Brompton Road. It was Felix's landlord and friend, the journalist Marmaduke Smithers, who had introduced the ladies to Lily; one of the women is his cousin.

Giving the impression that he was choosing his words with care – not an impression he usually gives – Marm had explained that the rooms on the middle floor of 3, Hob's Court would suit the women perfectly. At present, he said, they were living at their club, where all the rooms were small singles, each with a narrow bed, a little wardrobe, a desk and a chair.

It had taken Lily a few moments to understand what Marm was *not* saying. Diplomatically she told him that the sofas, tables, chairs and the large bed in the two-room accommodation on offer in her house could be arranged as the women pleased, and that the middle landing would be theirs alone.

Just before Lily met them, Marm told her the women had studied at Cambridge and Oxford respectively, although naturally, since they were women and not men, had not been allowed to take degrees. The fact of their being at such alarmingly intellectual establishments at all had been sufficient to overawe Lily. Marm had arranged for the two women to make a preliminary visit to view the accommodation one evening after they had finished work. Mrs Clapper had gone home, and Lily, wishing she had asked her housekeeper to stay, awaited their arrival with some anxiety.

She opened the door in answer to the discreet knock and saw two figures who at first glance looked very similar: both dressed in plain, well-cut costumes of good cloth, one in navy, one in clerical grey; both wearing modest felt hats, one on top of tidily arranged hair of a nondescript brown arranged in a neat bun, the other pulled down hard over grey hair cut in a rather savage chin-length bob. Both faces wore the same tentative expression. Even as Lily ushered them into the outer office and settled them, she was sensing an air of doubt and nervous expectation: the thought flew into her head that both these women *really* wanted this encounter to go well . . .

'Bernice Adderley,' one of the women said as Lily sat down opposite them. She held out a hand, shaking Lily's in a forthright way.

'How do you do,' Lily responded. Miss Adderley had small dark eyes that were presently studying Lily very closely, and this scrutiny, accompanied as it was by a severe – if not stern – look, was at first disturbing. But then Miss Adderley smiled. The brown irises almost disappeared as the eyes crinkled around them, and Lily noticed that all the lines on Miss Adderley's rather plain face seemed to go upwards.

'Dorothea Sutherland,' the other one said, and Lily's hand was grasped in a second handshake.

'How nice to meet you,' Lily responded. Miss Sutherland had a weatherbeaten sort of face and a wide mouth. She wore small gold-framed spectacles on her large, straight nose, and – unless it was an effect of the lenses – had very large, pale grey eyes. She too was closely scrutinising Lily; unlike her companion, she did not smile.

Nobody seemed to know what to say next. Perceiving that the women were waiting for her to speak, Lily leapt up and said, much too brightly, 'I expect you would like to see the rooms!'

One of the women muttered something terse that sounded like *why else have we come*, but Lily was leading the way through the hall to the stairs and could not be sure.

She reached the first-floor landing and hurried to open the three doors leading off it. 'Please, take your time,' she said. 'I will wait downstairs.'

Back in the outer office, she castigated herself for her unprofessional manner; what must the two women think of her? Too anxious to sit down, she paced up and down, listening to the footsteps above, trying to make out the quietly muttered words. 'I hope they like the rooms,' she muttered. 'I want them to move in!' And then, straight away: 'Do I? Do I really want two strait-laced, prim strangers living in the house? Might they not prove as irksome as the Little Ballerina?'

She was chuckling at the thought that *nobody* could be as irksome as the Little Ballerina when her visitors came back into the room and said that the rooms were suitable for their requirements and asked how soon they might move in.

Settling into their new accommodation, the women were polite, scrupulously correct, businesslike and reserved. Just the behaviour that Lily had anticipated and, perhaps because of this expectation, that was why at first she saw no further. Once her new tenants were installed, Lily assumed from their reticence that they wanted to be left alone, and she was happy to oblige.

In the middle of the night some six weeks after the women moved in, Lily was awakened by a groan of agony, quickly suppressed. Rigid with alarm, she lay quite still, alert and listening. The groan came again, and this time she realised it was coming from the floor below. Then there was the sound of someone vomiting.

She was torn between the nurse's reaction of wanting to rush down and offer her help, and the discreet landlady's response of pretending she hadn't heard. As she lay wondering which impulse to obey, there was a soft tap on her door and a quiet voice said, 'Miss Raynor? Are you awake?'

Lily leapt out of bed, pulled on her wrap and ran to open the door. Dorothea Sutherland stood on the landing. Her bobbed grey hair was in pins and she wore a rather masculine-looking woollen dressing gown over a long nightshirt. Her face was pale, her expression deeply anxious.

'How can I help, Miss Sutherland?' Lily asked calmly.

Miss Sutherland closed her eyes briefly. 'Thank you,' she whispered. 'I understand that you are a nurse?'

'I trained as a nurse,' Lily agreed. She was about to add that she had specialised in battlefield wounds and midwifery, but since neither seemed relevant, she didn't.

'Miss Adderley has been taken ill,' Miss Sutherland said. 'She tried to discourage me from coming to find you, but she . . . I . . .' She stopped. Lily was distressed to see that her lower lip was trembling. Suspecting that a woman like Miss Sutherland would hate to display weakness, she pretended she hadn't noticed.

'Sudden illness is often less alarming for the sufferer than for the witness,' she said gently. Miss Sutherland gave a low moan. 'If you think Miss Adderley will forgive you, however,' Lily added, 'let's go down to her immediately.'

Miss Sutherland ran down the stairs two at a time.

Lily found Miss Adderley lying half out of the bed, her face contorted with pain, a fist pressed so hard to the right side of her forehead that her knuckles were white. Swiftly going to kneel beside her, Lily laid her back against the pillows and checked for fever and for any obvious signs of illness or injury, then said, 'Miss Adderley, if you can speak, will you tell me what has happened? I can see your head hurts, and—'

'It is as if there is a knife stuck into my forehead, above my eye,' Miss Adderley gasped. '*I can't see!*' she added in an anguished wail.

'And you have been sick.' It wasn't a question, for the evidence was in a large bowl on the bedside table.

'Yes.' It was a whisper.

'Do you suffer from migraines?' Lily asked.

'I do, and one came on this evening.' A pause. 'I fell asleep, but then I woke up just now and I couldn't see. Black spots obscured my vision, and then the lights began.' Miss Adderley groaned, and the groan turned into a sob.

'Describe the lights,' Lily said.

'They are like a brilliant zig-zagging cloud; they flow right across my eyes, they have jagged edges that are yellow and flame red, and the light within is so bright and— *aaah!*'

Beside the sick bowl, Lily spotted another, filled with water and with a folded flannel beside it. Quickly wringing out the flannel in the cold water, gently she put it on Miss Adderley's forehead.

'The lights are called an aura,' she said. 'They are a symptom of migraine that—'

'But I've never lost my sight before!' Miss Adderley wailed.

'You haven't lost it now,' Lily said firmly. 'It is usual for the aura to persist for twenty minutes or half an hour, then it goes away and your sight returns to normal.'

Miss Adderley lay quite still for a few moments. Then she said, 'I believe you are right, Miss Raynor.'

Lily smiled. 'I know I am.'

Miss Sutherland, unaffected by migraine and thus temporarily more capable of clear thought than her friend, said, 'You are also a sufferer, Miss Raynor?'

'I am. Only the classic headache and nausea when I was younger, but recently the aura has developed.'

Miss Adderley had begun to relax. Now she rolled onto her side, and Miss Sutherland gently tucked her up. Lily got up and headed to the door, beckoning to Miss Sutherland.

'She will sleep now,' she said. Miss Sutherland nodded. Lily frowned. 'What does she take for the pain?'

'Laudanum.' Miss Sutherland's expression suggested she did not approve.

'Laudanum is highly addictive,' Lily said. 'If it would not seem interfering, might I suggest an alternative?'

'Oh, Miss Raynor,' Miss Sutherland breathed. 'I *wish* you would.'

These days Lily wonders how long the initial state of careful ignoring of each other by tenants and landlady would have gone on had Bernice Adderley not had a migraine. For the moment of necessity-born intimacy effected a definite easing of the polite reserve between tenants and landlady; now it is not only brief and courteous greetings that are exchanged when Lily encounters one or both of her tenants in the hall or on the stairs. Tentatively they have begun to extend the conversations, and Lily has been wondering whether to suggest a little tea party one Sunday afternoon for Miss Sutherland, Miss Adderley, Marm, Mrs Clapper, Felix and herself. She thinks about it now, decides to talk it over with Felix before issuing the invitations, and just as she does so, the street door is flung open and she hears the sound of Felix vigorously wiping his boots on the cocoa nut matting.

She knows it is Felix, and not only because he is one of only five people who has a key to the door and the other four are either at work or already inside the house. There's something about the way he bursts in, she thinks; as if he comes accompanied by a cloud of energy, and it gets displaced and pushed ahead of him even as he's closing the door. She smiles; she always seems to smile now, when Felix comes in.

'How did the meeting go?' she asks as he hurries through the outer office and into the Inner Sanctum. 'Were they satisfied with the report? Have we done enough?'

He grins. He is reaching into the inside pocket of his coat. 'Have *we* done enough?' he queries. 'Hmm. I seem to recall that it was *I* who spent far too long in a dismal street corner café much too close to Lime Street station.'

'I wrote the report,' she replies. 'And I spent as much time at Euston, watching this end of the operation.'

He extracts an envelope from his pocket and puts it on her desk, then flings himself into the chair they keep for visitors. 'Yes, my dear Lily, they were satisfied, we did more than enough, and to prove it, here's the cheque.' He taps the envelope. '*Oh*,' he groans, leaning back, 'let's just pray this is the last one!'

She opens it and extracts the cheque. Reads the amount. Looks up at him. 'This,' she says, 'is more than we agreed.' It is in fact considerably more.

His smile widens. 'I know. It rained in Liverpool all the time I was there. The extra money is a new bonus.'

'Don't tell me. The Bad Weather Bonus?'

'Precisely.' Then abruptly he sits up straight, staring at her keenly and frowning.

'What?' she demands.

'There's a group of people dithering about at the top of Hob's Court,' he says. 'They look as if they might be trying to find us, so I hurried on home to make sure I got here first.'

She leaps up, trying to tidy her hair and wipe the ink stain off her middle finger at the same time. 'Why didn't you say?'

His grin is back. 'I just did.'

TWO

Even as the three elderly people nervously approach the chairs Felix has swiftly set out and, having made a surely unnecessary amount of fuss deciding who will sit where, finally make up their minds and settle down, Lily can see they are related, and probably siblings.

Two are women, one perhaps in her early seventies, the other younger; the third is a man of the older woman's vintage. It is the elder sister who speaks for them.

'My name is Alethea Fetterplace,' she begins. She is clad, Lily observes – or perhaps iron-clad describes it better – in well-tailored black bombazine into which she has been corseted so tightly that she sits bolt upright and her bust protrudes like a shelf. The bombazine is a little rusty at the hem and the apex of the folds. In what appears to be an attempt to enliven the dense black, Miss Fetterplace has added a frilled fichu in violet and a vivid purple ribbon trim on her steel-grey bonnet. Her fine grey hair is parted in the middle and severely drawn back from the lean face with its high cheekbones and wide mouth. Her hands, in black lace mittens, are long-fingered, their top joints bent with arthritis. She has sharp blue eyes and a look of being interested in absolutely everything.

'This is my younger sister, Miss Frances Fetterplace,' she is saying. She turns politely to the woman sitting on her left. 'We usually call her Fanny, or Baby.'

Lily turns to the younger sister. Miss Frances Fetterplace has made sure that she is sitting in the middle. She risks a glance at Lily from under lowered eyelids and ventures a shy little smile. Lily is not fooled for a moment, for she has met women like 'Baby' Fetterplace before. She may be in her mid-sixties, but she is still reliant on the methods that have undoubtedly served her for a lifetime to bend her siblings to her will: coyness, girl-ishness; the impression that she is frail, in need of protection, prone to nervous exhaustion and not really capable of coping with the rigours of the world; and a winning, dimpled smile. She is even more tightly corseted than her sister. The waist within the subtly shining mauve silk of the bodice has an unlikely narrowness which, thinks Lily the former nurse, accounts for Miss Frances's continuous, gentle puffing. The gown has frills, tiny embroidered flowers, bands and borders wherever they can be crammed on. The bodice of the gown has a low neckline, and Miss Frances has arranged at least three floaty scarves around her wrinkled throat as if to counteract the autumnal chill in the air. A fringe of little curls has been arranged to peep out from beneath the brim of her pert little hat. Thinking that their rich gold and glossy sheen are unlikely, if not impossible, for a woman of Miss Frances's age, Lily wonders if the false curls are attached to her head or to the pert little hat.

'And this' – Miss Fetterplace leans forward to point beyond her sister – 'is our brother, Thomas William Gainsborough Fetterplace. He—'

'We call him Dukey because he has a big nose like the Duke of Wellington!' Miss Frances puts in, going off into a tinkling laugh and clapping her hands like a delighted six-year-old.

'That will *do*, Fanny!' hisses her sister.

Lily studies the Fetterplace brother.

He has a round face, the flesh plump, smooth and shiny, as if he has been blown up from inside. He has wide, pale-blue eyes under bushy, permanently raised eyebrows, which make him look as if life constantly surprises him and he finds it alarming and very difficult to fathom. He has the same wide mouth as his elder sister, but his is somehow loose, moist, and the lips are in constant motion as if he is keeping up a private running commentary on what he is observing. He is dressed in an old-fashioned but stylish coat, waistcoat and trousers in heavy black wool made for long wear; he has removed his shiny silk top hat, releasing dandelion-seed white hair that instantly springs up into an almost perfect sphere.

Lily returns her eyes to the eldest sibling. 'How may the World's End Bureau be of service, Miss Fetterplace?' She notices that Felix has quietly pulled up a chair and is sitting behind the siblings, slightly to their right. Lily can see him – and notes he has his notebook open and his silver pencil poised – but none of the Fetterplaces can unless they turn round.

Miss Fetterplace draws a breath and says, 'Our name is an ancient one, Miss Raynor. Our lineage dates back to William Odo Fetterplace, who was born in Normandy and came over with William the Conqueror in 1066, to whom he was a close and trusted companion. So much so,' she adds, 'that the Conqueror awarded him an estate in Norfolk as a reward for his loyalty.' Lily exchanges a swift glance with Felix, who makes a subtle hurry-up gesture, circling his free hand; they have encountered clients who insist on declaring their full family histories before, and it's always tedious.

'The surname is Anglo-Norman, d'you see,' Miss Fetterplace is saying, 'and "fete place" means an usher whose honoured role it is to escort people to the places prepared for them within a royal court or an aristocratic dwelling.'

Lily observes that Felix shakes his head and raises his eyebrows.

'Now of course we have no means of *verification* of this account of William Odo,' Miss Fetterplace admits, 'although we can be sure that he was of no little importance, for the family thrived, the estate grew and by the time Henry the Seventh was crowned—'

'In 1485,' Felix supplies promptly, earning a snorting chortle from Miss Fetterplace's brother.

'When Henry the Seventh was king,' the determined monologue continues, 'there is a record of a courtier named Edmund Fettyplace, whose son and grandson followed his lead and served in turn Henry the Eighth, his son and heir, Edward the Sixth, and his daughters, Mary and Elizabeth.' She rattles off more names and dates and pauses for breath, but before anyone can make a contribution, goes on. 'Now we do not know which of those Tudor ancestors received the honour of such a fine reward, but one of them was granted the tenure of a little house in a tucked-away court to the west of the Tower.'

'Your ancestor must indeed have given the most loyal and outstanding service,' Lily says. Felix mouths something that could well be *sycophant*.

Miss Fetterplace nods smugly as if to say, 'naturally'. 'The house is now known as number eight, Mary Rose Court,' she goes on, 'and it is where we, as the family's last descendants, still reside. It is situated in a row of ten, divided halfway along by a passage. The Court leads off a cobbled lane situated to the west of Great Tower Hill. All Hallows Church lies to the south; it is a *very* old church, and the bones of its foundations have stood there since the seventh century.' She leans forward, lowering her voice to a whisper. 'It was Edward the Sixth's chantry, you know.' She pauses. 'And it is where the victims of executions on Tower Hill were taken, their corpses still warm.' Her sister gives a rather dramatic little gasp of horror. 'The church's boundaries to west and north are Seething Lane and Fenchurch Street,' she says, resuming her normal tone. 'We live very quietly and simply in Mary Rose Court, content in our serenity and happy to be overlooked by the rush of life.'

'It sounds a most delightful residence, Miss Fetterplace, but—' Lily begins.

Miss Fetterplace takes not an iota of notice. 'The houses were built when King Henry the Eighth was young and preparing to embark on the path of matrimony with the first of the six wives,' she says, her voice louder now. 'The dwellings have been enlarged and much altered over the centuries, but the ancient essence of them is unchanged. We each have a very generous garden, although sadly these are without exception somewhat overgrown nowadays.' She makes a rueful face. 'None of the residents are in or anywhere near the first flush of youth, d'you see, and it is rare – unheard of, really – for anyone to embark on a project of any kind.' She pauses, frowning. 'I suppose one might say that the dead were left to enjoy their long peace, were it not rather too whimsical.'

Lily is on the point of asking what she means by that, and whether the gardens occupy land once belonging to the churchyard, when Thomas Fetterplace makes a sudden loud noise, apparently expressive of what *he* thinks of whimsy. His elder sister glares at him.

'We thought we should attend to the rose bed that runs along the inside of the wall at the end of the garden,' Miss Fetterplace resumes, 'which divides our property from All Hallows. The rose bed has been sadly neglected of late, but—'

'Not a rose bed but a mass of brambles and nettles!' puts in Thomas.

'We felt it incumbent upon us to effect restoration,' Miss Fetterplace continues, 'because—'

'It's so *old*!' her sister pipes up. 'Mother loved it when she was a little girl because she said the house always smelt of roses. Grandmama insisted it was always tended to perfection, Grandpapa's father Edmund always made a little ceremony out of the first cut of the autumn pruning and—'

'I am sure, Fanny,' Miss Fetterplace interrupts firmly, turning to her sister with a formidable frown, 'you have given an adequate description.' Turning back to Lily, she says, 'Family tradition tells us the rose bed was first created in the Tudor or perhaps the early Stuart era. It features in an oil painting of the garden, the work of a Dutch master, and it is included in a work of 1715, by a French artist, of the parterre that existed at that time.'

She pauses briefly to gather her thoughts. Felix takes the chance to say, 'The rose bed, then, has always been a prized and much-loved feature of your garden, and this is why you thought to restore and replant it.'

All three siblings struggle to turn and look at him – unsuccessfully – and they chorus, 'Quite so.'

'We managed to clear the tangled growth,' Miss Fetterplace continues, 'and we dragged it away to one side and burned it, in the most splendid bonfire. Then my brother—'

'Took m'spade and went out to cut the first trench,' Thomas says loudly across her. 'Went right on digging. Hard work, mind; any amount of roots and stones, all mixed up with the underlying clay. Old bricks, broken pipes and shards of willow pattern china, I found them all, I dug them out, I went on digging.' He eyes Lily, shoots a glance at Felix, returns to Lily. 'And then deep down in the earth I found an upturned bowl, colour of old ivory.'

There is a dramatic pause.

'Loosed the soil, eased the end of m'pick under it, levered it out,' he goes on. 'Only it wasn't a bowl. It was a skull.'

While he is still fixing Lily with wide-open, slightly mad eyes, Miss Fetterplace says with the force of one determined to tell the rest of the tale, 'And there was a small, fine-boned skeleton.'

It is clear that Thomas is expecting a reaction. 'A skeleton!' Lily exclaims obligingly. A soft bell-like sound has just rung in her head; she ignores it.

Miss Fetterplace leans forward, and the bones of her corset creak audibly.

'Now I dare say that a clever young woman such as you, Miss Raynor, is already drawing the obvious conclusion?' she says confidingly.

'I . . . well, given where the house is, and the fact that your ancestors had the connection to royalty, I suppose one might suggest that, er, it could be that—'

Fanny Fetterplace's impatience gets the better of her. 'Oh yes, Miss Raynor, *yes!*' she gasps. 'The skeleton could be that of someone *important!*'

Aware that all three are waiting eagerly for her to comment, *expecting* her to comment, as if they have given a very obvious hint and are waiting for her to pick it up, Lily is temporarily at a loss. She shoots a look at Felix, who mouths, *age*.

'Does it appear that the bones have lain there for some time?' she asks.

Miss Fetterplace nods approvingly. 'They were some way down in the earth,' she replies, 'and deep yellowish-ivory in colour.'

'Was there evidence of any garments?' Felix asks.

Once again Miss Fetterplace tries to twist round to stare at him. 'A good question, Mr—? I am sorry, I have forgotten your name.'

'Wilbraham,' Felix supplies. 'Felix Wilbraham.'

'There *were* fragments of cloth.' Miss Fetterplace's voice has dropped to a reverential whisper. 'It was—'

'*Velvet!*' Fanny Fetterplace shrieks suddenly. 'And also brocade! And a length of the most beautifully wrought decorative chain that I am *quite* sure is gold, and three perfect pe—'

'*Baby!*' her brother and sister cry together in a sudden display of anguish. Thomas shoots a glance at Lily. 'It's *secret*,' he hisses in an all-too-audible whisper.

Lily waits to see if anyone will comment on what has just happened. Nobody does; all three siblings are now looking at her with vapid smiles on otherwise expressionless faces.

'If we are to judge from the depth of the find, the colour of the bones and the rotted garments, then,' Lily says briskly, 'it appears that the interment is not recent.'

'Not recent,' Miss Fetterplace agrees.

'And do you . . .' Suddenly the question she ought to have asked straight away pops into Lily's head. Cross that she has allowed herself to be drawn into the siblings' storytelling, she asks it now. 'What did the police say when you reported your find?'

All three Fetterplaces look down into their laps. Eventually Thomas mutters, 'Told the constable of the watch. He didn't take much interest. Said there were bones dug up all over Tower Hill, and to cover them up again and leave them where they were.' His eyes skitter furtively to Lily and back to his elder sister. Lily is almost sure he is not telling the entire truth. Or even a small portion of it.

'That sounds like wise advice,' she says neutrally. 'Would it perhaps be sensible to take it?'

Frances Fetterplace's head shoots up and she fixes Lily with a horrified stare, eyes so wide that the whites are visible all around the irises. It makes her look more than a little mad. 'Oh, Miss Raynor, but we *can't*!' she cries on a sob.

Thomas leans over to comfort her, leaving his other sister to answer Lily's question. 'Sensible, yes,' she says sadly. She glances at her brother and sister. Then, leaning towards Lily and lowering her voice as if this would make her words inaudible to them, she says, 'But there have been . . . *occurrences*.' Her eyes plead for Lily's understanding, but Lily shakes her head, asking for more. 'Oh, dear,' Miss Fetterplace mutters. 'At *night*,' she hisses. '*Noises*. And once Dukey saw a flicker of light, very swift, as if a lantern beam had been uncovered and quickly covered again.'

'And these noises and lights were at the end of your garden?' Felix asks.

'Well . . .' Miss Fetterplace hesitates. 'Possibly our garden, possibly the churchyard. It is so very close, as we told you. Only the old wall separates our property from sanctified ground.'

'We think . . .' Thomas begins hesitantly. But his elder sister hisses, '*Dukey!*'

'Can't be sure quite where they come from,' he mutters, with the finality of someone closing a subject they don't want to talk about any more.

'He can't have the bones,' Fanny pipes up suddenly. Her brother turns to face her and gives her a ferocious scowl, which Fanny ignores. 'They are *ours*!' she screeches. 'She is ours, she's our *kinswoman*!' There are two spots of furious red high up on her round cheeks.

'Baby! Now that's *enough*!' the siblings protest, their voices drowning the last words. Miss Fetterplace grasps her sister's arm, her fingers gripping tightly. Fanny subsides, still muttering.

Lily studies the three old faces. They are all worried, she thinks. They are all scared. She looks at Felix. He nods.

'How would you like us to help?' Lily asks.

Visible relief floods the siblings. Miss Fetterplace mutters her thanks and Frances whispers fervently, 'Dear Miss Raynor, you are the answer to our prayers!'

For the next quarter of an hour, Lily asks questions and Felix jots down the answers. Watching him write, Lily reflects that what the siblings seem to want is someone to take their fears seriously; to go and inspect this skeleton that has turned up so embarrassingly in their ancient, long-neglected rose bed and tell them what they ought to do about it.

Once or twice, Felix looks up and catches Lily's eye. She is quite sure he is querying something, but she can't think what. They complete the financial arrangements – Thomas hands over a cheque for the deposit and an initial sum for expenses and politely requests an invoice, which Felix assures him is the Bureau's usual policy – and now the siblings are tackling the long and involved process of getting out of their chairs, adjusting their many garments and making sure they have all their possessions. There is quite a lot of muttering among them and Lily thinks all three still look worried. She catches Felix's eye and his brief nod informs her he has noticed too.

The siblings are already on the steps, with Lily and Felix in courteous attendance, when Lily says gently, 'Is there something else you wish to share with us?'

All three old heads turn to stare at her. Miss Fetterplace looks alarmed. Fanny gives a little shriek and punches her brother. 'I *said* we should tell!' she hisses angrily. 'I told you she'd guess anyway!'

'Of course she hasn't guessed,' Miss Fetterplace says scathingly. 'But I suppose perhaps we should . . .'

She pauses, frowning. Then she says in a rush, 'My brother described how he found the bowl of the skull and the rest of the skeleton.' She bites her lip. 'What he did *not* make clear is that the two were not attached.'

While Lily and Felix are absorbing that, Fanny Fetterplace gathers herself and says in a furious whisper, 'They cut her head off! Up there on the high scaffold, and until the last she looked for the mercy that did not come!'

Miss Fetterplace briefly grasps her sister's hand. 'My sister has a vivid imagination,' she says repressively. Then, with a glance at her brother, she adds a curt, 'Good day, Miss Raynor, Mr Wilbraham.' And, an elbow nudging each of her siblings, she ushers them away.

Back in the Inner Sanctum, Lily and Felix sit either side of her desk.

'What do you think?' she asks him.

'I think they are hiding something,' he replies instantly.

'Aah,' she says slowly. 'Was that what you were trying to tell me while we were sorting out the finances?' He makes a noncommittal noise. 'Well?' she prompts.

He frowns. 'Perhaps that's what it is,' he says after a moment. 'But I . . .' He pauses. 'Lily, I'm not sure I can describe it, but I sense something very odd about this business.'

'A head and a decapitated body in an old, abandoned garden,' she says. 'A suggestion that someone else knows about the bones and has gone looking for them. And a childlike, fanciful woman who keeps hinting that the skeleton is that of someone important. Odd, yes. It's most certainly *odd*.'

He is shaking his head. He glances at her ruefully. 'You'll think I'm letting my imagination get the better of me.'

She grins. 'I'll try not to.'

He pauses again, for longer this time.

'It's very apparent that the siblings are scared,' he says eventually. 'Now you might say that's only to be expected, three ancient people in an echoing old house that's been there for centuries hearing nocturnal noises and seeing flashes of light. But I think there's more to it than that.' He has been staring down at his notebook, turning his pencil from end to end, but now he looks her full in the face. 'Lily, my instincts tell me that something very dark is going on here.'

THREE

Lily and Felix both have cases that have reached their conclusion and require time for the preparation of reports and the submission of final accounts. It is therefore two days later that they reconvene to discuss the Fetterplaces' skeleton.

'I want to pay a surprise visit to number eight, Mary Rose Court,' Felix announces. 'If we . . .' He pauses and grins. 'If I'm right and they are hiding something, I'll surely have a better chance of spotting it if I go to see them than if we suggest they come here again.'

'You plan to burst in and start looking under the cushions?' she asks, amused.

He smiles. 'I was thinking of a more subtle approach. I'm going to try to speak to them individually. The brother clearly has something on his mind – did you notice the way his lips move all the time as if he's reassuring himself?'

'I did.'

'And as for the fluttery, girlish little sister, I'm sure I could charm her into whispering her secrets – she's probably been longing for a presentable young man to ride in on a white charger and sweep her off to safety.'

Lily is not sure where the warning comes from. But, as she looks into his smiling face, she has a sudden sense of threat so powerful and so dark that she gasps. 'Be careful,' she says. She can hear a slight tremor in her voice and hopes he hasn't noticed.

He has. He's Felix, she thinks, of course he has.

He gets up, eyes still on her. 'You sense it too.' It isn't a question. 'Don't worry, Lily, I promise to be as careful as both you and I want me to be.'

For a moment it is as if a sinister cloud has permeated the Inner Sanctum. Then, in what sounds far too like a determined attempt to dissipate it, Felix says brightly, 'And what do *you* plan to do next?'

* * *

They set out after lunch. Lily is on her way to Marmaduke Smithers' apartment. He is a journalist; a one-man campaigner for the poor and the unimportant; a fighter for social reform who never rests. He is Felix's landlord and Felix and Lily's good and trusted friend. He is also possessed of intelligence of a high degree and a retentive memory, and he has become Lily's first port of call when there is something she doesn't know about and wants to discuss.

Felix walks with her to the end of Kinver Street, one of the maze of lanes and passages between Royal Hospital Road and the King's Road, where Marm's apartment is to be found. Then, with a swift 'See you later' and her renewed warning to take care ringing in his ears, he sets off for Tower Hill.

For some reason he decides against the direct approach, which would have been to walk along the river almost to the Tower before turning left up Great Tower Hill, left into Great Tower Street and then left again into the network of little streets that included Mary Rose Court. Instead, he turns left much earlier, making his way along St Dunstan's Lane and following Great Tower Street until he reaches Seething Lane, which runs along the west side of All Hallows Church. Waiting until he is unobserved, he slips over the wall and lands softly in the long grass of the churchyard. Striding across to the northern wall, he follows it along to where a little wicket gate emerges on to Barking Lane. At one point, hurrying along in the lee of the churchyard wall, he notices a very unpleasant smell; he suspects he has trodden in the droppings of some small animal, or perhaps – sniffing again – the remains of whatever it caught for its supper a few nights ago. Then he is out in the open, and a left turn and then another one take him to Mary Rose Court.

He can see at a glance that the houses have seen better days. All of them could do with a coat of paint on their doors and window frames; one or two have at least one broken window pane, showing signs of a cheap and not very thorough repair. Some of the little front gardens contain mouldering, long-discarded bags of sundry rubbish, and one has a broken chair leaning up against the wall of the house.

But despite these depressing indicators of genteel respectability falling slowly into poverty, the houses were constructed back in the days when rich men built unstintingly with the best of available materials, employing the best craftsmen who worked with skill and an eye for beauty. Mary Rose Court remains a little gem of a place.

Felix lingers in the entrance of the dark and narrow little passage that divides the ten houses into two terraces of five and slowly looks around. It is clear that alterations have been made over the centuries to the original sixteenth-century architecture, and at first glance it is more typical of the Georgian than the Tudor era. The houses are narrow and each is three storeys high. The proportions are perfect; the symmetry pleases the eye. Each little front garden is bordered by black-painted railings, and steps lead up to the front doors. Suddenly Felix notices the silence: here he is not half a mile from the Tower, there is thundering traffic fighting its way through the perpetual congestion and there must be several million people within a ten-mile radius, yet here he stands in what could be the profound peace of the deep countryside . . .

Except that in fact it's not peaceful at all. There might not be anything to hear in this little world apart – and it really is an eerie, uncanny silence – but the air is alive with rumour, with tensions, with something like a constant scratching that is not perceived by the auditory system but the sensory.

Very deliberately, Felix forces himself to stand up straight. 'Stop being so fanciful,' he mutters. 'Find some courage!'

He steps out of the shadow of the passage and strides along to number 8.

Thomas Fetterplace opens the door to Felix's knock with an expression of surprise that swiftly turns to dismay. 'Mr— er, Mr . . . Wilbraham! Yes, yes, Mr WILBRAHAM, of the WORLD'S END BUREAU!' he shouts loudly, and in case either of his sisters has missed this very obvious warning, he turns back into the dimly lit hall and calls, 'Alethea! Fanny! Mr Wilbraham is here, isn't that a nice surprise?'

'I am sorry to arrive unannounced,' Felix says. He waits for Thomas to stand back and usher him in, but Thomas stands firm, holding the door with one hand and the frame with the other. 'I thought you would appreciate,' Felix adds boldly, 'that I need to see for myself the garden – the rose bed, in fact – and the—'

'Yes, yes, quite so!' Thomas makes nervous suppressing gestures with the hand not clinging on to the door. Then, as if accepting that having Felix inside the house is marginally better than outside on the street talking about gardens and rose beds and skeletons, he stands aside and says, 'I suppose you had better come in.'

He shows Felix into a dark and extremely cluttered room at the back of the long hall on the left, from which a tall window overlooks the wild garden – for someone standing, at least, Felix notes, for an out-of-control, extravagant tangle of ivy and Virginia creeper covers the lower part of the glass.

'Won't you please take a seat, Mr Wilbraham?' Thomas says politely. 'If you would excuse me just for a moment, I shall seek out my sisters and summon them to join us.'

He pushes the door to, but the latch doesn't engage. Even as the anxious sounds of his trotting footsteps hurry away along the hall, Felix has moved silently to push the door further open. He leans out through the doorway.

He can hear Thomas's nervous muttering, but at first the distance is too great for the words to be clear. Then – perhaps Thomas is coming back again – he makes them out.

'. . . must be *absolutely sure* we do not make any mention whatsoever of Father's papers, Alethea, for we cannot—'

There is a long, sibilant *sssssssh* as Alethea hushes him.

Now she is speaking, and amongst the flurry of nervous words Felix hears quite distinctly the whispered command to her brother: 'For God's sake, keep Fanny in her room!'

As rapid footsteps beat out on the chequered tiles of the hall, Felix pushes the door closed and shoots across the room. When Thomas enters a couple of seconds later, Felix is standing with his thumbs in his waistcoat pockets, back to the door, gazing out at the wilderness of the back garden.

'My sister Miss Fetterplace will join us directly,' Thomas says. He is more than a little breathless.

'And Miss Frances?' Felix asks innocently.

A deep blush floods Thomas's face. 'She . . . er, she . . . my sister is indisposed.'

Even ignoring the tell-tale blush, it is, Felix thinks, a paltry attempt at a lie. Only a few minutes earlier, Thomas announced he would seek out and summon his sisters, in the plural. It is an unlikely indisposition that overtakes a woman so comprehensively in so short a time.

Taking pity on his stumbling, red-faced host, Felix merely says, 'Oh, dear.'

An increasingly awkward silence falls on the stuffy, cluttered room. Thomas's eyes hold a pleading expression, which Felix interprets as a silent prayer that he will wait patiently for Miss Fetterplace and not do anything rash such as suggesting he and Thomas use this time of waiting to go and have a look in the rose bed.

Felix makes a small drama out of extracting his gold half hunter and inspecting it. 'I do think, perhaps, that we—' he begins.

Then the door is flung back on its hinges and Miss Fetterplace flows like a tidal wave into the room, wide black skirts brushing the little tables and the low, crowded shelves, her face a mask of determination. 'Mr Wilbraham, how good of you to call,' she says, as if this were a social visit. 'What a lovely day! A treat to see the sunshine!' she ploughs on. Barely pausing for breath, she continues, 'But, really, to have made the effort to come all the way from *Chelsea*!' She lays the stress as if Chelsea was off the north coast of Scotland instead of a mere five miles away. 'We may live quietly, Mr Wilbraham,' she adds with a patently forced chuckle, 'but we do understand how valuable time is to people who work so hard and so relentlessly as you and Miss . . . er, Miss . . .'

'Miss Raynor,' Felix supplies.

'There is absolutely no need for either of you to visit us in person again,' Miss Fetterplace says firmly. '*We* will come to *you* from now on.'

Felix is not fooled by the forceful words. Miss Fetterplace's chin is wobbling, very slightly. He strongly senses she is afraid.

'As you wish, Miss Fetterplace,' he says easily. She seems to slump a little with relief. 'But since I am here now,' he goes on, 'I will take a turn down the garden and have a look at what you have uncovered.'

Miss Fetterplace opens her mouth a few times like a landed fish, but no words emerge. She sends a frantic appeal to her brother, who drops his gaze and pretends he hasn't noticed.

Felix crosses the room, goes out into the hall and turns towards the back of the house. 'This way, is it? Shall I go on ahead to the rose bed?'

Thomas gives a soft moan and drops his face in his hands. Miss Fetterplace, shocked into action, hurries after Felix and manages to get herself between him and the garden door, which he has just shoved open.

Reaching down, she knocks his hand away from the latch – quite violently – and pulls it closed again. 'I am afraid that is impossible,' she gasps. She sends another agonised look at her brother, who has trotted after them, and this time he comes to her aid.

'It's our sister, you see,' he begins, his eyes begging for Felix's compliance. 'She . . . I'm afraid this is—' He stops, squares his plump shoulders and says firmly, 'The finding of the decapitated skeleton has been too much for her nerves. She has become deeply disturbed, and she is obsessed with the . . . er, with the *presence* of the bones, and although we try to discourage her, she persists in trying to go out into the garden to have another look, although the distress it causes her is . . .' Apparently words fail him, and he pauses. 'We feel – Alethea and I feel – it is best that we to try to ignore the existence of the, er, the discovery, and make pretence that there is nothing to see.'

He and his sister look hopefully at Felix.

Short of manhandling them out of the way, he realises there is nothing he can do. He is not fooled for a moment by this talk of Fanny's strange and worrying obsession with the bones, for her reaction two days ago when she was sitting on the edge of her chair in Lily's Inner Sanctum was breathless, thrilled excitement at the thought that the bones might belong to someone *important*.

He takes a few paces down the hall, away from the garden door. Both old faces still look anxious, so he says, 'Well, I wouldn't want to be the cause of a single instant's distress for poor Miss Frances.' Hope dawns pathetically in the siblings' eyes. 'And in any case, I am sure there is little to be ascertained from my inspecting a heap of old bones!' he adds cheerfully. The Fetterplaces move quickly aside as he heads back to the street door. 'My colleague, Miss Raynor, and I propose to make enquiries as to missing persons in the vicinity of Tower Hill,' he continues, casting round for any other steps he and Lily might take in the absence of the one glaringly obvious one of inspecting the skeleton, 'and we will inform you straight away if—'

There is a sudden eruption of noise from the floor above.

A door bursts open, little footsteps trit-trot along the hard floor and patter down the stairs, and Fanny Fetterplace's curvaceous and firmly corseted body swings out as she hangs on the newel post and jumps down into the hall, her eyes blazing with accusation as she fixes them on her sister and then her brother.

'You didn't tell me *he* was here!' she screeches, pointing a finger trembling with rage in Felix's general direction. 'You've been *out there*, haven't you? All of you, in the garden, digging around in the rose bed? And *you didn't take me*!' The scream is now so high-pitched and so impossibly shrill that Felix fears for the rather lovely stained-glass semicircle above the front door.

'But, Baby, dear, we haven't,' her sister says. 'We—' She shuts her mouth tightly on what she had been about to say.

Fanny rounds on her. 'Haven't you?'

'No,' Miss Fetterplace repeats.

Fanny looks at Felix. 'Is that true?' she demands.

'It is,' he says.

Now Fanny looks different. The signs of an overgrown child's tantrum smooth from her face and instead she looks haughty, disdainful – cruel, even.

'Yes,' she says slowly, staring at her siblings in turn. 'Look at you, the pair of you,' she hisses. 'The dear Lord above only knows what plans and plots you get up to, you silly old people and, goodness, you have made some blunders recently! But this . . . this . . .' She pauses, her face working. 'We have a skeleton in our garden,' she says, enunciating every word as if talking to idiots. 'Her poor head was cut off, there are remnants of gorgeous garments, and those three famous pearls and the precious length of gold necklace! We have Father's family papers' – her voice has risen to a screech – 'and we have *proof* of the link through the aunt's marriage to Edmund Fettyplace, *our* Edmund!' There is spittle on her plump lips. 'We *know* who she is, and now we fear someone else does too! She's in danger, such danger, and what do the pair of you do? You make half-hearted arrangements for some private enquiry agency to investigate, but I *know* what you'll do, you'll bury the bones again and you'll just tell me everything will be all right!' She gives a loud, agonised sob. 'You're cowards, the pair of you!' she hurls at them. 'You're scared of *him*' – both siblings gasp – 'and what he'll do if he knows you've been out there again! You're not—'

It is enough for Miss Fetterplace. Fanny is still shouting, but now she is being steered by the determined arms of her sister back along the hall and up the stairs. There is a brief exchange of furiously hissed words, then a door is closed with a bang and the only sound is Fanny's wailing.

Thomas gets out a large spotted handkerchief and mops his brow. Glancing towards the stairs – Miss Fetterplace has not returned – he says, 'My younger sister has always been a little temperamental.'

As soon as Felix is seated on the top of a westward-bound tram, he gets out his notebook and pencil and begins making detailed notes while the scene at number 8, Mary Rose Court is fresh in his mind. He looks forward eagerly to talking it over with Lily; he's almost sure that she will agree wholeheartedly with his proposal for what to do next.

By some means or other, he resolves to return to the Fetterplaces' garden after dark one night with a lantern, find his way to the rose bed and see what is in there for himself.

The silent, intent watcher who has noticed Felix's arrival and departure in Mary Rose Court and its immediate vicinity is still standing motionless, his eyes on the spot where Felix finally walked out of sight, some time after he has gone.

The Barrow Man has become fanatically possessive about his secret place in the lee of the churchyard wall. When he discovered it, he believed it was an answer to a prayer. Not that he ever prays; he hasn't done for years. The northern boundary of All Hallows churchyard has long been abandoned to nature. The nearest line of graves is some twenty paces away, and there is no reason for anyone to venture up here under the ancient wall. The rampant grass, shrub and sapling growth is untrodden. The Barrow Man is always careful to come and go along the faint track right beside the wall; he too makes sure to leave the long grass and the undergrowth undisturbed.

So how, he asks himself, has someone managed to find his hideaway?

But they have.

He has found the footprints, going *right through* the minuscule remains he left on the path when he came a few nights ago. It caused an explosion of fury so great that it was some minutes before he returned to himself. The red cloud invaded his head, his hands went to the knives in their sheaths on his belt and, as the height of the storm raged through him, his head filled with images of extreme violence, the damage that he hungered to inflict running in a series of flashes across his sight.

When he is calm, he thinks back to what has just happened.

How he levered himself up onto the churchyard wall separating the wild gardens of Mary Rose Court from his secret place. How he ducked behind the lowest branch of the alder tree that grew there and peered up at the house.

There was a man standing at the window looking down the garden. A tall man, broad in the shoulder, with dark blond hair and well-cut clothes. He stood with his thumbs in his waistcoat pockets.

You, the Barrow Man thinks now. It was you.

For some reason, the visitor chose first to approach Mary Rose Court via the rear. Having tried and failed – was that right? – he had gone on down the track, emerged onto Barking Lane and then walked up to the front door.

Why did he come here first, the Barrow Man asks himself. Again and again.

Because he knows about you, the cruel, ever-critical voice inside his head replies. He knows what you collect, where you bring them, what you do with them here. He'll be your downfall.

The Barrow Man's calm, expressionless face twists into a smile of utter bestiality.

'Not,' he says softly, 'if I am his downfall first.'

Lily is having a very nice afternoon with Marm Smithers. He makes it quite clear that he is pleased to see her, and this is verified by the preparations he has made. The living room of the shabby old Kinver Street apartment looks as if he might actually have taken a duster to it, and he has laid out a delicious tea with tiny potted-meat sandwiches, scones, chunky slices of treacle-black Parkin and some dainty iced biscuits. Lily is already on her second cup of tea and eyeing the sandwiches with a view to taking a couple more.

When they have both had enough – more than enough, in Lily's case, and she is trying to suppress a burp – Marm clears away the tray and pulls a stack of thick files onto his lap.

'Now, Lily, you tell me that the decapitated skeleton was found buried deep in an overgrown rose bed in an abandoned garden on Tower Hill,' he says, riffling through the pages of the top file.

'Yes,' she agrees. 'No more information than that, although Felix has gone to the house this afternoon to have a look for himself.' Once again, the little shimmer goes through her; that dark presentiment of danger . . . She ignores it.

'Hmm.' Marm is reading. Lily waits. Presently he looks up and, with an apologetic smile, says, 'I have been checking my files for recent reports of missing persons in that area.'

'Your Lost Women files,' Lily says. Marm tries to keep a record of people – invariably women and girls – whose disappearances have, in his view, been less than adequately investigated by the police. The girls and women are usually poor, powerless, unimportant and usually stay alive by selling their bodies. The files just keep growing, but Marm does not give up.

He sighs. 'Yes. As always, plenty of cases of women not where they are meant to be' – he flips through more pages – 'but without exception all had been seen fairly recently; within the last few months or years.' He looks up suddenly. 'It *is* a woman? This skeleton?'

'Oh!' The question surprises Lily, as does her initial impulse to say yes. She thinks back. 'Fanny Fetterplace – that's the younger sister, the one they call Baby – referred to *she* and *her*, but they all seem to indulge her as if she's a fanciful child and I am not at all sure she is to be relied upon.' She pauses. 'But yes, I believe it is a woman,' she goes on. 'Thomas Fetterplace described the skeleton as fine-boned, and the remnants of fabric were apparently costly brocade and velvet. There was a piece of gold chain perhaps from a necklet.'

'Gorgeous fabrics were not the sole preserve of women in past ages,' Marm observes.

'No,' Lily murmurs. Something has just jogged in her memory, and she is trying to isolate it. Marm waits.

She looks up to see that he is watching her, smiling gently. 'You were deep in thought,' he says.

She grins. 'I was. I've remembered another thing; Fanny Fetterplace said they'd found something else in the rose bed, and before her brother and sister stopped her, I think she was going to say "three perfect pearls".'

Marm closes his files. 'Lily dear, much as I would like to help, I fear that your fine-boned headless skeleton is a great deal too old to feature in my records,' he says.

'How far do they go back?' Lily asks.

'Oh . . .' Marm thinks. 'To the early 1860s, I suppose. When I first came to our great city of London as a callow young man in the hope of earning my fortune.' He grins.

You may not have done that, Lily thinks, but you are a good man, decent and honourable, and I am proud to call you my friend.

She quite wishes she was brave enough to say it aloud.

'I suppose,' she goes on after a while, 'I shall have to wait to see what new information Felix brings back.'

'You could do that,' Marm says. She looks up, alerted by his tone. 'But I have another idea.'

'I can see that you are longing to tell me,' Lily observes. 'Go on, then.'

He leans forward, his thin face alight with anticipation. 'We do not know, of course, how long the skeleton has been in the ground,' he begins, 'but it was buried deep, you told me, remnants of costly fabric clung to it, and pieces of expensive jewellery were found with it. All of which suggests that it is probably not a recent interment.'

Lily wants to agree but she is not sure they can be certain. 'Rich people still wear expensive clothes and good jewellery,' she says. 'They always have done.'

'True,' he agrees. 'But, Lily, what we must remember is that we know how this poor woman died.'

'Of course,' Lily says softly.

Marm, who probably didn't hear, is still speaking. 'She was beheaded. Her skeleton was put in the ground, the detached head placed with it. What does that suggest to you?'

'Execution,' she says. 'Beheading.'

Marm sits back, nodding. 'And the place where the bones lie is very, very close to Tower Hill. Which was—'

'The place of state executions from the late 1500s to halfway through the last century,' Lily finishes for him.

They look at each other.

Then she says, 'Fanny Fetterplace is quite determined that her skeleton is that of an *important* person.'

And Marm replies thoughtfully, 'Perhaps she is right.'

After a moment, he gives himself a shake and says in his usual businesslike voice, 'What you need, Lily my dear, is a historian well versed in the doings of the rich and the powerful in the heyday of beheadings,' he says. 'How lucky, then, that both you and I know two people who include such an expert among their friends!'

Lily studies him. 'I believe you must be referring to my new tenants?'

He beams. 'Yes, indeed. Neither of them are likely to be able to offer much help personally, since dear old Bunty is a scientist and Dorothea's deep interest in the past takes her a great deal further back than the Tudors.'

Tudors.

As he says the infamous name, Lily hears again the very faint chime of recognition inside her head. It's been ringing quite frequently, right from the moment when Thomas Fetterplace said he'd unearthed the decapitated skeleton of a small, fine-boned woman in the tatters of sumptuous clothing with three perfect pearls among the bones.

She knows she is being totally illogical, finding a putative connection where surely one cannot possibly exist.

'. . . other experts in their field at the Pavie Institute,' Marm is saying, 'and, indeed, it seems to have become something of a refuge for people such as Bunty and Dorothea: highly intellectual, learned women who find it so hard to find employment worthy of their intelligence and their talents in this male-dominated world.' Marm sighs, and his face falls into lines of sorrow. It is not only poor, lost women whom he champions, Lily reflects, for he appears to be an admirer of the entire sex.

'And one of these experts is a particular friend of my tenants?' Lily prompts.

'Yes. Her name is Agnes Halligan, and although one might describe her as a polymath, for her interests are wide and deep, she was originally a classicist and medieval historian. Her specific field of study nowadays is, or so I understand, the factual and mythological history of the Thames in London, its immediate surroundings, the important buildings on its banks and the wealthy and influential people who lived in them.'

Lily wishes she knew what a polymath is. This Agnes Halligan sounds alarmingly intelligent, and only moments after hearing her name for the first time, Lily is already in awe of her.

Marm has leapt up and is busy writing. He covers a page, blots it and folds it into itself, adding a stamp and an address which Lily, screwing her head round to see, notices is her own.

'I'm writing to Bunty to suggest she and Dorothea ask Agnes round to tea tomorrow,' he explains. Tomorrow is Saturday. 'Yes, I know I could have given the letter to you to put under their door,' he continues, 'but I thought it would be more discreet if the suggestion came just from me, as I try to help a friend. That's you,' he adds helpfully.

'Tomorrow,' Lily says faintly.

That gives her less than a day to start on the herculean task of addressing the depths of her ignorance.

Lily begins as soon as she is back in the Inner Sanctum. She refuses Mrs Clapper's offer of a nice pot of tea and a plate of shortbread before she sets off for home and the dubious delights of Clapper, as she calls her husband. Lily's stomach is still uncomfortably full with all that she ate and drank at Marm's.

Felix has left a fair copy of his Fetterplace notes on her desk. Drawing a pad of paper towards her and inking her pen, she begins to read. Although she knows it is at present quite impossible to put an accurate date on the skeleton in the garden of number 8, Mary Rose Court, she cannot dismiss the idea of a Tudor connection. Fetching one of her reference books, she writes out some dates:

Henry Tudor, born 1457, reigned as Henry VII from 1485–1509;
Henry VIII, born 1491, reigned 1509–1547;

Edward VI, born 1537, reigned 1547–1553;
Mary I, born 1516, reigned 1553–1558;
Elizabeth, born 1533, reigned 1558–1603.

Then she studies Felix's notes on the Fetterplace forbears:

William Odo Fetteplace (she notes the earlier spelling), *1042–1078.*

There is a gap of several centuries, and then:

Edmund Fettyplace, 1448–1497, courtier of Henry VII; his son Arthur Fettyplace, 1471–1520, courtier of Henry VIII; and grandson, William (1515–1587), who served Henry VIII and the successive Tudor monarchs who ruled after him.

There, then, is the proof of the link between the Fetterplace family ancestors and the Tudors – if, that is, the family's version of their history can be believed. And, Lily recalls, Fanny cried out that the skeleton was *ours; our kinswoman.* At first Lily had taken that seemingly outlandish implication as no more than a hysterical rant; that Fanny, with nothing better to do all day than indulge her fanciful imagination and make up wild stories of old, forgotten grandeur, has decided to claim an actual familial connection with the body in the rose bed.

Lily is so deep in thought that she doesn't hear the street door opening and closing, and only realises Felix is back when she looks up to see him standing in front of her desk.

'It's taken hold of you too, then,' he says softly, pointing to his own neatly written page and her additions.

'Yes,' she agrees.

He pulls up a chair and takes out his notebook.

'This is going to sound fantastical,' he warns, 'and, truly, I am not saying I believe it, or even that Alethea and Thomas believe it, but I think Fanny Fetterplace is absolutely sure that the body in the rose bed is that of Anne Boleyn.'

He is giving her that look, Lily thinks. The one that says 'you're going to be scathing and dismissive of this, but listen anyway.'

'Anne Boleyn,' she repeats softly.

'Fanny said they cut off the head on the high scaffold, and right till the end the victim looked for mercy that didn't come,' he says. 'The old tales say that Queen Anne went on believing Henry would pardon her, even as the swordsman swung the blade.'

'They do say that,' she murmurs. She had always thought that, assuming the story was true, this forlorn hope had probably been the only means by which poor Anne had managed to put one foot in front of the other and take the long walk.

'And just now she said more!' His face is alight with eagerness. 'Fanny, I mean. She said they had proof, that their father left papers indicating a marriage between Edmund Fettyplace and "her aunt".' When Lily doesn't answer, he adds impatiently, 'She clearly meant the woman in the rose bed's aunt!'

'Did Anne Boleyn have an aunt?' Lily asks mildly.

Felix emits a strangled sound of frustration. '*I* don't know! Do you?'

She shakes her head. 'But I know of someone who does.' Then, smiling now, she tells him who she is to have tea with tomorrow afternoon.

FOUR

Felix is preoccupied the next day, and fears he is not giving the sympathetic attention to Lily's anxiety about her forthcoming tea party that she feels he should.

He is planning to return to Mary Rose Court tonight. For one thing, the conditions are excellent, with a good possibility of clear skies for the full moon. For another, he doesn't think he can bear to wait any longer.

He cannot convey to Lily the complex blend of high excitement and anticipation that rages in him. She had listened attentively to the full account of his visit to the Fetterplace siblings on his return yesterday afternoon, which, once he had calmed down after making his dramatic initial announcement, he had to agree sounded rather dull, and clearly she has not been bitten by the same urgent desire to find out the truth. When he made his grand revelation – his plan to return to the ruined garden under cover of darkness – she merely said, 'Good idea.'

But, bless her, she must have noticed the effect of her disinterest, for later, when momentarily she had stopped fretting about not being nearly clever enough to meet someone as alarmingly knowledgeable and frighteningly intelligent as this friend of the new tenants, she came to seek him out in her grandfather's capacious old shed at the end of the garden to ask him to tell her again.

He had a sturdy bull's-eye lantern up on the workbench and he was carefully filling it with oil. 'I can get in over the wall at the bottom of the garden,' he said. 'It's the boundary of All Hallows churchyard, and I walked along it this afternoon.'

'Will the Fetterplace siblings or their neighbours not spot your light?' she asked.

'I don't think so,' he replied, carefully ignoring the fact that Alethea said Dukey saw lights, and hoping Lily had forgotten. 'The garden is a wilderness,' he added. 'And although some of the dense trees and shrubs are beginning to lose their leaves, there is still plenty of cover.'

But he knew without her saying so that she was concerned for him.

He continued with his task, pausing to wipe up a small spill.

Presently she said, 'Don't forget to fill your vesta case.' She pointed to the lantern. 'That will be of no benefit if you can't light the wick.'

He nodded, concentrating on the level of oil in the lantern. Then it occurred to him that, since she had taken the trouble to come out to find him in the shed, he ought to show a little more interest in this tea party she was going to. He turned to speak to her, and was surprised to see she had gone.

Lily is up in her quarters at the top of the house. She has twenty minutes before it is time to present herself at her tenants' door. There is, she thinks with a nervous smile, no excuse at all for tardiness.

She runs some water in the basin and washes her hands. Again. She has decided not to change; Miss Adderley saw her in the hall earlier and would perhaps think it odd if Lily were now to appear dressed in a different outfit. She peers into the looking glass to smooth her hair, which in fact is adequately smooth already.

She stands back and more of her appears in the glass. She loves this item of furniture, which belonged to her grandparents. A label on the back, brown with age, reads *Manufactured by James Parkinson of Liverpool*. The bevelled glass is oval, with a deep mahogany frame. It is very heavy, and small imperfections in the glass give minute and fascinating distortions. When Lily read *Alice Through the Looking-Glass* a decade or so ago, she was put instantly in mind of this mirror when Alice went through into the world alongside . . .

Returning abruptly to the present, Lily realises that if she isn't going to be late, she must hurry down the stairs immediately.

'Agnes, may I present our landlady, Lily Raynor,' Dorothea Sutherland is saying, one arm lightly on Lily's as she leads her over to where a tall, square-shouldered, stern-faced woman of about sixty stands in front of the hearth. 'Miss Raynor, this is my colleague and Bunty's and my friend, Agnes Halligan.'

Lily stares into a face whose bright, clear hazel eyes are staring right back. As the two take each other's measure, Agnes Halligan's severe expression softens. 'It is a pleasure to meet you, Miss Raynor,' she says. Her voice is melodious and pitched low. 'My congratulations on your beautiful house and on your business success.'

Lily feels herself blush. 'The house belonged to my grandparents,' she hears herself say. 'My grandfather and his forebears were apothecaries, and the business was run from here latterly.'

'I remember Raynor's Apothecary,' Miss Halligan says surprisingly. 'And an efficient and sympathetic young woman who worked here.' She is looking at Lily questioningly.

'Not me, of course,' she says, aware that it should have been 'not I' and worried that this erudite company will think her ignorant. 'It would have been my Aunt Eliza.'

Miss Halligan's smile deepens, revealing an unexpected dimple. 'Eliza Raynor. Yes, indeed.' Then, before Lily can nerve herself to ask for elucidation, Miss Halligan says, 'And now, instead of carrying on the family tradition, you are the proprietor of a private enquiry bureau.'

'Er . . . yes,' Lily agrees.

Miss Halligan leans closer and mutters, 'Well done.'

Tea is taken at the big round oak table that used to stand in Lily's grandparents' dining room. All three women put themselves out to make Lily feel at ease and, warming to them, she starts to relax. As they eat and drink, the conversation is of a general nature: the tenants say how much they like their new accommodation, and Dorothea Sutherland compliments Lily on the sterling qualities of Mrs Clapper. Lily relates one or two tales that illustrate just how long Mrs Clapper has been with the Raynor family, and amuses the women when she describes how her housekeeper will insist on referring to Lily somewhat morbidly as 'the last of the Raynors'. Miss Sutherland smiles in rueful sympathy, and Lily notices for the first time that she has rather large teeth that stretch out like a slice of orange peel.

When everyone has eaten enough and the teacups have again been refilled, Agnes Halligan taps gently on the table and, looking straight at Lily, says, 'I understand that you have a problematical new case, Miss Raynor, and that I might be able to help with some historical background.'

Needing no second invitation, Lily embarks on what she hopes is a succinct and comprehensible account of the problematical new case. Even as she hears her own voice speaking, she is aware that she has shaded her account of the decapitated skeleton, emphasising the depth of the burial, the fragments of costly cloth, the length of gold chain and the three perfect pearls. And, of course, since Felix was not allowed to inspect the bones yesterday, they only have Thomas Fetterplace's description to go on. He of all people is surely the most likely to emphasise what he *wanted* to find rather than what he *did*.

'Of course,' she says in conclusion, 'the body might well be that of a recent victim of violence, and the objects found nearby have nothing to do with her.'

Miss Halligan has been making notes in a neat hand on a small rectangle of paper. Now she looks up, and the light hazel eyes regard Lily intently. 'How long since the garden was abandoned to nature?' she asks.

Lily casts back to the initial meeting with the siblings. *Grandmama had insisted on roses in the house, Grandpapa's father had always initiated the pruning* . . . Adding two generations to the ages of the siblings, she says, 'A hundred years, perhaps.'

'Hmm.' Miss Halligan smiles faintly. 'Not a *very* recent murder victim, then.'

Lily can't think of an intelligent response to this, so she says nothing.

Miss Halligan makes another note, then puts down her pencil and says, 'If you will permit, ladies, I will state what I sense all of us are thinking. We may be quite wrong – in fact we undoubtedly are – but unless we set out this unlikely hypothesis and test it, it will always be there in the background.'

'Test to destruction, that's the scientific way,' Miss Adderley says approvingly.

Miss Sutherland is frowning. 'If I perceive accurately what you allude to, Agnes, then I must agree that it is *highly* unlikely.' She catches her friend's eye. 'But by all means, let's hear it, and then we may begin to demolish it!'

Three heads turn towards Miss Halligan, and Lily says politely, 'If you will, then, Miss Halligan?'

She folds her hands on top of her notes and, without any apparent preparation, begins to speak.

'I believe I speak for us all when I say that, on hearing the details of this fine-boned, beautifully dressed and bejewelled woman whose head had been cut off, the name that flew instantly to mind was that of Anne Boleyn.'

'I think that is probably my fault,' Lily says immediately. 'It is, as I have implied, who Frances Fetterplace believes the skeleton to be.'

'Yes, we understand that, Miss Raynor,' Miss Halligan says. 'But, speaking for myself, I admit that my thoughts were tending that way even before you told us of Miss Fanny's fixation.'

'And why on earth we should think of her and not one of the hundreds of other poor women who met a similar death under the brutal regimes of the past, I have no idea!' fumes Miss Sutherland.

'Quite, Dotty,' murmurs Miss Halligan. 'Nevertheless, may I take it that it was Henry the Eighth's second queen that we pictured?' There are soft sounds of assent.

'*Pictured* is right. It's because of that portrait,' says Bernice Adderley. 'The one where those dark eyes stare challengingly out of the canvas, dark hair under the bejewelled cap framing that pale face, and the famous pearl choker with the gold B hanging from it and the three little pearls.'

'The very image,' agrees Miss Halligan. 'To make a very obvious objection: a woman on the scaffold about to be beheaded by a skilled French swordsman will *not* be wearing any sort of necklace.'

'One of her attendants could have placed it with her body afterwards,' Miss Adderley suggests. 'As a gesture of love, and respect, so that there would be some honour in death, some mark of who and what she had been.'

They all digest this for a moment. Lily can't help thinking that already the scales are weighed heavily in favour of a positive identification.

There is something she has been meaning to ask and now,

taking advantage of the momentary lull in the conversation, she says, 'Yesterday my associate Mr Wilbraham called on the Fetterplace siblings. Fanny became rather over-excited, I gather, and claimed that, among certain papers left by her late father, there was proof that one of the Fetterplace ancestors – Edmund – married someone she referred to as "her aunt", which Felix – Mr Wilbraham – understood to mean the skeleton's aunt.'

Miss Halligan frowns. 'Anne Boleyn's parents were Thomas Boleyn and Elizabeth Howard, daughter of the Duke of Norfolk. Undoubtedly both had sisters, and I imagine it would be possible, if not somewhat tedious, to find out if one of these women married a man called Edmund Fetterplace.'

'It was spelt Fettyplace in Edmund's time,' Lily says.

There is a small pause while everyone appears to think about that.

Then Miss Adderley says briskly, 'Agnes, you, Dotty and probably Miss Raynor too may be familiar with Anne Boleyn's story, but I'm afraid I am not. Would you please enlighten us?' There are murmurs of agreement.

'Very well,' Miss Halligan says. 'Henry the Eighth was desperate for a male heir. His first queen, Katharine of Aragon, suffered many stillbirths and miscarriages, and after twenty-four years of marriage, produced one surviving child, Mary, who—'

'Bloody Mary,' says Miss Sutherland.

'Yes,' Miss Halligan agrees, 'although why she alone should have been awarded that epithet in an age of brutal and bloodthirsty monarchs, I have never known. Sadly for Katharine, the King's growing conviction that the lack of male children was a sign of God's displeasure at a cursed union coincided with his overpowering lust for Anne Boleyn, who was one of his wife's waiting women. Anne played a clever hand; she assured him she could give him sons, but refused to admit him to her bed until they were man and wife.'

'Clever and brave, not to say foolhardy,' remarks Miss Sutherland.

'But Anne was already pregnant, in fact, when she became Henry's queen in 1533,' Miss Halligan goes on. 'When her daughter Elizabeth was born in September of that year, Henry hoped the healthy child was a sign of better things to come. But, like Katharine before her, Anne could not carry a male child to term. In February of 1536, she miscarried. The more malicious and lurid contemporary accounts say it was a shapeless, formless chunk of flesh. The more charitable and compassionate said the foetus was recognisably male. With it, Anne knew, went her last chance of survival as Henry's queen. One wonders just how soon she understood that as well as losing her crown, she would also lose her life.'

She pauses, looking round at her audience. The other two are, just like Lily, spellbound.

'It was to be a brief three months,' Miss Halligan says softly. 'On the nineteenth of May, Anne ascended the scaffold beside the White Tower and the skilled French swordsman removed her head with one stroke. Her ladies hurried forward, wrapping the body and the severed head in white cloth and taking their tragic burden to the Chapel of St Peter ad Vincula, which lay within the precincts of the Tower of London. No coffin had been supplied, and Anne was put in a chest of elm that had held arrows. The chest was placed in the chancel, close to the recently interred remains of her brother, Lord Rochford.'

'But how could—' Miss Sutherland begins.

'Patience, Dotty.' Miss Halligan puts a hand briefly on her friend's. 'Now, bringing the tale forward by three and a half centuries, six years ago workmen were summoned to inspect the floor of the chapel's chancel. The remains of several bodies were unearthed. Records were consulted, and it was concluded that the placing of one of the bodies – that of a female with gracile bones aged between twenty-five and thirty at the time of death – matched the place of Anne's deposition as described. However, this is not at all certain; the so-called proof was that Catherine Howard, Henry's fifth wife, who suffered the same fate as Anne, was also buried under the chancel, and between them were two men, the Duke of Somerset and the Duke of Northumberland. But many others had also been placed there. Margaret Pole, Countess of Salisbury, five years after Anne; Lady Jane Grey in February 1554; Jane Rochford, wife of Anne's brother George, in 1542.'

Lily has been watching Miss Halligan, very impressed by her ability to rattle off these facts and figures, these names from the far past. She wonders how much of what she has just learned will be available to pass on to Felix later. Not very much, she concludes.

Miss Halligan glances round her audience, and it is as if the calm eyes are quietly summoning her listeners' attention once more. 'But,' she says softly, 'there is a persistent rumour that of these five beheaded female bodies which the workmen had been informed would be there under the floor, only four were present. It was concluded that it was the body of Catherine Howard that was missing.' Again, she looks at the three women listening to her. 'But, really, after more than three hundred years, how on earth could anyone know?'

After a brief, thoughtful silence, Lily says, 'What happened to the four bodies?'

Miss Halligan turns to her. 'The Queen – by which of course I mean Victoria, our present queen – commanded that they be exhumed and re-interred in coffins marked with the identity of the corpse that was believed to be within.'

'And so somewhere beneath the chancel floor in this Chapel of St Peter ad Vincula, there is a coffin that claims to hold the remains of Anne Boleyn?' Miss Adderley, Lily reflects, is a woman who likes a fact to be plainly stated.

'Presumably so,' Miss Halligan agrees. 'Now,' she goes on firmly, 'the remains may very well be those of Anne Boleyn. But did those who found her simply decide the body was hers because they expected it to be – because they expected to find her there? I can see at least two other possibilities. First, Anne was never there in the first place because her relatives, heartsore, grieving, and determined that the Tudors and the state should have no more of her, smuggled her body away. Second, that at some point in time another corpse was substituted, either directly after her death or in 1876.'

After a moment, Dorothea Sutherland says, 'I understood that the Boleyn family home was at Hever, in Kent. Would her family not have taken her there?'

'Hever Castle passed to Henry after Anne's father died in 1539,' Miss Halligan said. 'Admittedly the family were still in possession when Anne was executed, but even the most wildly optimistic of them must have known that the glory days were over. Besides,' she adds prosaically, 'Hever is more than thirty miles from London. A long way to bear a coffin in conditions of utter secrecy.'

Lily has been following a thought of her own. 'May I say something?' she asks.

The women turn as one to stare at her. 'Of course!' Miss Halligan says.

'I was just wondering,' she begins, nervous under their scrutiny, 'if, even given we believe Anne's body could have been removed after her death, it would have been possible to bury it in what is now the Fetterplace siblings' garden.'

Miss Halligan's bright eyes narrow, and she nods her approval. 'Good question,' she remarks. 'And would it?'

Frantically snatching the relevant facts from her memory of what the siblings told her, Lily says, 'There was a definite connection between the Fetterplace ancestors and the Tudor court. An Edmund Fettyplace was courtier to Henry the Seventh, and later descendants served Henry the Eighth and all three of his children. One of these forebears was awarded the house near Tower Hill where the siblings now live.'

'Then we have our answer, surely?' Miss Adderley says. 'We cannot but—'

'Of course!' Lily exclaims. 'I apologise, Miss Adderley, for interrupting you, but it has just occurred to me – the Fetterplace house is in Mary Rose Court, and I may be wrong but wasn't the *Mary Rose* one of Henry the Eighth's ships?'

'She was indeed,' Miss Halligan says. 'Launched in 1511, if memory serves, sank in the Solent in July 1545.'

'You're probably not going to name a newly built row of houses after a ship that's sunk,' Miss Sutherland points out, 'so we may perhaps assume that Mary Rose Court existed in 1536, and that one of the Fetterplace courtiers was in possession of it.' She stops suddenly. 'Or am I making a false connection? Guilty of seeing what I *want* to see?'

'Like those who claimed the body was Anne's because they expected to find it,' murmurs Miss Adderley.

'I think, Dotty,' Miss Halligan says, 'that we are *all* seeing what we want to see. But, goodness me, what a tale this is!'

Miss Adderley pushes her chair back with a loud scrape and says, 'I for one need some more tea! Anyone else?'

As Miss Sutherland gets up to help, Lily finds herself alone at the table with Miss Halligan. Observing that the older woman is deep in thought, Lily keeps quiet.

But then the brief silence is broken.

'Heads,' Agnes muses softly. Turning to look at her, Lily sees that her eyes have glazed sightly. 'They have their own power, you see,' the quiet voice goes on. 'The Druids, the Celts and many other earlier peoples believed in the crucial importance of the head, and, post mortem, the skull.'

Briefly wondering at the relevance of this, Lily thinks: beheadings. The headless skeleton in the rose bed. Of course.

'The Thames was a sacred river,' Miss Halligan says. 'The repository of sacrificial objects, as well as the bodies of the dead, often separated from their heads. And what a place to hide what you wish to conceal! One cannot but wonder how many victims have been quietly disposed of in the Thames' dark and fast-flowing waters.'

'I know a man who regularly fishes out corpses,' Lily remarks. 'His name is Alf Wilson, and he works with the river police at Wapping. He and his men call themselves the Disciples.' Miss Halligan smiles. 'I asked him once if many people fall in and drown, and he said practically everyone who falls in drowns. He told me the bodies receive such a battering that frequently they are in pieces by the time Alf and the Disciples fish them out.'

'As we were just observing,' Miss Halligan comments. 'The Thames is a good place to discard a body.'

That, Lily thinks, is just what Alf Wilson says.

Miss Halligan is looking at her with new interest. 'What a fascinating life you lead, Miss Raynor,' she murmurs.

We have been to dark places, Lily thinks as the four of them make short work of the fresh pot of tea. She is quite relieved when, putting her cup down, Miss Halligan announces that it is time for her to leave.

FIVE

Felix and Lily stand in the outer office. It is late: darkness fell some time ago, and the moon has not yet risen. Felix has dressed in warm clothes, and wears his big old topcoat as an outer layer. It is in a shade of grey almost indistinguishable from black. He also has a thick black scarf and a woolly cap that is capacious enough to pull down over his eyebrows. He is wearing his stout boots, his vesta case is in his pocket and the bull's-eye lantern stands ready by the door.

He wishes he didn't feel so apprehensive.

I'm not apprehensive, he confesses to himself. I'm scared.

He has been trying to hide it from Lily, but he fears she knows him too well. She has just said, with a pretence at a light, casual tone, 'Of course, there's no need for you to do this unless you really think it's necessary.'

The trouble is that he *does* think it's necessary, and so does she. Until one of them finally inspects the skeleton with their own eyes, there can be no way forward.

It was nice of her to make the comment, though.

As he checks the oil level in the lantern yet again, she says, 'I've been thinking about what you heard Miss Fetterplace say to her brother, about their father's papers.'

He manages a smile. 'It was actually the other way round; he was speaking to her. He said they must be *absolutely sure* not to mention Father's papers.'

'There you are, then!' Her voice is too bright. 'It's probably nothing! All this sense of mystery and dark deeds is because they're trying to get away with a minor fraud of some sort, and they don't want you calling in unannounced and snooping around.'

He bites down the obvious comment that they wouldn't be hiding evidence of fraud out in the rose bed, which was the location they *really* didn't want him to investigate. She is doing her best, he thinks. He is flooded with a surge of emotion, which is no help at all just now.

'Perhaps,' he says kindly. 'But they are afraid, Lily. They are so afraid.'

And, he thinks as he opens the front door and steps out into the night, there is only one way that he and Lily can begin on the long road to finding out why.

Trams run less frequently at this time of night, and Felix has quite a long wait for the first leg of his transport to Tower Hill and his late-night return to the wilderness of garden behind number 8, Mary Rose Court. When finally he reaches his destination and is lurking in the darkness between the gas lamps in Great Tower Street, he considers his options.

His initial plan is to walk along the Court and turn left down the narrow passage between the two terraces of houses, then turn right and locate the section of wall behind number 8. He has understood from Miss Fetterplace's description that the residents of Mary Rose Court are ageing gentlefolk who turn in early, and so he is disconcerted not only to find several houses showing lights, but one where the guests leaving some evening entertainment are standing on the doorstep, still chattering brightly and showing no signs of imminent dispersal.

He retraces his steps. Returning to Barking Lane, he turns right, and then follows the boundary of All Hallows until he finds a place where he can climb over; he does not use the wicket gate he found earlier because it is situated right under a street lamp. Then he hurries between the forest of ancient gravestones and across the grass until he is under the rear wall of the churchyard. Number 8 is three houses along from the central passage; locating it after quite a long search – the whole area is wildly overgrown and, remembering those talkative guests, he is reluctant to uncover the bright light of his lantern – he thinks he has the right place.

He levers himself up into the lower branches of an alder growing right by the wall. He is behind the house two along from the central passage: number 7. Straddling the wall – which, since the land slopes down towards the river, is alarmingly high above the ground on the churchyard side – he shuffles along to the next-door garden.

For several long moments he sits and listens. He thinks he can make out voices, some way away. There is the faint sound of hansom cabs driving away.

Then all is quiet.

He waits some more.

He realises with dismay that he is afraid.

It is a haunted spot. It is so close to Tower Hill, and the brutal scaffold where so many men and women met their deaths. Knowing even as he did so that it was not a good idea, this morning Felix had looked up the history of the Tower Hill scaffold in one of Lily's huge reference books, discovering that the last public execution was in 1747, the victim someone called Simon Fraser, the Lord Lovat.

Only a century and a half ago, Felix thinks now . . .

There isn't a sound on the chilly autumnal air. Slow swirls of mist have begun to rise up from the grass.

And that stench that he detected yesterday still lingers. Only faintly, but nevertheless it is an awful smell: rotten, suggestive of decomposition, of maggot-ridden flesh.

He turns his mind away from thoughts of death and looks up at the house. It's definitely the right one; he can make out its neighbours to the right, and beyond them, the dark and narrow little passage between the two terraces. Looking down, he can see straight away where the rose bed has been dug over. Apart from anything else, it is the only part of the long garden that is free from the stranglehold of vigorous weeds. Someone has left a spade stuck in the loose soil, and to the left the burned circle indicates the location of the bonfire.

He sits quite still, reflecting on how the clearing of the old rose bed has only served to show up what an unkept, tangled mess covers the rest of the large garden.

He knows he is postponing the next move. Telling himself that the sooner he gathers his nerve and gets on with the task he has come here to do, the sooner he can get away, he pushes himself forward off the wall and jumps down into the soft earth of the rose bed.

Now that he is on the ground, he appreciates that the greenery running rampant through the garden rises higher than he had thought. He can no longer see the ground floor windows of number 8, so, unless someone upstairs decides to part the heavy curtains and fold back the shutters, it is safe to use the bull's-eye lantern for some badly needed illumination. He opens the little shutter and, enhanced by the thick glass of the lens, the beam of light shoots out. He looks up anxiously at the house, but the upper windows are still black. He reassures himself that the Fetterplace siblings look like the sort of people who shut themselves firmly up at night; fearing that any slight movement of air to improve the atmosphere in the bedchamber would lead swiftly and directly to terminal pneumonia, they probably make a habit of drawing the curtains tightly as soon as dusk begins to fall. They probably nailed up the window frames decades ago.

Pointing the light down at the ground, slowly he shines it along the length and width of the rose bed.

The skeleton is in a depression at the far end, some three feet below ground level and covered lightly with loose earth.

Felix's initial impression is that it must have been a lengthy task for Thomas Fetterplace to dig such a huge hole. And he's hardly a young man. Following on instantly from this comes the worrying thought that it must have taken something quite extraordinary to prompt the old man to embark on so arduous and demanding a task.

Just for an instant, Felix has the strange sense that he has *become* Thomas Fetterplace, and he recognises that what is driving him on is fear.

Very firmly, Felix dismisses that troubling illusion.

He sets the base of the lantern in the soil so that the beam of light fans out into the depression. With both hands free, he brushes off the covering of earth and begins a thorough examination of the skeleton, from its truncated upper spine to the delicate little feet. The bones are slight and quite small. He works through them: collarbones, ribs, radius and ulna, humerus, femur, tibia, fibula. So far, so good.

Although he is all but sure the skeleton is that of a woman, now he concentrates on trying to view the bones with impartial eyes. The remains of a small, slim woman might well look quite similar to those of a boy, he reminds himself. Among his preparations for this night's work, he asked Lily if there was a way of distinguishing male from female skeletons, and she gave him some pointers. Now, as he begins a closer examination of the body in the earth, he senses Lily's warm, friendly presence beside him, and instantly he feels better. Just for a moment.

She told him to check the pelvis, describing how the shape was different in the two sexes. The skeleton before him has a wide, roughly oval opening. A woman's, then?

Lily also told him to check the brow ridges.

Which, of course, means inspecting the head. Which is no longer attached to the body but lying a short distance apart.

In a brief and violent instant out of place and time, suddenly he *knows* what it means to have your head cut from your body. To kneel there in the straw which will absorb your blood, trying to stop the terrible, terrified trembling, praying that the rustling sound that abruptly breaks the hushed silence means the swordsman is sliding his weapon out from where he has concealed it from your horrified eyes. Praying that the *whoosh* of something heavy whistling through the air is the blade's sharp, bright edge aimed straight at the back of your neck; that the split-second of hot, white, pure burning agony will be over in a heartbeat . . .

Felix returns to himself. He is shaking all over, and sweat has broken out over his torso.

He crouches there for a few moments, waiting for his heart to stop its frantic pounding.

Then he checks that his hands are steady and reaches down to the pale dome just visible beside the skeleton. He cleans off the loose soil and, his touch gentle and reverential, he raises the skull. He has had to fight his reluctance; checking over the bones was relatively easy, and concentrating on remembering their names helped him to keep his emotions under control. But that was before, he thinks; before that ghastly image of horror that has just taken over his mind.

He is not at all sure he can manage such a degree of self-possession any more . . .

Now he is holding the head in his hands. The seat of the mind, and also the place that bore the face. This, he reflects, is the part of the body most personal to whoever once inhabited it.

He gazes at the skull.

It is beautiful. The brow ridges are almost flat, the nasal bones are narrow, the cheekbones are high and gently rounded, the chin is small, pointed and perfectly shaped.

This was a woman. Without any doubt at all, he *knows* it was. He can almost picture her. She was daintily made and very lovely. He imagines a small mouth above that pretty little chin; she is smiling, such a mischievous, intelligent, amused smile, as if she has just thought of the funniest, silliest prank to play on some unsuspecting companion.

He stares into the empty eye sockets, imagining dark eyes that glitter with laughter.

He wonders how long ago she died. Looking down, he can see the remnants of cloth that Thomas Fetterplace described. His obliging mind turns them into a deep-sleeved gown with a long, sweeping train and a high-collared cloak lined with fur. He nudges the lantern slightly, and the light flickers off something that gleams. It is a length of gold chain; it is fine – fit for a long, slender neck – but its weight speaks of high value.

And there, shining like three more tiny full moons in the real moon's light, are the little pearls.

They are perfect.

Reverentially he picks one up, turning it over in the beam of the lantern. He knows it is real, but remembering being told once long ago how to make quite sure, he wipes it thoroughly and rubs it against one of his front teeth. Its surface feels gritty.

Still turning the pearl over in his fingers, he touches something that interrupts its smooth roundness. It is a small circle of gold; the sort of fitting that allows a pearl to be suspended from a chain.

Or a golden letter B.

Again, the thought seems to come to him of its own volition.

He places the pearl back with the other two, arranging the length of chain beside them.

He is still holding the skull in his other hand. The eye sockets are empty now; that sudden sense of the presence of the living, breathing, laughing woman has gone. With infinite tenderness he places it back where it belongs, carefully aligning it with the severed bones of the neck.

He looks at the cut for some time.

He has read of executions. He has been horrified by the descriptions of axemen having to make several attempts before the head was off. He has always hoped that the poor victim would be unconscious after the first one.

Still studying the severed neck, he knows this woman was not killed by some clumsy oaf who needed two, three or four swings of the axe. The delicate bones of her neck were efficiently and cleanly severed with a single cut.

He stands up, more shaken than he likes to admit. He replaces the soil covering, arranging it over her as if it was a soft blanket. He steps out of the rose bed, brushing the dirt off his hands and knees, then picks up his lantern.

He stands quite still for a moment. 'Goodbye, pretty lady,' he says very softly.

Then he places the lantern on top of the wall, scrambles up after it and, closing its shutter to cut the light, recovers his breath before jumping down into the churchyard.

He lands awkwardly a yard or so out from the wall, in the long grass of the churchyard. He is all at once deeply and overwhelmingly afraid. Straightening up, he reaches back to collect his lantern. He knows it is unwise to show a light, but he cannot help himself: he opens the little shutter and the warm, golden beam shines out.

His terror recedes, but only fractionally.

He is still in the grip of *knowing* that something is lurking; even as he was jumping down from the wall, he sensed its presence. Something has changed since he climbed the wall and entered the Fetterplace garden. Something is there now that wasn't there before. It is dark, malign, and he feels its cold, pitiless consciousness brush against his own. He tries to chide himself for his fancies. 'Stop being an over-imaginative fool!' he mutters.

His words die on the air as if something has greedily sucked them in.

The silence of deep night returns, but as he stands there, ears straining, he can sense once more that strange scratching that is half a sound, half a sensation perceived in the skin. It is profoundly alarming.

He stares out into the deserted graveyard. At first all he can see in the moonlit grass are the haphazard gravestones.

His eyes rake over the scene, one way and then back again. He looks along the path that runs along the foot of the wall, first to the right, then to the left.

Something has changed . . .

Yes. He has it now. There is a large object in a place where before there was nothing but the faint outline of the rough track. It is in shadow, and hard to make out. It looks like a barrow. Its long handles point up at an angle at the back. But a dark shape, like a bundle of sticks, blurs the outline of the handles, as if whatever was thrown into the barrow was too big to be contained and had spilled out to the rear.

A stab of pure fear runs through him.

He tries to reassure himself. It's the sexton's barrow, he thinks. Left here with his tools, ready for an early start tomorrow morning.

Then why didn't I see it earlier, before I clambered over the wall to get into the garden?

He takes a step towards the barrow. It is as if he has suddenly become very heavy, with legs of solid metal and stone weights on his feet. He can hardly move.

And there, just for a second, right before him stands the figure of a man. Dark clad, standing in the deep shadow, and a flash of light so brief that he might have imagined it.

The figure vanishes.

Slowly, so slowly, Felix approaches the barrow. Stops.

Several impressions assault his senses all at once. A sight . . . something he can't interpret as it appears and disappears several times in rapid succession, as if a light was flashing on and off, never on for long enough for him to make sense of what he is seeing. A smell . . . butcher's shop smell, hot, heavy with iron. A touch . . . something brushes against his outstretched hand, something wet and very cold. For the briefest of moments, the white oval of a face, the nose and mouth obscured, and the top half bisected by the shallow black vee of heavy eyebrows. A sound . . . very close behind him, a weighty object that whistles as it flies through the air.

In his mind's eye he sees an axe swinging down.

But no, his wild thoughts cry silently, that was the skeleton, and anyway it was no crude axe blow that severed the head but a sword, expertly wielded by a highly skilled executioner and . . .

Then, just like that, everything stops.

There is nothing.

Some hours later, as the bright moon starts to slide down the western sky, a man is scuttling through the graveyard of All Hallows. He is heading for home, and taking a familiar route where experience tells him he is very unlikely to be seen. He really doesn't want to be seen. His business is his own, and he does not welcome others' interest.

He runs along behind the northernmost graves, dodging occasionally round those that are out of alignment. He tries not to look up to his left, to the overgrown grass and the gnarled old shrubs that grow beneath the boundary wall. Something lurks up there in the shadows. He would not go anywhere near the haunted, accursed spot if it wasn't for the powerful need to keep his movements hidden.

The more lurid of the rumours press for his attention. He pushes them to the back of his mind. 'Home, hurry on home,' he murmurs, his teeth chattering from a mixture of cold and dread.

Then, as yet again his disobedient eyes turn in the one direction he really doesn't want them to, he sees a dark shape.

It lies at the foot of the church wall.

Go on. Run for home, pretend you didn't see anything, he orders himself. None of your business, you don't want to go over there poking your nose in, you don't know what'll happen if you're seen.

The dark rumours see their chance and flow back into his mind.

He is on the point of tucking his chin into his chest and hurrying on his way. But just at that moment the clock of All Hallows Church strikes the hour: one, two, three, four.

And the man's conscience wakes up.

He has attended services in All Hallows. Not very often, but enough to keep alive the sense beaten into him in childhood of a vengeful Old Testament God who is ever watchful, who spots every example of unchristian behaviour and punishes it. 'Vengeance is mine, saith the Lord, and I will repay,' the man mutters to himself.

Forcing every single step, he walks slowly across the unkempt grass to the churchyard wall. The object lying beside the little path is a body. Beside it is a lantern, on its side. The man touches it: the glass is cold, the flame long extinguished.

He kneels down beside the body. It is big, tall, broad: a man. His clothes are good quality, and he wears a heavy topcoat, now soaked with dew. Bending forward, he puts the back of his hand to the motionless face. That too is cold.

This fellow's dead, he thinks. Nothing I can do for him. He straightens up and hurries away.

He has managed to reach the wicket gate that gives onto Barking Lane when the vengeful God comes back. This time the bearded face wears a thunderous expression, and a huge hand extends a forefinger that shakes with rage.

And, perhaps prompted by this furious celestial vision, the man experiences a sudden strange moment of compassion. Whoever lies there dead under the wall had been a fellow night owl, a companion in the darkness. Should his corpse be left there in the grass, wet, cold and abandoned?

The man wrestles with his better self for some time. Then he trots along to the lamp post on the corner, where there is often a night watchman. There is indeed someone standing there now, stamping his feet and muttering.

The man approaches him, scarf around his lower face, hat pulled down. At least, he reflects, let me keep my identity to myself.

'Body, up under the wall, top of the graveyard,' he mutters. He waves an arm in the right direction.

'Body?' repeats the night watchman dubiously. He is very tall, skeletally thin, and he feels the cold. Huddling into his thick coat, he gives an ostentatious shiver. 'You sure?' He grins. 'It's a graveyard, mate. Dozens a' bodies.'

'This one's not in a grave, he's lying on the path,' the man insists.

The night watchman's face still has its disbelieving expression. He sniffs audibly. 'You been drinking?' he demands.

The Skeleton in the Rose Bed 59

The man tries one last time. 'There's a body,' he insists. 'You're an officer of the watch. *Do* something!'

Then he turns and flees.

The night watchman is almost at the end of his shift. He really doesn't want to go investigating this unlikely tale of a body on the path under the wall. Especially given which wall it is: he too has heard the frightening rumours. He is strongly tempted to pretend that he hasn't just been told about this corpse. But two things persuade him: first, he has already been given a warning for failing to meet the high standards expected of the officers of the night watch, and second, he is so chilled and so bored that any activity is better than none.

He strides down to the wicket gate, enters the churchyard and hurries off across the grass. He veers off to the right, joining the path beneath the wall and following it until he spots the dark shape lying beside it. Crouching down, wheezing with the effort, he puts a hand inside the coat and under the jacket, feeling around for a pocket containing a wallet or some document that might reveal the corpse's identity.

His expression suddenly changes.

And, as if he has just been slapped, he jerks into action.

SIX

In the early morning quiet of an autumn Sunday, Lily is dreaming. She is in a narrow passage with high, unbroken brick walls on either side. There is someone else moving along the passage. She hears the sound of hoofbeats and the regular squeak of a wheel that needs oiling. But then in the way of dreams the image breaks up and she is in her Derbyshire grandmother's large kitchen eating a huge slice of gingerbread. Her grandmother stands over a bent and beaten old oven tray and she has a toffee hammer in her hand.

A hand is shaking Lily's shoulder, vigorously and persistently. 'Miss Raynor! *Miss Raynor!* You must wake up, for someone's knocking at the door!'

Lily opens her eyes. Dorothea Sutherland is leaning over her, woollen dressing gown wrapped close around her, its belt in a tight knot. Her bobbed grey hair is flattened on the left side of her head and her face looks naked without her glasses.

'The door?' Lily says, her mind still in her grandmother's kitchen. 'It'll be one of the lads, wanting his breakfast . . .'

Then her brain slips into gear. She knows where she is and the identity of the woman who has just woken her. The absence of traffic and people noise combined with the first faint hints of pale grey lightening the darkness prompt her to recall that it is Sunday morning. And very early.

'What time is it?' she mutters, reaching for her gold watch.

'Five and twenty to six,' Miss Sutherland says, just as Lily's eyes register what the watch hands are telling her.

And now whoever is knocking on the street door renews their efforts. Abruptly remembering that she has neighbours, Lily throws back the bedcovers, reaches for her dressing gown, slips her feet in her slippers and races for the stairs.

She jumps down the final three steps of the lower staircase and runs to the street door. Beset by a fear she cannot let herself think about, she fumbles with the lock and hears it turn. The door won't open. Through the threatening panic, Miss Sutherland says quietly, 'The bolts,' and reaches out to the top one even as Lily slides back the one at the bottom.

Flinging the door wide, she sees on the top step a beanpole of a man huddled in a heavy coat, anxious eyes staring at her from under a wide hat brim. Behind him on the street there is a cart with a bay horse in the shafts. A second, much bulkier man sits crouched on the cart bed.

'Got your Mister Raynor,' the man says in a hoarse whisper. 'On the cart?' he adds on a note of enquiry when she doesn't answer.

'Mr *Raynor*?' she manages to ask.

'Mr Raynor, of three, Hob's Court,' the man insists. 'This *is* Hob's Court?' Now anxiety and embarrassment are added to confusion in his long, bony face.

'Yes, number three,' Lily confirms. 'My grandfather used to live here, but he is dead.'

The skinny man frowns. 'What was his name?'

'Abraham Raynor. He was a pharmacist,' she adds, although cannot for the life of her think why.

The thin man shakes his head. 'No, the initial's L,' he says. 'L. G. And he's a private investigator of this add—'

Then Lily understands. And the fear comes thundering back, so strong now that she feels her legs shake.

When she started her business, she had cards printed. She can still remember how proud it made her to read the brief details:

World's End Bureau
3, Hob's Court, Chelsea
PRIVATE ENQUIRY AGENCY
Proprietor: L. G. Raynor

Only two people carry these cards.

Pushing the skinny man out of the way, deaf to his alarmed 'Steady there, miss!', Lily flies down the steps and round to the back of the cart. The crouching man looks up, meets her eyes. He doesn't exactly shake his head, but she senses he wants to.

He leans back slightly, revealing the long, dark-clad shape that his upper body has been concealing. The shape whose legs hang unmoving over the edge of the cart bed. Lily takes one brief look at the deathly white face and feels a silent moan of grief well up inside her.

She must have made some small sound, for the bulky man says swiftly, 'He's not dead. Very gravely injured, but he breathes and the heartbeat is steadier than one would expect.' He is studying her closely, and she recognises professional interest; he is a doctor, she thinks in a detached part of her mind, and he wants to know if I'm taking this terrible news calmly or if I'm about to faint.

'I am Lily Raynor,' she says. Her voice is cool and steady. 'This' – she indicates Felix's still body, and now fainting seems a distinct possibility – 'is Felix Wilbraham.'

'He is employed by this World's End Bureau?' The bulky man clearly likes to get his facts straight.

Lily nods. 'Yes.'

She seems to have frozen. Her body won't move and she can't think what to do next.

The bulky man smiles kindly. 'The name's March, Benedict March. I'm a doctor, and I live on Tower Hill. He' – he nods towards the skinny man, who has crept back down the steps – 'is one of the regular night watchmen, and this is by no means the first time he's summoned me to a victim of violence.' Lily fumbles for the right response, but Dr March has no time for social niceties. 'We must get the patient inside,' he says in the sort of voice nobody argues with, 'for he is very cold, he has lost a lot of blood, and although I did what I could for him at the place of the attack, I now need light, hot water, somewhere to lay him flat and, preferably, the assistance of a skilled nurse, although I imagine I'll have to do without that unless you happen to have such a person lurking in your basement.'

He is moving into efficient action as he speaks, positioning the skinny night watchman at Felix's feet and shuffling round so that he can lift the head and shoulders. When Lily tells him quietly that she is a trained nurse, he smiles very briefly and nods. Lily steps forward and places her hands under Felix's hips, and together, slowly and gently, the three of them slide him off the cart and up the steps. Miss Sutherland has already propped the door fully open, and now she takes up a position opposite

Lily, taking her share of Felix's considerable weight, and they all shuffle to the foot of the stairs.

'Where to?' pants the doctor.

'Top floor,' Lily says firmly.

She has already worked it out. Felix is going to need a great deal of nursing if he is to recover – she has utterly shut her mind to any alternative outcome – and her large, airy rooms on the second floor will provide the necessary space and quiet.

Trying to protect the inert body from hitting walls, banisters or newel posts, the mismatched quartet carry Felix to the top of the house. Bernice Adderley has not been idle; she seems to have grasped the situation, and when the doctor, the night watchman, Miss Sutherland and Lily finally carry Felix into Lily's bedroom, Lily notes that the bed has been neatly made, the covers turned back in a perfect triangle, the pillows plumped, and all the giveaway signs that the bed and its immediate surroundings were very recently occupied by a woman have been discreetly tucked out of sight. Risking one swift, anxious glance at the wash hand stand, Lily gives a sigh of relief as she spots that the stockings and drawers she rinsed out last night and hung on the towel rail are no longer visible.

She catches Miss Adderley's concerned face and mouths, *Thank you*.

For the next unknowable amount of time, Lily has far too much to fill her mind to worry about personal linen drying on a towel rail. Her two tenants, far from exhibiting annoyance at being so rudely awoken and complaining about not expecting *this* sort of thing in a respectable house, have efficiently carried out the requests that Dr March has barked out. Between them they have arranged a steady supply of hot water – no mean feat when the fire in the range would have needed stoking to full heat and the heavy cans of water then borne up two flights of stairs – and some intelligent searching through the linen closet on the middle landing has resulted in a stack of clean towels and tea towels.

Lily has taken in her tenants' activities at the very corner of her mind; the remainder of her attention is on Felix's awful wound, and Dr March's skilled hands as he sets about treating it. Lily decided after the first couple of minutes that no better saviour could have been found, for it is clear that Benedict March knows exactly what he is doing. In a brief pause as he and Lily stop to stretch their backs – her bed is far from ideal as an operating table – she says as much, and with a brief grimace he mutters that he served as an army doctor for twenty years. 'I've seen more head wounds than you could shake a stick at.'

Then they go back to work.

Lily, still in her nightdress and dressing gown, sits in one of the armchairs in the sitting room next to her bedroom. Dr March occupies the other one. They have just drunk two cups of tea apiece, and already cleared the tray of sandwiches, small sponge cakes and shortbread that Mrs Clapper brought up to them ten minutes ago. 'Nothing like high drama,' Dr March observes as he shoves the last little cake whole into his mouth, 'for sharpening the appetite.'

While Lily and Dr March devour their refreshments, Bernice Adderley is sitting with Felix.

He is still unconscious.

Lily is trying not to think about that. Dr March has told her that it is only to be expected after such a vicious blow to the skull, and Lily knows from her own experience that the profound sleep of deep unconsciousness is the body's way of healing itself.

She is also fighting to shut out images of Felix's utter stillness and the blue-white pallor of his almost translucent flesh.

She notices that Dr March is looking at her. 'Good woman, your housekeeper,' he remarks lightly. 'Does she always come in on a Sunday?'

Lily, aware that he knows exactly what she is trying not to think about and is attempting to distract her, says, 'Not usually, no. She goes to church on Sunday mornings, but I expect she thought God would understand that she was needed here. She is very fond of Felix,' she adds, and the simple little statement temporarily undermines her.

'The lady with the mannish hair and the alarmingly intelligent eyes went to fetch her, I gather,' Dr March remarks.

Lily finds herself smiling at the description. 'Miss Sutherland,' she says. 'Yes, she very sensibly decided we could all do with Mrs Clapper's ministrations.'

There is a brief silence.

Lily tries hard not to revert to thinking about Felix, but finds she can't stop herself. 'What happened?' she says very softly, as if she doesn't want Felix to hear. 'What do you know?'

Dr March sighs. 'Not very much,' he replies. 'The night watchman – his name is Billy Simpson – was approached by a man who said he'd found a body. Simpson went to check and found Mr Wilbraham's unconscious body. He believed that— er, that life was extinct. He felt inside the coat for some personal item that might contain a clue to the body's identity and found a wallet. To his amazement he thought he detected warmth. Believing this might mean the corpse still had life in it, he hurried to seek me out. When he finally got round to checking inside the wallet, he found the card with your name and address.'

'And you brought Felix here,' Lily murmurs.

'Billy Simpson was in a bad state when he came to find me,' Dr March is saying, 'and it was hard to make much sense of his incoherent ramblings.'

'Well, he had just found an inert and badly wounded body,' Lily says.

Dr March shoots her a sharp glance. 'He's used to finding the victims of violence. It is part and parcel of his job.' Perhaps sensing he has spoken too harshly, he says more gently, 'He was afraid, Miss Raynor. Terrified. Something had scared him badly, and he was still in shock when he came to my door.' He pauses. 'It was brave of him to have returned to the bod— to your friend,' he corrects himself quickly. 'It took a lot of courage, and he was shaking all over when we reached the spot.'

'Where was this?'

'Underneath an old wall that divides the churchyard of All Hallows from a residential street. The gardens of the houses back onto the churchyard.'

'Mary Rose Court,' Lily murmurs.

'You know it, then,' Dr March says. He meets her eyes, quickly looking away. 'An unsavoury spot,' he mutters. 'Bad air.'

'Bad *air*?' she echoes. She is reminded of the belief of early medical men that disease was caused by foul miasmas.

Dr March is shaking his head. 'I don't know why I said that, for it is hardly a scientific term.' He tries to smile but fails. Then he says in a rush, 'It was a *foul* place. I smelt blood, and also a faint but distinct stench of putrefaction. Either could have been caused by a dead animal – a fox's kill, for example, for there are plenty of both foxes and their small prey in the grounds of All Hallows.' He stops. Then he says very quietly, 'But for a fox to kill a rabbit or a vole is part of the natural world. And what I felt on that path under the ancient wall was . . . there is no other word for it. It was evil.'

There is a brief, tense silence.

Then Lily says, 'Could he . . . is it possible that the injury could have been caused by Felix banging the back of his skull on the wall? If he'd fallen, for example?' Dr March is already shaking his head, but she presses on. 'You see, he had to get into the garden of one of the houses in Mary Rose Court. We are conducting an investigation at the request of—' She remembers client confidentiality and stops. 'Felix's intention was to search under cover of darkness, and in order to maintain a secret approach, he would have climbed over the wall.'

'Instead of knocking on the front door,' Dr March says. 'Yes, Miss Raynor, I understand.'

'Well, what if he slipped and fell?'

The doctor looks at her, his expression kindly. 'Miss Raynor, the head wound was caused by a wooden object. You *know* this,' he adds with sudden passion. 'I am sorry to remind you, but you picked the splinters out of it. If he had banged his head on the wall, there might have been fragments of stone, although in any case the angle was wrong for it to have happened that way.' He frowns. 'Someone crept up behind him, or perhaps rose up out of a hiding place, swung a very heavy wooden object with great force and caught Mr Wilbraham on the back of his crown. Over the occipital lobe, as no doubt you will recall from your anatomy classes.'

'There are trees growing along the wall, and . . .' She pauses.

'*No*, Miss Raynor,' he says firmly. 'Your colleague was attacked. Apart from the head wound, he has sustained extensive bruising to the ribs and the lower back. Probably at least one rib broken or fractured,' he adds, more to himself, 'although there is no more I can do than bind him, and let nature do the rest.' He frowns slightly.

'But if he fell, he could have damaged his ribs!' Lily cries.

'Those bruises were caused by a foot in a stout boot,' Dr March says firmly. 'Whoever the attacker was – and I would put money on his being a man – he felled your friend, almost certainly thought he had killed him, and so we may well adjudge that the kicks were from sheer brutality. From rage, perhaps?' he continues. 'Possibly Mr Wilbraham disturbed someone engaged on a task he preferred to keep to himself; some task that we may surmise gave him satisfaction of some kind? I smelt blood and rotting flesh; possibly our man traps animals and enjoys observing their suffering? That is of course only conjecture, although to my mind it could explain the fury that was behind not only the blow to the head, but those savage kicks to the torso: our man was up to something dirty, or shameful, and undoubtedly illegal, and then your colleague popped up and spoiled the night's fun.'

'Fun?' she whispers.

'My apologies, Miss Raynor,' he says instantly. 'I was being thoughtlessly insensitive.'

You were, she thinks. But, reflecting that the doctor's skill and experience with near-fatal wounds has probably saved Felix's life, she doesn't say it aloud.

Silence falls, as if both of them have all at once run out of things to say. Lily realises that she is exhausted; also, that she has not yet washed and dressed, let alone undone her hair from its night-time plait and arranged it properly. And, just as she becomes aware of her unkempt state, she hears footsteps on the stairs. There is a tap on the door and Mrs Clapper says in a penetrating whisper, 'Miss Lily? Are you there?'

'Yes, Mrs Clapper,' Lily replies. She is, she reflects with a small smile, hardly likely to be anywhere else. 'Come in.'

Mrs Clapper notices the tray with its empty plates and cups, and gives a nod of satisfaction. 'I'll take that down with me,' she says. 'Miss Lily, I wouldn't have come up except there's someone downstairs, and he's very eager to see . . .' She jerks her head towards Lily's bedroom. 'Told him I'd come and ask,' she says, her voice thick with emotion.

'Who is it, Mrs Clapper?' Lily thinks she knows, but, since he is the very person whose presence she would most fervently wish for, she hardly dares hope she is right.

'That Miss Adderley went to tell him,' Mrs Clapper is saying. 'Says she reckoned he'd want to know, then he insisted on coming back here with her, and now he . . .'

More footsteps echo on the stairs and come hurrying across the landing. The tread is even heavier than Mrs Clapper's, and she is by no means light on her feet.

Lily is already at the door when it is opened.

Marm Smithers is white-faced from shock and the lines on his face are as deep as chasms.

Lily manages to say, 'He's not dead, Marm. He hasn't regained consciousness, and he is very badly wounded, but he is still alive. He's *still with us.*'

Then Marm gives a strangled sound and opens his arms, and Lily falls against his chest and into a hug so tight that she can scarcely draw breath. She can hear herself sobbing – great gulping sounds that come up from somewhere deep inside her – but she doesn't try to stop. She is also well aware that she is hardly dressed to receive company, but that doesn't seem to matter either. She can feel Marm's thin frame shaking, and guesses that emotion has overtaken him too.

Presently she hears Benedict March make some comment about it being healthy to give vent to the tension and the distress of the past few hours, and that sweet tea is what is needed.

And Mrs Clapper says in a remarkably sanguine tone, given the circumstances, 'I'd better make a fresh pot, then.'

The Barrow Man sits concealed in one of his riverside hiding places, legs drawn up to his chest, head resting on one bony knee. The sun is struggling to evade the gathering clouds. He thinks it will rain soon, but for now the weather is fine.

He is thinking about disposal.

For there is always the problem of disposal.

It has ever been the case. In his boyhood home, there was a small patch of garden that went with the cottage, although, like everything else, it was under the tight and rigid control of his fierce father. But the cottage belonged to a large estate – his father worked for the extremely wealthy and dissolute man who owned it – and so there had also been access to fields, woodlands, tracks and secret pathways, as well as an enchanting little chalk stream and a long stretch of canal bank. To his child's eyes, the land ran on for ever.

Then, the difficulty was not the spiriting away of the remains, but the ever-present necessity of evading the perpetually intrusive eyes of those who had the care of him.

Quite often the intrusive eyes belonged to the very wealthy man. He had a title – he was a marquess – and there had once been a wife, although after a while she did not inhabit the Big House any more. The marquess liked to watch nature, he told the child who lived in the cottage. He liked to feel the cool water of the chalk stream on his naked flesh, he explained when the boy came across him in the shallows without his clothes on. And it was good for the body and the soul, he said to the burgeoning adolescent with the first downy hairs on his chest, to give way to natural appetites just as the birds and the bees and all wild creatures did.

His father was a *very* angry man. The humiliations and petty cruelties that had been heaped upon him in his lowly state had been passed on down the line to his wife and son, and they were always magnified considerably in the process. In short, he was a sadist and a domestic tyrant.

He was also a religious fanatic. The long hours of his working life belonged to the marquess, but his evenings and nights belonged to himself, and in these times he pored endlessly over the Old Testament, committing to memory vast chunks of Genesis, Deuteronomy, Leviticus and the rest, so that he had a quotation – usually an extensive one – for every occasion. The fundamentalist order in which he was a preacher was obscure and had few members, but its adherents all swore an oath to raise their sons – daughters did not count – in total accord with the order's tight and unforgiving doctrines.

The boy that he had been could not turn to his mother as a refuge from his father's harsh regime. She worked as under housemaid up at the Big House and, apart from the fact that she was exhausted at the end of each day and in no mood to bear witness to her only son's distress, she was in any case too afraid of her husband to have risked his wrath by comforting her child.

When he was almost fifteen years old, on the fulcrum of the change from child to young man, his mother died.

The boy knew his father had killed her.

He would have told them how and when, and probably why, except nobody asked him.

All at once he was hurled out of his childhood and the only home he had ever known, expelled from the freedom of the great estate, the secret ways through the woods, the silent, slow waters of the canal which had always held out the tantalising promise of escape.

He found himself in a prestigious college in a Wiltshire town, and it was some time before he discovered that this very costly education was funded by the wealthy man. The marquess's conscience appeared to have prompted him into this uncharacteristically altruistic gesture: he had been carrying on a rather diverting flirtation with his comely under housemaid, and when her husband found out that she had sat on the wealthy man's lap and let him fondle her, he beat her to death with the flat iron she was using on his worn old shirts.

Like the boy, the wealthy man too could have told them how, when and why the woman had died. But when they came to ask him if he could shed any light on her death, he had a wall of very expensive lawyers standing before him and quite soon the questions ceased.

A certain notoriety, however, attached to the case. The wealthy man decided it would be better for the boy to have a fresh start untainted by the recent past. Accordingly, when the boy was enrolled in the college, the name by which he had been known for fourteen years was quietly put aside and he became Hubert Percy Godwin.

He had not told anybody about the marquess's love of the natural world and all its aspects. He was keeping that dirty little secret to himself. For the moment.

The boy now known as Hubert Godwin had absorbed much from his years in the local primary school. The well-learned lessons in how to stop the victims of his bullying from telling tales, how to subtly put the blame on others when one of his experiments left awkward evidence, and how to keep a bland, serene expression on his face while his thoughts turned to savagery, now served him well, and for a time he relished the new freedom. There was a sudden and steep upward curve in his range of experiments, for the school was very well equipped, with up-to-date laboratories affording access to instruments and chemicals never available before. And, by the most delicious irony, those who taught him observed his enthusiasm and, gratified by it, *encouraged* him.

If only, he often thinks now, they had known.

In biology they actually *taught* dissection. The Barrow Man has vivid and enduring memories of the rabbit pinned out on the board, its belly slit and splayed open to reveal the internal organs; the frog whose nerve had to be stimulated to make its foot jerk. Duplicating those experiments alone at night, his confidence grew rapidly as he moved to larger and larger creatures.

And larger creatures, of course, meant that he had to dispose of a steadily increasing mass of skin, bone, slippery internal organs and putrefying flesh. The stress of finding a way of smuggling it all away to somewhere nobody would find it began to affect him, and it was to this that he attributed the sudden rash and ill-planned event that was his undoing.

He'd never liked Matron's cat.

They expelled him.

He slipped quietly away.

After some unenthusiastic attempts to trace and find him, the wealthy man and the college decided that he wasn't really worth the trouble. His father had no opinion on the matter. Having murdered his wife and by his own actions had his son removed from his control, there was nobody left to torture and terrorise, and quite soon he lost his mind and was confined for life inside the tight security of a mental asylum for the violently insane.

Hubert Percy Godwin was never again seen or heard of in the vicinity of the college, or anywhere else for that matter.

The boy was then seventeen. He was, he decided, a man, and he would set out on this exciting road of opportunities with a new name. He could not enact his plan without money, of course . . .

He paid a brief visit back to the place where he was born and, very late one night, called on the marquess. When, a long time later, he left, he didn't have to worry about money any more.

So many names, the Barrow Man thinks now, so many places. His pattern of regularly moving on eased the ever-present disposal problem slightly, for there was no chance of being held responsible when remains were uncovered if he was a hundred miles away and had yet again changed his name.

Waterways always called out to him: perhaps it was the lingering memory of the chalk stream and the canal that bordered the wealthy man's estate. Living on, or beside, a river, a canal, a watery area such as the Broads, had featured regularly in his peripatetic life. Sometimes he wonders if all the other waterways were a mere prelude to the greatest one of all. For sure, now that he is once again beside the Thames, he has found a bond with it that he knows in his deep heart is too strong to sever.

And there is a problem.

He feels the anger that is his sole inheritance from his father begin to stir. Unlike his father, he is not its slave but its master. He sits quietly, feeling the red cloud grow and broil within him. He smiles faintly – he has just envisaged a scene of savagery so perfectly architected that it is almost beautiful – and slowly the rage decreases and is subsumed into him.

There will be a solution to the difficulty of disposal, he tells himself silently.

Of that he has not the slightest doubt.

SEVEN

The day seems endless.

Lily is so tired by eight o'clock in the evening that she doesn't even question why Mrs Clapper is not only still there, but has just brought a tray bearing poached eggs on toast, a large helping of sherry trifle and a glass of stout into the Inner Sanctum and deposited it on Lily's desk.

Lily tries to recall if she ate anything at midday and cannot. She tucks into the delicious food and decides it doesn't matter.

'You get that stout inside you,' Mrs Clapper says sternly. She is standing on the other side of the desk, arms folded, and Lily knows she won't move until every last scrap has been eaten or drunk. Lily quickly finishes the eggs and the trifle, then turns to the glass of stout. She's not sure she's ever drunk it before, but it tastes good.

'Now,' Mrs Clapper says as Lily puts the empty glass on the tray, 'we need to do some planning, Miss Lily.'

I know, Lily thinks wearily. But I'm not sure I can.

'I've thought it through,' Mrs Clapper continues, 'and I've asked the others, and we think it'll be simple enough to have someone sitting by Mr Felix all the time. Till he's better,' she adds, trying to sound cheery and optimistic.

'How would it work, Mrs Clapper?' Lily asks dubiously. 'We can't ask Miss Sutherland and Miss Adderley to help, for they are my tenants and—'

'Wasn't no need to *ask* them,' Mrs Clapper interrupts.

'But they hardly know him!' Lily cries.

Mrs Clapper sighs. 'They can see the need, can't they?' She eyes Lily closely for a moment, then mutters, 'They *like* it here. Like the freedom to be how they are. They want to *help*, Miss Lily!'

Lily understands quite a lot from those few words. She also perceives that Mrs Clapper has quietly picked up the nature of Miss Adderley and Miss Sutherland's relationship and, as she seems to do with most of life's small surprises, has taken it in her capacious stride.

'Both of them work for their living,' Lily points out.

'They do, but they don't work at the same time all the time, if you take my meaning.' Mrs Clapper, Lily thinks, has certainly been busy. 'Plus there's you and me and that Mr Smithers,' Mrs Clapper continues. 'Yes, I know you both have to work too, Miss Lily, but Mr Smithers says he can write whatever he writes sitting beside Mr Felix just as well as in his own rooms, and I dare say there are tasks you can do up there rather than here at your desk?'

Lily tries hard to think up more objections, then suddenly wonders why. 'It's a splendid plan, Mrs Clapper,' she says instead. 'I take it you have prepared a schedule?'

Mrs Clapper looks abashed. 'Well, it was Miss Sutherland who wrote it all down, on a page with lines and boxes, and the day and night all divided up.'

'Wonderful,' Lily murmurs. Then, fighting her exhaustion and squaring her shoulders, she asks, 'When does my shift start?'

Mrs Clapper gives her a kind smile. 'You, Miss Lily, are not to watch the patient till early tomorrow. You are to go to bed. You've been up since before dawn, so I'm told; you've assisted that fat doctor in mending Mr Felix's hurts; you've washed out his bloodstained linen – though the good Lord alone knows why you didn't have the sense to leave that to me – and you've been running up and down stairs all the rest of the day, trying to do seven things at once.'

It is true, and for a moment Lily's fatigue gets the better of her and she closes her eyes. She senses Mrs Clapper's silent sympathy from across the desk. 'I am a little weary,' she admits. 'But I haven't even thought about where I shall sleep.'

'All taken care of.' There is a note of smugness in Mrs Clapper's voice.

Lily's eyes spring open.

'But Felix lies unconscious in my bed!' she cries. 'I can't climb in beside him!'

'Course you can't!' Mrs Clapper looks shocked. 'Miss Lily, your bedroom has a connecting door to your sitting room, but it also has a door straight onto the landing, for all you don't use it. Now, what the ladies and I have done is make you a shakedown bed in your sitting room, and if you keep the connecting door firmly closed, people tending Mr Felix can go in and out through the *other* door, and you'll be as private as you please!'

Lily is greatly moved. 'When did you and the ladies do this arranging, Mrs Clapper?' she asks with a smile.

Mrs Clapper looks bashful. 'This afternoon, while you were with Mr Felix. We noticed you were taking forty winks – and no blame in that, Miss Lily – and Miss Adderley suggested we get on with it while you weren't looking.'

The thought of a bed – even a makeshift one – in a room where she can be alone and sleep undisturbed is such a heavenly vision that for a moment Lily feels like weeping.

She stands up. 'Thank you very much,' she says gravely. 'I shall fetch a jug of hot water and retire straight away.'

'Water's already up there.' Now Mrs Clapper undoubtedly sounds smug. 'That Mr Smithers had orders to take it up just now.'

Lily finds that, without her conscious effort, her feet have already begun to take her towards the door. But one last thought occurs to her. 'You must go *home*, Mrs Clapper!' she exclaims. 'You're not even meant to be here on a Sunday! What will your husband be thinking?'

'Clapper knows where I am, why I'm here and why I won't be home much for a day or two,' Mrs Clapper says stoutly. 'I'm having the first night shift, then I'll nip back and get some sleep while Miss Adderley takes over.'

'You can't . . .' Lily begins.

But Mrs Clapper gives her a look, and she subsides.

Lily wakes to full daylight.

She stretches, looking around. Her sitting room looks much the same. It is large enough for a narrow bed to have been laid out in the corner without having to move the chairs beside the hearth, the small table and the little desk where Lily sometimes studies papers and reads. The arrangement that Mrs Clapper and the tenants contrived for her has proved surprisingly comfortable, and she suspects she has Miss Sutherland or Miss Adderley to thank for the large number of plump cushions arranged under the thin mattress.

The long sleep has restored her. She gets up and walks soft-footed to the door onto the landing, thinking that she will go down and fetch more hot water. But someone has forestalled her: a large, covered jug sits quietly steaming on the other side of the door. She washes, dresses and does her hair. Looking at her gold watch, she sees that it is just after seven o'clock.

She goes out onto the landing. With no idea quite who or what to expect, she quietly opens the door to her bedroom and steps inside.

Felix lies utterly motionless. He is still pale, but she thinks she can see very faint signs of colour in his cheeks. The bandage around his head that she replaced late yesterday because of breakthrough bleeding still looks pristine. That, surely, is a hopeful sign . . .

Marm Smithers is sitting on the far side of the bed, watching her.

'Good morning, Lily,' he says softly. 'Did you manage to sleep?'

'Yes.' She feels slightly guilty. 'For hours, in fact. I feel much better.'

He smiles. 'Very glad to hear it.'

'What about you? I thought Miss Adderley was going to take the second half of the night shift?'

'She did,' he replies. 'I went home, then relieved her soon after five so she could sleep before going to work.'

Lily wants to express her huge gratitude to him, but it occurs to her that Felix matters as much to him as to her. To say thank you would be patronising and wrong.

She goes round to sit in the second chair placed beside him. For some moments they both study the steady rise and fall of Felix's chest.

'I think he looks a little less pale,' Lily ventures.

Marm goes 'Hmph,' then adds, 'Well, he's not *more* pale.'

Absurdly, Lily wants to giggle. 'Has he stirred?'

'He was restless in the small hours, according to Bunty. Muttering something about blood and a charnel house smell, but he didn't make much sense, apparently.'

'Oh, dear,' Lily whispers. 'If his mind is rambling, that isn't a good sign.'

'Dear Lily, he was barely conscious,' Marm says. 'He was probably dreaming. But it was *good* that he was briefly less deeply asleep, because Bunty managed to get him to drink a cup of water.'

'Yes, that is good,' Lily agrees.

She can't think of anything else to say and nor, it appears, can Marm.

After quite a long silence broken only by the faint but regular sound of Felix's soft snoring, Marm says, 'He went back to the house in Mary Rose Court the night before last, didn't he?'

'How did you know?' she demands. I could have stopped him – *should* have stopped him, she thinks. And Marm holds me responsible for what happened.

Marm sighs. 'Lily, it isn't your fault.' He appears to have read her mind. 'You told me that Felix was going to the Fetterplace house in the afternoon, but if he'd tried to investigate the rose bed then he'd have had the three siblings watching every move, which would have greatly restricted what he could and couldn't do. It was obvious that he'd have to return under cover of darkness to have a proper poke around. And of course' – he glances at Felix – 'we have no idea if he discovered anything.'

'Someone didn't want him there,' she says in a small voice.

'Which suggests he must have found something he shouldn't have done,' Marm adds. 'He's in the garden, digging in the rose bed, and he finds, what? This skeleton the Fetterplace siblings uncovered?'

'Yes, I imagine so,' Lily agrees. 'Was that the something he shouldn't have found? But it makes no sense' – she answers her own question – 'because the Fetterplaces had *already* uncovered the bones and the bits of cloth, and the length of gold chain and the pearls, so it wasn't a secret anyway.' She is aware she is gabbling, but Marm nods his understanding.

'I don't know, Lily,' he says. 'Was Felix finding the bones and the grave goods somehow more important than three dotty old people finding them? Did whoever was trying to keep the grave hidden know, or guess, who and what Felix is, and decide they had to stop him?'

'I believe the assailant thought he was dead,' she says quietly. 'Dr March said the kicks to the ribs and back had the force of brutal rage behind them. As if, having slain his man, the attacker was taking his revenge.' It is still a very distressing thought.'

Marm winces. He stares at Felix. 'What did you see, my friend?' he murmurs. 'What did you uncover that mattered enough for someone to try to kill you?'

There is, of course, no answer.

As Lily stands up to leave – she needs to make herself some breakfast, and then somehow set about arranging her day's work – Marm touches her hand. 'I won't keep you,' he says, 'but when I returned to Kinver Street last night, I brought this back with me.'

He reaches down beside his chair and straightens up again with a copy of *Alice Through the Looking-Glass* in his hand.

She grins. 'Is that your reading matter for the next few hours, Marm?'

He returns the smile. 'I once read that even quite deeply unconscious people may be able to hear what is going on around them,' he says. 'Now I have no idea if that is true – certainly, it seems unlikely – but Lewis Carroll is rather a favourite of mine. And look!' He points towards the large, oval mahogany-framed mirror on the wall opposite the bed.

Lily smiles. 'Yes. It makes me think of venturing through looking glasses too.'

'What could be more perfect?' Marm goes on. 'It is some time since I read *Alice*. If Felix can hear, he'll know that someone is with him, and perhaps it will help him find his way back to us.'

For a moment Lily can't speak. Then, hoping the threatening emotion will no longer be quite so obvious, she says, 'It's a very good idea, Marm. Make sure you mark the place you reach, then whoever takes over from you can continue the story.'

They exchange swift farewells. She creeps away across the room, and very gently begins to pull the door closed behind her. Just before the latch clicks home, she hears Marm's melodious voice begin to speak.

'One thing was certain,' he says, 'that the *white* kitten had nothing to do with it – it was the black kitten's fault entirely.'

Fighting the strong temptation to return and listen, she hurries away.

* * *

The Skeleton in the Rose Bed 79

It is late, and the night is growing cold. A distant clock, loud in the utter stillness, has just struck eleven.

Lily sits at Felix's desk in the outer office. She has been there for some time, although she has been dozing and so cannot tell exactly how long. She sat with Felix for much of the afternoon and long into the evening. Today has been hard, for both of her tenants had to go to work, and Marm has had demands on his time that have removed him from number 3, Hob's Court for much of the day. Lily and Mrs Clapper have watched over Felix between them. Even in the late afternoon, when first Miss Adderley and then Miss Sutherland came hurrying home full of apologies and ready to stand their shifts at the bedside, Lily could see how exhausted they were and sent them away to rest. Only as evening turned to night did she finally agree to Miss Sutherland's almost angry suggestion that *really* she ought to leave Felix to others' vigilance and go to bed.

Yet here she still sits, in Felix's chair.

She gives her tired mind a poke and asks herself if it is anything other than indolence that prevents her from getting up, checking that the house is secured for the night and making her way up to her bed. Presently she answers her own question: 'I do believe I am waiting for something,' she murmurs.

Her eyelids droop and she slips into a half-sleep. She is still aware of her surroundings. The outer office is so very familiar, and filled with Felix's lively spirit and the echo of his laughter, and it is a comfort just to sit here. She can see him, over-watering the potted plants to make up for recent neglect and making some self-mocking comment about the poor captive things never knowing whether it's going to be famine or feast. The scene shifts and they are back in France on that endless train journey; she has just tended to his damaged shoulder and there is a moment that shines out from her memory like a beacon light because everything was different after that . . .

Someone is knocking at the street door.

Shaken back to the present, she is confused and thinks, it can't be the night watchman and Felix on the cart, because that has already happened, and he isn't dead, and I . . .

The knock sounds again. It is a soft knock, she realises, as if someone doesn't want to rouse the whole household but is merely making a gentle sound to see if anyone is still awake downstairs.

She leaps up, straightens her hair and her clothing and hurries to open the door.

A bulky figure stands on the top step, made taller by the top hat. In the small amount of light spilling out from the hall, she meets his deep eyes. He smiles briefly, then says, 'I have need of the apothecary.'

They were the words he spoke to her at their first meeting.[2] She is profoundly moved that he remembers too.

'As I told you that night,' she says softly, 'there is no apothecary here now.'

He smiles, a flash of white teeth in the midst of the dark beard. 'And then it was you I had need of, as it is now.'

She steps back, making room for him to come in. But he looks uneasy. 'This is your home and your place of work,' he mutters.

She understands. He doesn't really know this version of her; he knows the woman who leaves her formal garb and her restricting corsets behind her as, dressed in a simple cotton gown and an old bonnet, she slips through the back door, down the garden and out through her grandfather's shed, to escape those things that distress her and cause her such pain in her professional life in favour of a few hours, or sometimes days, on the water with Tamáz Edey and *The Dawning of the Day*.

'Come through the house. We'll go down to the shed,' she says.

He nods. She closes and bolts the door, then leads the way along the hall. On through the kitchen, where she picks up the shed keys, and the scullery, where all is pin-neat and spotlessly clean, ready for Mrs Clapper to begin her work when she comes back in the morning. They stride the length of the long walled garden. Her grandfather's shed is extensive; it runs the width of the garden, and forms the rear wall. There is a door out onto the street beyond, but she always keeps it locked and bolted. She unlocks the door on the garden side, and she and Tamáz enter. She takes a lantern off a hook just inside the door, and even as she looks round for the vesta case that she knows is

---

[2] See *The Woman Who Spoke to Spirits*

here somewhere, he has reached for his own battered old case that he keeps in a waistcoat pocket and is holding a light to the lantern's wick.

Her grandfather's old workbench runs along the wall. She pulls out two stools tucked underneath it and she and Tamáz sit down.

Tamáz breaks the silence.

'I know about your colleague,' he says. 'How is he?'

She doesn't ask how he knows. Tamáz has a network of contacts that seems to cover most of London, and he absorbs information as if he was breathing in air. 'Still unconscious, although several times he has stirred and gulped down some water.'

Tamáz nods. 'You have help and support in caring for him?'

'Yes.'

He studies her closely, and his tight expression softens into compassion. 'He is strong,' he murmurs. 'Such a blow to the skull would have killed many men. Yet he is here, still breathing, and drinking water.' He pauses. 'I think,' he adds, 'that if this assault was going to end his life, it would already have done so.'

She has no idea why she is suddenly filled with hope. Tamáz is not a medical man, and he hasn't even seen Felix's terrible head wound. Yet his few words have comforted her more than anything else that has happened in the past day and a half.

She reaches for his hand, and instantly he grasps hers. 'Was that why you came?' she asks. 'To tell me Felix will recover?'

'I cannot say that for certain, cushla,' he warns her softly. 'I can only share what is in here.' He puts his free hand over his heart. 'But no, that is not why I wanted to speak to you.'

She waits.

'There is a darkness around the river,' he says after quite a long pause. 'Many have been sensing it, but because it is so frightening, it is not spoken about. People who live on the water see things. They *feel* things.' He stops, frowning. 'The water is our home and our element. We know when all is aright, and we are swift to pick up when it is not. When evil is present.'

She tenses at the word. Still holding her hand, he feels the change. He looks at her enquiringly.

'Somebody else said they sensed evil. It was at the spot where Felix was found.'

'And where was that?' he asks.

She smiles swiftly at herself. She had imagined that, all powerful as he so often seems, he'd have known already.

'In the shadow of the old wall that runs along the north side of All Hallows churchyard, over near Tower Hill,' she says.

He nods. Then it feels as if he has slipped away from her, down deep into his thoughts, his long accumulation of knowledge and his memories. She waits, and presently senses that he is back with her.

'Is there paper and ink in this Aladdin's cave of a shed?' he asks. She opens the drawer that is attached to the underside of the workbench and extracts a pad of paper, an old quill pen and a lidded ink pot that from its weight she can tell is still quite full.

Then she watches as Tamáz begins to draw. His hand moves swiftly over the paper – he is left-handed, she notes – and the pen strokes are sure. He has a definite artistry, and very soon she knows what he is doing.

'It's a map of the Thames,' she says.

He nods. 'It is.' He says no more, concentrating on his map.

After perhaps ten minutes, he puts down the quill. 'This is the course of the Thames,' he says. 'Here is Chelsea, where we are now, and on upriver are Chiswick and Barnes, and further westwards the Grand Union Canal leads off on its long journey to the Midlands and the northwest. Downriver are Westminster, Southwark, the City, the Tower, Wapping, the docks, Limehouse and Greenwich beyond.' He glances at her. 'That way is the mouth of the river, where its accumulated waters pour out into the sea.'

'I know,' she murmurs.

'Of course you do.' That quick smile again. 'Now, here are the places where boatmen congregate.' He points to the basins: Limehouse, which she knows, the one just along from here at Chelsea Creek where no doubt his boat is presently moored, and others whose names she does not know. 'These are the tributaries of the Thames.' Now he indicates several wiggly lines that lead into the river from the north and the south.

She frowns. 'I don't know about these tributaries.'

'Few people do. Their names are largely forgotten, except when they are used in street names such as Fleet Street. But once the Black Ditch, the Peck, the Neckinger, the Walbrook, the Westbourne and the Wandle were vital parts of London. In a wiser age their waters were honoured with sacrifices, and those who lived by them and depended on them knew that to pollute them was a sin against the natural order.'

He has sparked another recent memory.

'A very learned woman told me that the ancients believed in the power of the skull,' she says slowly, trying to bring Agnes Halligan's words to mind. 'She said the Thames was a sacred river, and a repository of sacrificial objects, heads and bodies.' She looks up from the map to stare at him. 'Did that not count as polluting the sacred waters?'

'No,' he says. 'It was a way to honour the dead; both your own dead, and the bodies of your worthy enemies.'

She hears his words, but she is thinking of what else Agnes Halligan said. *What a place to hide what you wish to conceal! One cannot but wonder how many victims have been quietly disposed of in the Thames' dark and fast-flowing waters.*

The atmosphere in the familiar and homely old shed is all at once dark with foreboding.

And Tamáz says in a low voice, 'Now it is different. Now the river is dishonoured, for what is happening is violent, despicable and foul.'

'I think,' she says nervously, 'you had better explain.'

He nods to say he has heard, and then falls silent. After some minutes, he says, 'The boatmen and their families tying up in the Limehouse canal basin noticed first. The initial thought was that there had been an incident upriver, and some quirk of the tide had swept what was borne on the water into the basin, where the objects became trapped because, as you will recall, there is no flow of water through the canals, or not enough to be of any significance. But then it happened again, in a basin to the west, and yet again, elsewhere. It could no longer be written off as accident and coincidence, and at last the people who live on the water began to speak of it among themselves.' She is about to ask what this river detritus consists of when he says with sudden passion, 'It is our *home*! We honour the water because of that, and also for its own sake, for it is the life-giver and one of the most powerful forces known in this world. For someone to treat it as a convenient repository for the results of their brutality is anathema.'

'Are they . . . is it heads that have been found?' she asks nervously.

He stares at her. 'Heads, yes. Also pieces of torso. Lumps of flesh and, once, a shoulder and breast.' He pauses, his eyes unfocused.

'And you're quite sure they are not simply the victims of accidents?' she asks. Her mouth has gone dry and it is not easy to speak. She is aware how savage the Thames is to those who fall in. More often than not, bodies are torn to pieces with a ferocity that suggests the river strongly resents their presence in its waters.

'They are not, cushla.' He doesn't elaborate.

She doesn't speak for a moment. She is thinking about something he just said. 'The boatmen in the canal basins noticed first,' she said. 'So what about now?'

He sighs. 'Now, the pattern has changed.' He points again to the map. 'The human detritus is being deposited in the lost tributaries. To begin with, in the Black Ditch.' He points to the short curve that goes inland east and then west from Limehouse. 'The latest finds suggest it is now the Walbrook.'

He moves his finger to indicate an almost straight line that extends roughly northwards out of the river, east of the Fleet and west of the Tower.

Lily feels a cold sensation in her chest.

'The Walbrook,' she repeats, her voice barely audible.

'It has its source in Finsbury and its course leads right through the most ancient areas of the City,' Tamáz says. 'It once ran beneath, or perhaps in a channel through, the wall that the Romans built around their great town of Londinium. They worshipped close to its banks in their Mithraeum, which was the temple dedicated to Mithras, the soldiers' god. Many battles were fought in the vicinity, and in the manner of those warriors of old, the dead of both sides were treated with honour.' His finger traces down the line of the Walbrook. 'Nearly two thousand years later, almost in our own times, workmen digging a ditch came across a vast number of skulls – three hundred or more – in the sad remains of what had once been the Walbrook. Some say they were from a great battle between the Romans and the Celts; some say they were the dead from Boudicca's revolt. But they had been placed there deliberately, in a river that flowed into the mighty Thames, and their skulls as the seat of wisdom and courage were honoured with offerings of shields and ritually broken swords.'

She shivers.

Still staring intently at the map, her eyes have moved slightly to the right: to the Tower, and Tower Hill beside it.

She looks up and meets Tamáz's steady gaze.

He says quietly, 'You must be very, very careful. There is danger, and darkness, and deeply evil intent.' Very gently he touches her chest, where the gift he once gave her hangs on its chain beneath her clothes. 'The witch bottle has power, and you have told me that it has protected you more than once. But this, cushla, is a peril too great for it.'

Now he grasps her upper arms, pulling her close. The lantern's light is full on his face, and she can see his fear for her in his expression. 'I know what is in your heart, and I sense that almost all your thoughts are elsewhere.' Briefly he inclines his head towards the house. 'But for now he cannot help you.' He pauses. 'I know the waterways,' he continues. 'I have some small understanding of the river. Evil has come here unasked, but the river will not lie passive before it.' His grip on her arms tightens. 'Lily, you must let me help you, for the danger is far too great for you to face alone.'

Tamáz has gone.

Lily let him out of the rear door of the shed, and his footsteps did not go away until she had locked and bolted it.

She sits for some time in the shed, staring at his map, trying to summon the calm, steady spirit of her grandfather. Then she returns to the house.

Lily goes into the bedroom. Bernice Adderley sits beside Felix's bed, knitting what looks like a sock, the three needles flying.

'I wonder that you can see to work in such a low light,' Lily says softly, moving to stand beside her.

Miss Adderley chuckles. 'You're not a knitter, I take it?' Lily shakes her head. 'Thought not. I don't need to see, my dear.' After a moment she adds, 'It's not time for you to relieve me, is it?'

Lily says, 'No, but nevertheless I think you should go to bed.'

'But . . .' Miss Adderley jerks her head towards Felix's long, still form.

'I too am going to bed now,' Lily says. 'I shall open the connecting door between the two rooms, and I am quite sure I shall hear if Felix moves or makes a sound.'

Miss Adderley eyes her dubiously. Then she says, 'Well, you were a nurse, and no doubt learned to attune yourself to your patients. You're quite sure?'

'Yes.'

Miss Adderley rolls up her sock, sticks the needles in the ball of wool, and gets to her feet. 'It was the sheep that made me think of this,' she says, waving the knitting.

Lily is at a total loss. 'The sheep?'

'In *Alice Through the Looking-Glass*!' Miss Adderley's tone suggests it should have been obvious. 'Chapter five, "Wool and Water", and the sheep in the little dark shop with her elbows on the counter!'

'Chapter five already!' Lily says. 'You have been progressing well.'

'Dotty and Marm, mainly,' Miss Adderley says. 'However, I did catch Marm reading Tweedledum and Tweedledee, and he was *most* effective. Dotty and I were chuckling away, and we all thought even poor dear Felix had a faint smile on his face!' She reaches for Lily's hand and squeezes it. 'Just wishful thinking, I expect.'

'I expect so,' Lily agrees. Her heart gives another small leap of optimism.

'Now, you promise to call me if you need me?' Miss Adderley says.

'I promise.' But I won't need to, Lily adds silently.

Shortly after the door has closed and the sound of Miss Adderley's feet on the stairs has faded, Lily is undressed and in bed. The door between her sitting room and the bedroom is propped open, and the two doors onto the landing are closed.

'Just you and me, Felix,' she says quietly. The words provoke a frisson. 'I'm going to go to sleep now, but I shall be right here if you need me. Goodnight.'

She closes her eyes. Sleep is ready to absorb her, and she doesn't hold back. She knows she ought not to put such faith in Tamáz's words, but she can't help herself.

Because she too is filled with the conviction that Felix is going to get better.

EIGHT

Lily stirs out of some serene and instantly forgotten dream to a thin beam of early light filtering between the curtains. As soon as she is properly awake, awareness comes crashing back.

Felix!

Leaping out of bed, not pausing to gather up dressing gown or shawl, she races through the connecting doorway and stands panting beside the bed.

He is fast asleep. His breathing is steady and deep and, when she rests a hand lightly on his forehead, there is no hint of the fever that Dr March warned about and that she has been dreading since early on Sunday morning. That was the day before yesterday, she calculates; surely, if infection was going to set in, it would have happened by now?

Still staring intently down at him, she realises what she should have registered instantly: he has moved. Last night he still lay as he had originally been placed – on his back, wounded head supported by soft pillows and a folded towel in case the bleeding should start up again. Now he lies on his right side, facing her. His right hand lies palm uppermost beside the pillow, and his left arm is outside the covers.

She touches his left hand. It feels cold. Very gently she raises the arm, draws out the bedclothes and, lowering the arm, covers him up to the shoulder. He mutters something. She waits, stock still, to see if he will say any more. His breathing slows, and she judges he is now deeply asleep.

Hardly aware of what she is doing, she bends over him and kisses his cheek. Very briefly – the expression there and gone in an instant – he smiles. He says, quite distinctly, 'Lily.'

She waits again. But he neither mutters nor moves again. Heartened, encouraged more than she can say – more, probably, than is wise – she tiptoes away to prepare for the day.

* * *

It is Dorothea Sutherland who sits with Felix for the early morning shift. Returning to the bedroom to speak to her, Lily is moved by the sight of the upright figure with the large book on her lap. Miss Sutherland is reading the chapter about Humpty Dumpty and, Lily thinks, she must be very familiar with the story, for her eyes frequently move from the page to Felix.

Not wanting to make her jump, Lily quietly clears her throat. Miss Sutherland spins round, sees her and exclaims in an excited whisper, 'He opened his eyes! I am *sure* he did, for he looked straight at me!'

Lily goes to stand close to her, and Miss Sutherland grasps her hand. 'Did he show any sign that he recognised you?' Lily asks. She tries to keep the urgency out of her tone, but she doesn't think she succeeded.

Sure enough, the bright joy in Miss Sutherland's face fades and she shakes her head.

'It is early days yet, Miss Sutherland,' Lily says. 'We must keep our hopes up.'

There is a small silence. Then Miss Sutherland says quietly, 'Miss Raynor, Bunty and I are happier and more settled in this house than anywhere we have lived before, and already it feels like home. Now that this frightful attack has happened and we are all pulling together to do our best for our patient, might we dispense with strict formality? My name is Dorothea, or Dotty' – she blushes, as if the latter revelation embarrasses her – 'and Bernice's friends all call her Bunty.'

'And I am Lily, which of course you know,' Lily says instantly. 'Yes indeed, Dorothea.' She can't quite manage Dotty yet. 'I should be delighted.' She glances at Felix. 'Although we can't ask him just now, I'm quite sure he would rather be informal too. He always says that when people call him Mr Wilbraham he instantly thinks he's in trouble, especially when they're frowning.'

For a moment Felix's cheerful presence seems to fill the room.

Dorothea nods in satisfaction. Lily senses she would quite like to return to Humpty Dumpty, and so she says briskly, 'I have an errand to run this morning, and I imagine I shall not return till after midday. Mrs Clapper will be here presently, and Marm said he would be back around mid-morning. Would you . . .'

'My morning is free,' Dorothea says. 'I will happily lead Felix on through Looking-Glass Land until Marm arrives. Good day, Lily.'

Mrs Clapper has arrived early again and she is in the kitchen. Lily, already in her outer garments and ready for some walking, quickly outlines the plans for the day and then makes her escape before Mrs Clapper can launch into a long conversation. She hurries to the street door, pauses briefly to make sure she has pen and notebook in her small leather bag, and goes out into the morning. Descending the steps, she reaches down to check her left boot.

She is smartly dressed in a well-tailored navy-blue skirt and a tight-fitting jacket with a peplum, with a hip-length woollen coat against the chill of the bright day. It is as well her skirt is long and sweeping, for her boots do not live up to the elegance of the rest of her outfit. They are not elegant at all: they have stout laces and reach to her knees, and they look exactly like a labourer's work boots, which is what they are. Made of well-greased and waterproofed leather, they are strong, supple and extremely comfortable. The low heels allow Lily to run in them without turning an ankle.

When she purchased them, she took the left one to a cobbler in a distant part of town and asked him to sew a long, narrow channel down the inside of it, of a size to accommodate the rigid horn sheath she provided. The cobbler did a neat job and the pocket is hard to spot from the outside, with the stitching only just visible. In its sheath inside the channel lives a long, fine, very sharp boning knife that belonged to her grandmother, worn from years of sharpening, its brass handle bound with red leather.

Lily gives the left boot a little pat for luck and hurries on her way.

Thanks to Joseph Bazalgette and the embankment he engineered to cover his new and desperately needed system of sewers, it is possible to walk beside the river more or less all the way from Battersea Bridge in the west to Blackfriars Bridge in the east. It is a distance of a little under five miles, but Lily is a fast walker and she is in dire need of exercise and open air. And it is early still; only a quarter to eight. Adding on an extra half an hour of travelling after she leaves the Victoria Embankment, it will still only be around ten o'clock when she reaches her destination. She draws a deep breath, turns to her left and starts walking.

The river police depot at Wapping is very much as Lily remembers it from her two previous visits. It is small and cramped, full of far too many objects that clutter up the space, and the sturdy timbers that support the wooden platform it sits on are constantly assaulted by the force of the tidal flow, first one way, then the other. When Lily first met Alf Wilson, he trotted out what was clearly his usual joke about him and the other officers referring to themselves as the Disciples, because they were fishers of men – in their case, dead men. And women, and children – the Thames is not fussy and drowns pretty much anyone who is unlucky enough to fall into its mighty and powerful waters.

Alf is alone in the depot and seems genuinely delighted to see her. Perhaps, she thinks wryly, it is a quiet morning for body-recovering. Unless, of course, all the other Disciples are out doing exactly that.

'I've just put the kettle on,' Alf is saying, 'and I dare say you'd welcome a cup of tea, Miss Raynor?'

'I would indeed, Mr Wilson—'

He interrupts, frowning. 'Now what did I tell you about calling me that?'

'Sorry! Yes, Alf, I'd love some tea. I've just walked here from Chelsea.'

'*Chelsea!*' His friendly brown eyes round in amazement, as if she'd told him she'd marched down from Edinburgh. He is busy spooning rather a lot of tea leaves into the old Brown Betty, and now he reaches for the merrily boiling kettle. 'In that case, you'll be wanting a couple of the missus's rock buns and all. Chelsea, now! That's where you have your bureau, if I am not very much mistaken?' He puts several more vowel sounds into *bureau* than is strictly necessary, as if he relishes saying the word. 'The World's End Bureau' – there he goes again – 'number three, Hob's Court, Chelsea. You gave me your card. Remember?'

In case she doesn't, he points to the lower border of the large map of the river on the wall, where her card has been carefully positioned right in the centre so that anyone looking at the map can't fail to notice it.

'Makes me and the Disciples that proud to know you, all those times we see your bureau mentioned in the papers,' he says. It happens only rarely – Lily and Felix prefer to keep their heads down – but she doesn't like to correct him.

He prises open the battered old tin and urges her to take at least two rock cakes. She recalls from experience that the missus can't honestly be said to have a light hand with her baking, but Lily is so hungry that she wolfs them down, although some discreet dunking into her mahogany-brown tea minimises the risk to her teeth.

'Delightful as it is to see you, miss,' Alf says presently, 'I know full well that a busy woman such as yourself isn't here just to pass the time of day.' He studies her, frowning slightly. 'And yet it's odd that you should turn up here today.'

Knowing full well that he's longing to explain, she obliges by saying innocently, 'Really, Alf? And why is that?'

He pauses for what is, for him, quite a long time. Then he says in a far more sombre tone, 'You know what we do here, miss? I told you, didn't I, first time you came, how so many of the corpses and parts of corpses that fall and are pushed or deposited into the river end up hereabouts, and it's our job to retrieve them and see they're decently tended to?'

'You did, Alf. I seem to recall that the figure was more than a hundred and fifty per year.'

He shakes his head, drawing in a whistling breath through his teeth. 'It's considerably more than that now. Everybody wants to go boating on the river, see, 'specially in the spring and the summer, so there's all those as don't see the *danger* of little boats in addition to all the rest. You'd think,' he adds, 'that the *Princess Alice* disaster back in seventy-eight would have put them off, but folks are foolhardy and won't take heed.' He shakes his head again. 'But that's not what's strange, miss.' He pauses, almost as if he is reluctant to go on. Then in a rush he says, 'Thought maybe I should tell you, what with you being a Private Investigator' – she can hear the capital letters –

'that there's bits of bodies fetching up here. Been going on a while now – three months, maybe more? At first it was animal carcasses, the smaller ones neatly bisected, the larger creatures all cut about to buggery and . . . Sorry, miss,' he says sheepishly.

'It's all right, Alf. Please, go on.'

'Then it got an awful lot worse,' he says quietly – she can hear the dread in his voice – 'because it started to be *human* remains. Now I know what you'll say, miss' – she hasn't been planning to say anything – 'that it's surely nothing new for us to find bits of bodies, but like I told you before, there's not much mistaking a corpse that's been battered apart by the river, because it'll have been thrown against anything and everything in its path, from floating logs and the keels of heavily loaded barges to the piers of the bridges.' He pauses, frowning. 'When it's accidental-like, the damage is random and rough-edged, but these body parts are different.' He shoots her a swift glance as if to make sure she isn't about to faint.

'Please, continue,' Lily says calmly.

'So far, we've found two heads, although one was just the empty scalp, a couple of arms, the left side of a torso, two . . . er, two chests' – he indicates his breast – 'three feet and several upper and lower legs. In almost every case, the cuts are as clean as if they'd been done with a very sharp cleaver, which perhaps they were.'

Lily waits a moment to make sure her voice will be steady – it is a ghastly catalogue – and says, 'Were all these parts in a similar sort of state?'

He understands straight away what she means. 'Some were much more decomposed than others,' he replies. 'With a few of the limbs and partial limbs, we could only tell what they were by the bones.'

'What on earth can be happening?' she says. She hadn't meant to voice the thought, but Alf responds eagerly.

'That's what we all say!' he exclaims. 'It's not right – it's not *Christian* – to go cutting up bodies for your own amusement, now is it, miss?'

'Is that what you think, Alf? That whoever is doing this somehow derives satisfaction from it?' She is amazed.

Now he looks embarrassed. 'Well, I suppose it could be some lunatic killer who can't think how else to dispose of his victims,' he mutters.

But she is still thinking about what he said about amusement. Knowing she must be very diplomatic – for she is sure that Alf believes life's more sordid aspects must be kept well away from the delicate eyes and ears of the fair sex – she says, 'Are you suggesting that a certain sort of killer might derive erotic pleasure from cutting up his victims' bodies with such skill?'

At first, he can't meet her eyes. She feels his discomfiture coming off him in waves. Then he raises his head, looks straight at her and says quietly, 'Well, we've yet to fish out any bits from a male body.'

It is only by chance that the Barrow Man observes the blonde woman with the upright carriage, the workman's boots and the clear green eyes leaving the Wapping depot of the river police authorities.

His glance had gone straight past, but then, his attention drawn by the sight of a woman in that place, his eyes return to her.

But he is not looking closely at her, for he has much to think about. He is . . . *disturbed*, he decides, deliberately minimising the level of his anxiety, because when he had returned to the path under the graveyard wall the night after he had attacked the intruder, the body had gone.

He can still remember far too vividly how he had reacted when he understood the body wasn't where he had left it. His heart had pounded so hard and so fast he thought he might pass out, and he had felt sick, his limbs shaking, his hands sweating. It was anger, he tells himself firmly now. *Anger*. Anger with himself, for he knew even at the time that he ought to have made sure the corpse was out of sight, and it had been both lazy and foolish to think it would be safe where it was. He had relied on the fact that people hardly ever ventured along the path, and never by night. Only someone had.

He was even more angry – murderously angry – with whoever had removed the body. It wasn't that he had planned to experiment on it, for he has no interest in male flesh. However, for reasons of his own he had very much wanted to have a closer look at the dead man.

As if that was not bad enough, the corpse thief had also trespassed into the Barrow Man's private, secret place. And his very presence had violated that precious ground. *Polluted* it.

For a while his fury rises to such a pitch that he is not sure he can contain it.

Gradually, he calms himself.

And then remembers his other worry, for he is still much troubled and angered by the disposal problem. He had believed he'd found the perfect solution: the old Walbrook river ran in its covered-over course quite close to the wall behind the overgrown gardens, and when he discovered the long-forgotten access that time had clearly forgotten, it felt as if providence had detected his dearest wish and was delivering it right into his hands. It was good, he'd thought, when fate by her generous actions indicated how thoroughly she supported the *rightness* of what he was doing.

For nearly a fortnight he has been indulging in his pleasure in the well-thought-out scheme. The hidden place he has contrived in the overgrown corner of the churchyard is ideal for his work. The deep shade of the trees and the dense vegetation under the wall at the north end are perfect. When he is ready to release material he has finished with to the uncaring waters of the great river, all he needs to do is to fill his barrow and follow the short and well-concealed route along the paths and the narrow back roads to where the Walbrook runs beneath the innocent feet of those who walk above. You would think, he tells himself, trying to control the rising red rage, that once he has discarded the pieces he has no further use for, that would be the end of it.

But then, keeping his ears open for rumours and murmurs as he always does, he has discovered that it isn't.

In the past he has been careless. It was a sharp lesson but no surprise when the people who lived on the water began to whisper of what was turning up along the canals and in the canal basins. He has berated himself harshly for being so *stupid* as to forget that canals do not have a through-flow of water; what is thrown into them tends to stay there.

But his seemingly miraculous discovery of the secret access to the Walbrook ought to have been the answer!

It was, for almost two weeks.

Now the talk has started again, and this time it is concentrated upon the sudden increase in a particular kind of detritus that is being washed up around Tower Bridge and Wapping. Disturbed, he has returned to his stack of information on tides and currents. He can find no answer – it is a field of study in which he has very little prior experience – and he is left with the depressing and disturbing conclusion that his Walbrook solution is imperfect, and he must work out a better one.

His silent, fiercely contained rage has its focus on the officers of the river authority who are so devastatingly efficient in hauling the river's offerings out of the water. Which is why, on this Tuesday morning, he is standing in a doorway at the end of a filthy, narrow passageway, watching the comings and goings at the Wapping depot.

The fair-haired woman in the heavy boots is standing looking down at the river, half-turned away from him.

He stares at her.

How easy it would be to dispose of her.

He has never thrown a living human body into the water, but there is a first time for everything. How would it be? He lets his mind make pictures. He would creep up behind her – he can walk almost silently when he has a mind to – and before she was even aware of him, one arm would be tight around her waist, the other hand hard and firm over her mouth and nose. Unable to breathe – for his right hand is prodigiously strong – already she would be thrown into a panic, and very quickly she would fall limp against him. Should anyone witness his actions – unlikely, for there isn't a soul about in this dingy and sordid little corner – he would adopt the lazy drawl he learned to mimic in his college days and shout, 'I say, you there! I need your help – my poor dear wife has fainted!' He is smartly dressed, and that, together with the imperious tone, would demand instant obedience from whatever underling rushed to his aid. Then he would say, 'Hold her up, man, come along! Look after her while I go for assistance. Look sharp!'

Yes. That would serve, if he was disturbed.

If not, there is a short flight of stone steps a little to the left of the fair-haired woman. They are covered in slime and a foul-looking sort of bright green weed, but with care he could carry her down to the water and, under the high wall, who would there be to watch as he lowered her into the water and held her head under until she drowned?

Still staring at her, he focuses his power. He imagines his fierce thoughts narrowing into a thin ray of light, so bright that it might be a stream of fire: a sharp beam of malice aimed straight between her shoulder blades.

He has seen his victims wince when the beam hits them. But not this time. Something strange has happened. For his invisible dart suddenly gives quite a hard jolt, as if someone has raised a shield to block it. Instantly, without conscious thought, he cuts it off.

For he keeps ever in mind the old myths of mighty warriors who perished because their deadly powers were somehow reflected back on them. He must not take the risk of that fate befalling him.

He wonders what can have caused this unexpected rebuff. It is as if she bears an amulet, a protective charm . . .

Deliberately he turns his thoughts away.

He returns to the image of her pale face seen through water as he drowns her, eyes and mouth wide open in terror.

The violent images fill his head, and his body responds as it always does. Briefly he closes his eyes, the more to enjoy it.

When he opens them again, she has gone.

Ah well, he consoles himself, it would have been merely a kill. His barrow is a long way away, and so he could not have transported her off to the forgotten place in the churchyard where he performs his work. He could possibly have hidden the corpse until darkness falls and the streets empty, but there is little in the way of a truly foolproof hiding place in the immediate vicinity.

Thinking of that small, well-concealed structure that is his work place reminds him that he has tasks requiring his attention. As he turns and slips away, his mind already leaping ahead to his work, he reflects, not for the first time, how harsh it is that nobody will ever understand that he carries out his experiments in the interests of science. That has always been the driving force, right from the days of childhood in the small garden, the wide estate, the surrounding countryside and the canal bank. When he was young and had little cunning, often he was caught and punished. Even at the college, as he grew towards manhood, those erudite and wisdom-loving men who ought to have known better shrank from him and condemned him as an ignorant brute devoid of human sensitivity.

He never let any of them put him off.

It is fascinating work, and he still has so much to accomplish. As he strides away, his mind is so fully engaged on his project that he almost forgets about the fair-haired woman in the rough boots.

Almost.

On leaving Alf Wilson's depot, prompted by a strong impulse that she does not question, Lily pauses to stare down into the powerful surge of the khaki water. Out of nowhere she has a sense of utter horror. She imagines cries of desperate anguish; she sees faces with wide-open mouths and terror-filled eyes struggling in the water; she smells a stench so vile that she wants to retch.

Unthinkingly she grasps through her clothing for the witch's bottle that lies over her breastbone.

As soon as her alarmed heartbeat has slowed down, she turns and hurries away.

She finds herself emerging from one of the small roads that wind around St Katharine Docks, looking up at the Tower. She has been striding along without thinking, but now, realising that she is close to Tower Hill, she decides to go and have a look at Mary Rose Court. She turns to her right, following the line of the forbidding walls, and, passing Trinity Square, tries to recall Felix's description of the location. Presently she comes to a narrow lane that turns off to the right: a plaque reads *Mary Rose Court*. The houses are on the left: two terraces of five dwellings, the houses tall and narrow. She enters the Court and, keeping to the shadows, walks soft-footed along it. She calculates from the house numbers that number eight will be the third house from the far end. Before she reaches it, she spots a dark little passage running between the first and the second terraces. Nobody can have passed along it for some time, for weeds and small shrubs have pushed their way up among the broken paving slabs and litter has been blown in and is entangled in the greenery. Advancing a few paces along it, Lily sees that someone has shoved a stained old mattress behind the brambles along the left-hand side.

She edges her way along the passage. The first few yards are the worst, for after that the rampant plant growth thins out, and now the few species which are hardy enough to survive with so little light are thin and strangled-looking.

She is frightened.

Go back, the voice of sense tells her sharply.

She goes on.

Light flows into the further end of the passage. She stops, peering out. To right and left a high wall extends. She leans forward, and sees that a narrow path runs along behind the houses. On the far side there is a line of trees standing in deep undergrowth, and beyond that is a churchyard.

'All Hallows Church,' she says softly.

She looks out over the wide, empty space. There are signs of activity lower down the long slope, closer to the church. But up here at the northern boundary there is not a soul to be seen, and the few jagged, crooked gravestones suggest long abandonment. Lily experiences a wave of the strangeness and poignancy of places where once there was human activity but now are deserted.

She steps out onto the path. She is shaking slightly; the fear is increasing. 'But *why* am I so frightened?' she whispers. There is a smell in the air; it's very faint, but it's definitely there. It makes her think of rotten meat and seething maggots. She takes another step. Now she can see, looking to the right, that the path bends sharply inwards towards the churchyard, forming an angle. Alders grow densely just there, and there is a vast yew tree. It is not easy to make out, but she can see a small, low building crouched in the shadows, all but invisible.

She feels she ought to go and investigate it.

But she can't. She simply cannot move her feet.

She is muttering to herself, the growing sense of dread now

mixed with anger at her own feebleness. Struggling, she tries once more to move.

Then she hears the regular footfalls of someone coming along the path from her left. She darts back inside the passage and crouches down. Her face hidden by the dying leaves of a buddleia, she parts the brittle stems and looks out.

A man crosses the far end of the passage. He walks purposefully, head down, and she cannot see his face. She does not try; the moment he comes into view, she draws right back against the wall and, praying that he will not glance to his right, buries her face in her hands.

She waits for a long time after the footsteps have faded, still crouched down, still covering her face. I am like a child, she thinks with sudden clarity, believing that if my eyes cannot see, nobody can see me. Cautiously she stands up and, step by hesitant step, makes her slow way back to Mary Rose Court.

Lily arrives back at number 3, Hob's Court a little after one o'clock. As soon as she is inside and hanging up her coat and hat, she hears their voices: Marm, Bunty and Mrs Clapper are on the middle landing, and their distress is evident.

She races up the first flight of stairs and says, 'What's happened?'

Marm turns to her. He is pale, his frown deep. 'Felix has been awake,' he says.

'But that's . . .' she begins. That's wonderful, she had been going to say. But a glimpse at the three anguished expressions tells her it is far from wonderful. 'What is it?' she whispers. '*Tell me!*'

Bunty has a quick glance at the others and then says, 'He's had a wash and change of sheets, and Mrs Clapper brought up a freshly laundered nightshirt.' She pauses, nervous eyes reluctantly meeting Lily's. 'He has eaten a very small amount of food and, more importantly, drunk two glasses of water. We were—'

Mrs Clapper has been shaking her head, obviously wanting to interrupt. Now she can no longer contain herself.

'He might well have eaten and drunk, and that's all well and good.' Her mouth works, and for a moment it seems she can't go on. Then, dismay and profound distress creasing her face into harsh lines, she bursts out, 'Miss Lily, he's *bodily* present but *he's* not there!'

NINE

Tiger.
   Tiger Lily.
   Lily.
Lily, yes.
Felix smiles, although he doesn't know why.
The woman's soothing, melodious voice has been speaking of Tiger Lily. *Oh, Tiger Lily, I wish you could talk.* Then in a lighter tone with a note of tetchiness a slightly different voice replies, *We* can *talk, when there's anybody worth talking to.*
Felix doesn't know where he is.
He is lying in a wide bed with crisp sheets and soft blankets. His head and shoulders are supported by plump feather pillows, and he can smell lavender. He thinks someone said that lavender soothes headaches, and he can picture a hand holding a little bottle that sprinkled cool drops. How did they know his head ached so much?
His body hurts too. There is a steady pain in his ribs, which becomes acute if he tries to draw a deep breath. He thinks he must have bled a lot: earlier when there was all the fussing and he was being bathed with hot water and there were fresh sheets to lie in, he . . . But he has lost the thread of that thought. He tries to go back to retrieve it, but it has gone.
He gazes around the room.
There doesn't seem to be anybody there just now. That is quite strange, because it seems there is *always* someone there. He twists his head to the right and to the left, as far as the pain allows. To the left is a small bedside table and a chair. There is another chair set against the end of the bed. Behind him to the right there is a doorway, and the door is ajar. There is a second door in the wall on the right, and this has been propped open with a door stop. He can see two upholstered chairs set either side of the fireplace, and beyond them against the far wall is a desk with a wooden chair tucked under it. There is

what looks like a makeshift bed laid out on the floor in front of the desk. Straightening his head again – with some relief – he looks down the length of his body to the foot of the bed and the wall beyond. Over to the right there is a window. Straight ahead there is a large, oval mirror with a frame of dark wood.

'I expect it is mahogany,' he says aloud. His voice sounds very odd, and seems to echo inside his head.

He stares at the mirror. There is something about mirrors . . . someone was speaking about a looking glass. It was probably this one, then. He seems to recall being told that someone – a girl – had gone through the looking glass as if it were no more than soft gauze, to find herself in the different world of the room next door. He doesn't think he wants to follow her. It seems to be a dangerous place, because he's heard people talking about a volcano – *mind the volcano!* – and a queen flying through a wood, and a monster with jaws that bite and claws that catch.

But supposing the girl was Lily? If she was, then he has no choice, because he knows he has to find Lily.

Although he has no idea why.

He closes his eyes.

He dreams. Then he catches himself, for he has heard a king snoring and a man told him *you would be nowhere if the king was dreaming about you; just a thing in his dream . . .*

Am I nowhere?, the thought is alarming. Nothing but a thing in someone else's dream? His fear grows.

An image of fenders and fire irons suddenly fills his mind. He wonders if he was hit with a fire iron. Is that why his head hurts so much? There was a barrow and it had arms and legs sticking up out of it – this new image drives out the fenders and the fire irons – so perhaps the jumbled-up limbs meant that the king and the flying queen were in the barrow?

Something else occurs to him: it was a *red* king who was snoring, he recalls, and, come to think of it, the queen was also red. *Yes!* He thinks he has cried the word aloud, but he can't hear his voice so perhaps he didn't. But he is suddenly feeling much more cheerful, because he *has* remembered correctly: the arms and legs in the barrow were red, so they *must* have belonged to the king and the queen.

He wonders why they were in the barrow.

Perhaps they were hurt? *Somebody* must have been hurt, because he remembers smelling blood. There had been a battle – two rotund men had fought over a rattle with a sword and an umbrella – and then a monstrous crow like a vast black cloud had descended and made a hurricane with its wings that blew *another* flying queen through the woods . . .

Felix is afraid, although he doesn't know why. He tries to think about Tiger Lily again, because that makes him feel better.

Tiger.

Lily.

Thinking of Lily puts an image in his mind. But it's a woman, not a girl. Where is she? Felix would like her to be here, because she is strong and he trusts her. And there is more than trust . . . there is also an emotion that makes his heart feel strange. But what if she's gone through the mirror? 'Will I have to go after her?' he whispers.

But he can picture the arms and legs in the barrow and he can't face going back, because the king and the queen smelt of blood and there is someone or something through there that *hurt* him so badly and there was a white face with no mouth and thick black brows and his head feels as if it's full of dreams and he's so frightened because what if he's not *here* any more but through *there* already, trapped in someone's dream? If he can't escape – and how on earth is he to do that? – then how will he find Lily?

Someone is leaning over him. It is a man. He is big and bulky and dressed for the outdoors. He is vaguely familiar. He puts a large cold hand on Felix's forehead and mutters in a low voice, 'Slight fever. Only to be expected.' There is a brief rattling sound, then the low voice says, 'Give him these.'

Someone tries to force something through Felix's clenched teeth but he thinks it's a biscuit and it's *very* dry so it will choke him, and quite soon whoever it is gives up.

And a man's voice says, 'Leave them with me, Dr March. Lily will be here very soon, and she will manage it.'

Lily!

Felix *really* wants to stay awake if Lily is coming soon. But he feels sleep running after him like the huge black crow, as fast as the flying queen in the wood, and although he tries *with all his might*, he cannot outrun it and he feels himself tumbling, tumbling, and the cool sheets and the soft pillows embrace him and he falls back into the darkness.

Lily tries and fails to get to sleep. It is late – after midnight – and she is exhausted. But she is worried about the Fetterplace case. It is now nearly a week since the siblings engaged the services of the Bureau, and so far there has been no progress at all on the matter of the skeleton in their garden. Admittedly this is largely the siblings' own fault, since they refused to let Felix anywhere near the rose bed. Nevertheless, Lily's professional pride is at stake, and she knows she must evolve a plan of action.

It's just that it's so hard without Felix.

Stop that, she tells herself firmly.

The other matter preying on her mind, is, of course, Felix.

She listens for a moment, but there is no sound coming from the next room. She knows that sleep is the best cure, and it was a relief when Dr March's febrifuge worked its magic so quickly. The slight fever, however, is not what most concerns her.

Earlier, she went down to show Dr March out. 'My housekeeper told you that Felix had eaten a little and drunk plenty of water today,' she said, pausing in the hall.

'Yes, yes, all to the good,' the doctor replied. Lily detected impatience.

'What she did not add is that, even when sufficiently alert to sit up and stare around while he ate and drank, he showed no signs of recognition,' Lily hurried on. If she had hoped blurting it all out quickly would lessen the pain of the words, she was wrong. 'Mrs Clapper said "he's not there".'

Her voice caught, and the doctor's slightly cross expression softened. 'Miss Raynor, your colleague suffered a brutal blow to the head,' he said gently. 'Such an injury might well have killed him, so we must be thankful for Mr Wilbraham's thick skull.' He smiled briefly. 'These things take their own time,' he added, 'which I am quite sure you as a former nurse must know full well.'

He met her eyes. 'Will he come back?' she whispered.

'Now you know I cannot answer that,' he said firmly. 'But I would say the signs are good. He has come out of the profound unconsciousness, and his needy body insisted he take in food and water.'

'I think it was Mrs Clapper who insisted,' Lily said with a smile.

He returned it. 'And that, of course, expresses precisely why I am expecting Mr Wilbraham to recover.' He waited, eyebrows raised expectantly.

'Because of Mrs Clapper?' Lily asked, puzzled.

The smile broadened. 'Because of all of you, the two spinster ladies, Mr Smithers, Mrs Clapper and you. Not many patients have such devoted care,' he continued, 'and if your friend is aware of you all – which I am sure he is, for all that he doesn't yet know who you are – then no doubt he is as eager to return to you as you are to have him back.' He drew out a gold hunter, flipped open the case and groaned. 'Now I really must be on my way. Goodnight, Miss Raynor.' He stared at her for a moment, frowning. '*Talk* to him, and try not to worry.'

Try not to worry, she thinks now.

Easier said than done.

She turns her pillow, closes her eyes, but sleep is still as distant as the moon. Getting quietly out of bed, she picks up her notebook and pencil, wraps herself in her thick shawl and goes through to the bedroom. She sits down in the chair beside the bed, turning the lamp up a little.

She studies Felix. He is profoundly asleep, breathing deeply and steadily. His forehead is quite cool to the touch.

She opens her notebook and, after thinking for a while, begins to write. After only half a page she is already painfully aware how much she misses Felix in this process; normally they do it together, both of them throwing in ideas and drawing tentative conclusions. Now she's alone. She had not realised just how much she has come to depend on him . . .

Stop it, she tells herself.

She sets out an outline of each problem followed by a proposed plan of action. The first reads: *Problem One: Find some way of viewing the skeleton in the Fetterplace garden.*

Felix was refused access when he called at the house, for the surely insubstantial reason that any discussion of the bones upsets Miss Fanny. What nonsense, Lily thinks now. They brought the problem to us – what did they think it would lead to but a discussion of the skeleton?

Of course, Felix then went back by night. Lily has no idea if he managed to get into the garden and achieved his objective; it depends on whether his assailant came across him before or after he had climbed the wall into the garden.

It is too painful to think about that.

She forces her mind back to Problem One, and presently spots the obvious solution. She writes: *Plan of Action: call at 8, Mary Rose Court and catch Alethea Fetterplace on her own.*

She is not sure how to accomplish this, but surely the three siblings do not spend each and every minute of the day together? If the brother and the younger sister venture out, or if Miss Alethea sets off on a solo outing, that will be Lily's chance.

Problem Two, she writes: *Something sinister is going on in the vicinity of the path behind the Mary Rose Court gardens.* She adds: *Smell of putrefaction, dilapidated old shed hidden out of the way.*

She wonders if Felix made this discovery. If he disturbed whoever uses that path – she remembers the footsteps – and if it was this person who assaulted him.

'This *man*,' she whispers, for she cannot but think that the figure she saw passing by the end of the dank little passage must be connected. He scared her so much, she remembers reluctantly, that he must have been there for some sinister purpose . . .

Plan of Action, she hurries on. Then she stops, for she doesn't think she has one. After a moment she writes: *Ask Miss Fetterplace if she has observed any comings and goings.*

She hears a soft rustle of bedclothes; Felix has turned over. She puts down her notes and edges her chair closer. Dr March said she should talk to him, she remembers.

So, very softly, she says, 'Felix, I wish I could talk to you. I wish we could pool our thoughts on the Fetterplace business, and that I could ask you if you had the first idea of whether there really is something alarming going on behind the Mary Rose Court gardens.' She pauses, stretching out her hand to touch his. 'I had no idea how much I valued your original way of thinking and your sound sense until they were taken away,' she goes on. Then, in a rush, 'I don't think I can do it without you. Please, *please*, dearest Felix, come back!'

Felix swims up out of a dream.

Whatever the bulky man with the big hands gave him has worked. He feels better, and his head does not ache as much. The sense that he doesn't understand what is real and what is part of the dream has receded slightly, although he is still very confused.

But he knows that he is safe in this comfortable bed in the calm room with its single low-flamed lantern.

There's a woman sitting beside the bed. She has her fair head bent over a notebook and she is writing busily. She is dressed in a nightgown with a lace-edged frill at the neck, and has a heavy woollen shawl around her shoulders. He thinks that he must know her. She isn't a nurse, because if she was, she would be in uniform.

Nurse . . .

For some reason the word rings a faint bell in his memory.

The fair-haired woman is still writing. She is preoccupied, and hasn't noticed that he is watching her. He studies her. He realises he is smiling. He has no idea who she is, but he knows he can trust her. That he is safe when she is here.

After quite some time, he also realises that he cares for her. Very deeply.

In the morning, Lily stands at the end of the passage between the terraces in Mary Rose Court. After quite a long wait, the door of number 8 opens and Miss Alethea Fetterplace and her brother Thomas step out into the chilly morning air. Lily eases back into the passage until she is concealed, annoyed that the wrong combination of siblings has just left the house. But then the door abruptly opens again and there is Fanny on the top step, handkerchief clutched to her face, and she wails, 'Don't leave me all by myself, you meanies! *I want to come too!*'

Miss Alethea stops, irritation apparent in her very stance. Then she hisses to her brother, 'It's your turn, Dukey. I took her last time.'

'Yes, and look what happened!' he hisses back. 'Yes, I *know* she loves going on the river, but she always makes a fuss, sooner or later, and I simply *hate* it!' His tone changes to a wheedle as he adds, 'Couldn't you and I go on our own, just this once?'

Miss Fetterplace is clearly tempted to abandon her tricky sister and leave her to her wailing. But then there is a loud howl of anguish from Fanny, and she sobs, 'You're *plotting*! I *know* you are, so don't you *dare* deny it! I hate you, I HATE you! Don't leave me, you're not allowed to leave me, *take me with you!*'

The last four words are a furious scream. Curtains are already twitching as Thomas Fetterplace says angrily, 'Oh, very well, I'll go back and fetch her.' He rests a brief hand on his elder sister's arm. 'It's all right, Alethea. You stay at home, and I'll take her. It is, as you said, my turn.'

Miss Fanny, Lily observes with amusement, must have been fairly sure her tactics would embarrass her siblings enough for her to get her own way, for even as Thomas hurries back to the house, she emerges in hat and cloak clutching a small reticule. Lily waits in her hiding place until Alethea has gone inside the house and Thomas and Fanny are out of sight. Then she goes and knocks on the door.

'My colleague Mr Wilbraham is indisposed,' she says once she and Alethea Fetterplace are seated in wing chairs in a pleasant room overlooking the wild garden. A small fire burns in the grate, and its cheery warmth is welcome. 'However, when he was here last week, you told him that he could not examine the skeleton in your rose bed because of the distress it would cause to your sister.' Seeing Miss Fetterplace open her mouth to reply, she presses on relentlessly. 'Now, Miss Fanny is not here this morning, and so I must insist that you permit me to go down your garden and carry out a full inspection, since until I have done so, I fear I can make very little progress in this case.'

She hears the echo of her forthright words in the quiet room. She is embarrassed; she hadn't realised she was speaking so loudly and so crossly.

Miss Fetterplace waits courteously for a moment to see if her guest has any more to say, then, with a diffident smile, says, 'That is precisely the conclusion I reached too, Miss Raynor. Of course it is necessary for you or your colleague to view the skeleton, I do understand that, and I deeply regret that my brother's and my indulgence of Fanny and her ways has led to this unfortunate delay.'

A delay, Lily reflects angrily, which led directly to Felix being so badly hurt, since if you'd let him look at the wretched bones in the first place, he wouldn't have had to creep back by night. But Miss Fetterplace really does look as if she's sorry, and so Lily waits until she can speak calmly.

'Thank you, Miss Fetterplace,' she murmurs.

Her hostess bends down and rummages in the large bag she has deposited on the floor beside her chair. 'I have written to you, and here is the letter,' she says, holding it out to Lily. 'Look!' She points to the name and address. 'I have suggested in my note that we arrange a private meeting. And here you are!' she exclaims.

'Here I am,' agrees Lily. She stands up. 'Shall we begin?'

Her first sight of the delicate bones lying in their earthy shroud sets off a strong and unexpected surge of compassion. Lily can see straight away that the skeleton is that of a woman. A fine-boned woman, not very tall. The head lies where it would have been in life, and the severing cut is only apparent when she looks hard. The teeth are small and even, and only two are missing. The bones of the face indicate that in life the woman had a delicate, pointed chin, a broad forehead and high cheekbones. There is an unusual degree of symmetry, and she would have been truly beautiful. The arms are folded across the chest and the hands are small, with long finger bones. Something about the little finger on the right hand catches her eye, and briefly she bends closer for a better look, straightening up again with a frown. The pelvis tells Lily's experienced eyes that the woman bore at least one child. A mother, then, and almost certainly a wife. And the bones of the upper spine reveal with no doubt at all that the head was removed from the body by means of a single, clean stroke with a very sharp blade, wielded by expert hands.

Lily finds it rather difficult to turn her attention away from the woman's skeleton and onto the items that were buried in the earth beside her. She picks up the three little pearls, one of which is cleaner than the others, rubbing them with her fingertips. The action removes the dirt of centuries and brings a lustrous shine. Whoever gave them to the woman had a lot of money. Assuming the fragment of gold chain was another gift from the same man, its weight and quality support that conclusion. She is about to pick up the fragment of rich cloth when, out of nowhere, she suddenly realises that she is uncomfortably close to the path on the other side of the garden wall.

And now she appreciates that she is in a high state of alert. Her heart is thumping, her breathing is shallow and her palms are sweating. She thinks at first the fast-growing uneasiness is because she is crouching right beside a skeleton. She turns to look at it again, and once again sorrow and pity flood through her. She reaches out her hand and very gently strokes the skeleton's right cheekbone with her fingertips.

She understands that the old bones do not scare her at all.

How could they, when her heart is filled with distress over the poor young woman's awful death? Far from being repulsed and frightened by her pitiful skeleton, she would quite like to gather up what remains of the woman and give her a hug.

She knows then that the fear is because of whatever is infecting the path beyond the wall.

Gently she replaces the light covering of earth over the bones and the grave goods. She acts without thinking: her mind is fully engaged elsewhere.

She is in the garden of number 8. There are two more houses completing the row, and she can see from where she crouches that the wall continues after the last house, where it makes its sharp turn in towards the churchyard. And that is the corner where the half-hidden building stands, tucked away beneath the trees and among the brambles and the buddleia.

She looks across into the gardens of numbers 9 and 10. They are in much the same state as the one she is now in. The fences still stand, more or less, but it would not be difficult to find a way through. Then, assuming she could get over or round the wall, she would be only a few paces from the hidden building.

Slowly she stands up.

She ought to go and investigate it. She wants to – or, at least, a part of her does. The other part of her is shaking with fear because, although she is still in the relative safety of number 8's garden, with only an ancient and pathetic skeleton for company, already she is filled with anticipatory dread at the thought of emerging onto the path.

'Do it,' she whispers aloud. 'Go on, *do* it! You have to; there's nobody else.'

Not allowing herself any more thinking time, she edges through the first crumbling fence, steps over the second and finds herself on a dark little path overhung with the sweeping branches of a willow. She follows it, hoping it will end in an impassable barrier. But it doesn't. She reaches the wall, but here there are steps that lead up to the top and down the other side.

She climbs up and jumps down onto the path.

Close up, the building looks even more ramshackle. It is coated in green mould, dying greenery reaches up towards the eaves, the wooden planks of the walls are warped and the roof has several gaping holes. She edges round to the far side, looking for a door. Its planks too are bowed and bent. Leaning forward, she peers through the biggest gap, trying to see what is inside.

But the gap doesn't give any view of the interior. Right behind it is a second door, and this one smells of recently sawn wood. Hurrying now, tripping in her haste, she returns to the other places where there were big gaps, and in every case finds the same result: the ancient, rotting timbers of the original walls have been neatly and unobtrusively backed by new timber. What looks to the casual eye to be an abandoned wreck is only the outer shell of something very different. She looks up at the roof. Now she knows what to look for, she can see that this too has a new lining.

Whoever did this work has provided himself with a virtually invisible space in which to store secrets, or carry out some sort of clandestine work, without anybody knowing about it.

Lily can smell putrefaction; she thought she detected it as she reached the bend of the path, and now the stench is stronger and she wants to retch. Slowly she goes back to the door, trying the handle. It is locked.

Inside her head a voice says sternly: *get away from there!*

'But . . .' she begins.

Then her courage runs out. As panicky fear rushes in to replace it, she turns, flies back down the path to where the steps cross over the wall, pushes through two fences and a lot of undergrowth and comes to a stop, bent over, hands on her hips, gasping for breath, beside the rose bed.

She waits until her heartbeat and her breathing are almost back to normal. Then she tidies her hair, brushes the dead leaves and the seed heads off her skirt and, trying to assume a calm expression, walks back through the wilderness of garden to the house, where Alethea Fetterplace awaits her.

TEN

'I lost sight of you as you went up the garden,' Miss Fetterplace greets her. 'You found your way, did you? You have now studied the skeleton?'

'Yes, thank you,' Lily replies.

Miss Fetterplace is studying her anxiously. 'Dear me, Miss Raynor, but you look very pale! And how your hands shake! Oh, and your skirt is muddy at the hem – let me fetch a clothes brush, and I shall—'

'Please do not trouble yourself,' Lily says firmly. 'Better to let the mud dry, then it will brush off readily.'

Miss Fetterplace nods, then, still looking worriedly at Lily, says, 'Sit down, Miss Raynor. You look as if your legs will not bear you another minute! I will make a strong pot of tea, and you will feel better in a trice.' She heads for the door, and briefly she turns back. 'The remains of that poor lost woman are a disturbing sight, I know. I cannot look down upon them without a tremor in the heart, and the first time I saw them, I . . . well, suffice it to say I felt much as you do now, Miss Raynor.'

Lily, head resting in the corner of the wing chair by the hearth, closes her eyes and lets the warmth of the fire creep up her legs. She had not realised how cold she was. Only a short time ago, battling her way back into the garden of number 8, she was sweating from exertion and dread, and now the sweat has grown chilly on her flesh. She shudders.

Miss Fetterplace seems to think that Lily's trembling hands and extreme pallor are because she has been examining the bones. Lily has no intention of correcting the assumption. Whatever lies concealed within the ruined walls of the old shed is not for sharing. 'Even if I knew what was in there and *could* share the information,' Lily mutters to herself.

She can hear the encouraging sounds of a kettle coming to the boil and the clatter of cups and saucers. The quiet domestic sounds soothe her, and she senses herself backing away from the fringes of whatever horrors lie along the path and into the safety of the warm and comfortable room.

Miss Fetterplace is a conscientious hostess, and it is not until Lily has drunk two cups of tea and eaten one and a half rather stale ginger biscuits that she leans forward in her chair and, her face eager, says, 'Now then, Miss Raynor, what did you make of our skeleton?'

Lily has been expecting the question. Briefly she summaries her findings: the bones are those of a woman, young, slender and not very tall, who had borne a child or children and who was accompanied by fragments of jewellery and some cloth fragments of rare and costly quality.

'Yes, yes, and what age are the bones?' Miss Fetterplace demands.

'I cannot say with any certainty,' Lily replies. 'It is, I believe, very difficult to determine how long a skeleton has been in the earth. It was buried deep, I understand?'

'Indeed,' Miss Fetterplace confirms. 'Not a recent burial, for there were layers and layers of detritus above her.'

Lily notes the change of pronoun. Not for the first time, she reflects that the Fetterplace siblings decided that the bones were those of a woman long before anybody came along to confirm it. 'I have the sense that these are old bones,' she agrees. 'Apart from anything else . . .' She stops, not sure whether to go on, for what she had been about to say will be hard to hear for the strangely agitated woman sitting opposite.

'Go on, Miss Raynor,' comes the quiet order.

'The manner of death also suggests that the woman died a long time ago, for she was beheaded by a single, skilful stroke. It is a hundred years and more since anybody met their death in this manner,' she says.

'You say *died*, and *met their death*,' Miss Fetterplace says with sudden sharpness. 'She did not *die*, Miss Raynor. She was killed. Murdered, indeed, by the cold hand of the state acting at the behest of the king, and she . . .' With obvious difficulty, she cuts off the flow of hot words. She sits quite still for some moments, her breathing calming, then says, 'I apologise, Miss Raynor. My dismay overcame me.'

'I quite understand,' Lily replies calmly.

There is a short silence. Then, recalling something from the siblings' visit to the Bureau's office, she says, 'You told us when you came to see us that you believed the skeleton was that of someone of importance, and you hinted at royalty.'

Miss Fetterplace sighs. 'That is Baby's firm conviction,' she mutters. 'My sister, Frances,' she adds.

'I cannot be *sure*,' Lily says, emphasising the word, 'but I believe she may be right.' Trying to ignore the flare of hope she sees in Miss Fetterplace's face, she explains. 'Several factors point to this. First, the fragments of costly jewellery and fabric indicate great wealth, although we must bear in mind that these may have nothing to do with our skeleton.'

Miss Fetterplace shakes her head very firmly, presumably in denial. Mildly irritated by this certainty, Lily says, 'I do wonder, Miss Fetterplace, that you leave those lovely pearls out there in the rose bed, where they might attract the attention of an opportune thief.'

Miss Fetterplace's expression is stony. 'It is highly unlikely that such a person would climb over the wall and begin digging in the rose bed. And besides . . .' She stops abruptly, then adds in a whisper, 'They stay with her.'

There is a rather awkward silence.

Then, resuming her account, Lily says, 'Second, the bones, and especially the leg bones, are straight and their surfaces are smooth and not pitted, and both these factors point to an adequate, if not good, diet in childhood. No young woman raised in filth and dire poverty in the sinks of a great city could have bones like that. Third, the teeth are good. One or two are missing, but that could have happened since death, and the remainder are sound, with no sign of the wear that occurs even in young adults from grinding down food of poor quality, such as bread made from flour containing stones and other impurities. In the absence of flesh, it is, naturally, impossible to judge this woman's body shape, but I believe she was well fed from childhood onwards, which, once again, implies wealth and privilege.'

Miss Fetterplace's eyes are alight with excitement.

'So she is . . . she could well be a woman of high status,' she whispers.

And Lily has to agree. 'It is not impossible,' she concedes.

Miss Fetterplace nods, several times. Her lips move as if she is silently talking to herself, and Lily can almost feel the intensity of her thoughts. Miss Fanny, she thinks, said the skeleton was that of a kinswoman. Her brother and sister had quickly dismissed the claim, and Lily concluded that it was probably no more than Fanny's fanciful wishful thinking.

But as she runs through her mind what else was said at that initial meeting, she recalls talk of *occurrences* . . . Night noises, and a quick flicker of light as from a carelessly uncovered lantern. And the noises and the lights came from the direction of the end of the garden and the churchyard.

If only Felix and I had been able to discuss all this together, Lily thinks, her mind full of distress, one of us would have realised the importance of those occurrences. And then, like a blow to the head, she remembers what Felix said just after the siblings had departed: *I believe something very dark is going on here.*

Oh, Felix, she says to him silently, how right you were.

Miss Fetterplace's expression suggests she has snapped back into the moment. Eyes intent on Lily, she says gravely, 'There is something which we *must* address, Miss Raynor. If we are right and the remains at the end of the garden are indeed those of a figure of historical importance, it is possible that we are not the only people who know about them.'

'But . . .' Lily hesitates. 'But how *could* anyone else know?' she demands. 'The skeleton has probably been lying in your garden for centuries! You only discovered it recently, by accident, and . . .' But something in Miss Fetterplace's expression sends out a warning; suddenly she looks furtive. Guilty, even. And, for an instant, the resemblance to her sister is strong.

'I fear, Miss Raynor, that we were not quite truthful,' Miss Fetterplace murmurs.

'Go on.'

She draws a breath, then says, 'We told you that we felt it our duty to restore the rose garden, and Fanny explained in some detail how old it was, and how our mother and grandmother had treasured it.'

'I remember.' Lily's tone is cool.

'And then Dukey – my brother, Thomas – described digging right down through layers and layers of china fragments and old pipes, stones, broken bricks and roots, going so deep that in places he came to bare clay.' She pauses, looking questioningly at Lily as if expecting her to comment. 'Didn't you *see*?' she adds.

And then Lily understands.

'Didn't we see that it was too much,' she says slowly. 'That if your brother had dug as deeply as he was implying, it was not in order to clear the ground for a rose bed.'

Miss Fetterplace is nodding. 'Miss Raynor,' she says softly, 'we did not discover her skeleton by chance. We *knew* it was in the garden, and the rose bed was not the first place we tried.' She pauses, smiling faintly. 'Dukey was threatening to give up because he said it was worse than needles in haystacks, and he was afraid that, despite letting the weeds and the brambles proliferate, if we went on digging trenches, someone would eventually notice. Then Fanny of all people, silly, fanciful, nerve-wracked little Baby, said she believed the bones lay in the rose bed. And,' she concludes simply, 'she was right.'

'Why didn't you tell us this when you engaged the Bureau's services?' Lily asks.

Miss Fetterplace looks away. 'I apologise,' she says, although it is no explanation.

'You should have . . .' Lily begins.

But Miss Fetterplace isn't listening. 'Oh, Miss Raynor, don't you *see*?' she cries. 'We knew the bones were there, and we are all but certain whose they are. We had always suspected their presence, because of who she was and who we are.' And Lily hears Fanny's shrill screeching voice saying, "She's ours. Our kinswoman."

Lily waits. She knows what Miss Fetterplace is about to say, for she is thinking the same thing.

'If *we* know,' Alethea says very softly, 'then it is not impossible that others know too. And if they also know who she is, then that would account, would it not, for the noises and the flashes of light that we see in the night at the end of the garden.'

After another lengthy pause, Miss Fetterplace speaks again.

'I believe that when we sought you out, we gave the impression that our main concern was to find out why there was a skeleton buried in our garden and what we should do about it. But, Miss Raynor, we always knew she was there, and we need no advice on what we should do with her! No – we sought your help because we're not only going by the night noises and the flash of light; we *know* someone haunts the path at the end of the garden, and he will not stop until he has robbed us of our treasure.' Her face looks haggard. 'Miss Raynor, we are so *very* afraid of what he will do next.'

As Lily sits on the west-bound tram, she tries to put her thoughts in order.

The Fetterplace siblings did not engage the Bureau because they were frightened and disturbed at the discovery of the skeleton; they already knew it was there. Lily wonders *how* they knew about the skeleton. And how they came to the conclusion that the dead woman was related to them.

The siblings engaged the Bureau because of the figure who haunts the path between the gardens and the churchyard. They fear he too knows about the skeleton, and moreover who she is. Who she *was*. Lily thinks about the nature of that fear: it doesn't seem to be the case that they think he will take it away and in some way gain by revealing who she is; they are simply scared of him as a being.

If he is the person Lily believes him to be, she entirely agrees with them. She is so frightened of the *menace* he exudes that she is shaking even in the safety of the tram.

What does this man want with the skeleton? Does he think that the grave of a wealthy and important historical figure must contain a vast hoard of riches? If so – and assuming the Fetterplaces haven't found more jewellery and already hidden it away – he is wrong. Does he seek the fame and fortune that he believes will follow when he announces to the world he has found the body of a very famous victim of past violence? But will there even *be* any fame and fortune waiting for him?

Lily frowns, frustrated by her inability to see a clear motive.

The man who haunts the path by the graveyard wall is very protective of his patch, Lily muses. If, that is, she is correct in thinking it was the same person who attacked Felix so savagely in his fury at finding someone climbing the wall into – or out of – the Fetterplaces' garden in the middle of the night.

The tram trundles on. She will be at her stop soon. She puts her notebook away, tries to relax her mind and lets her thoughts drift.

She is sure that the haunting man's presence in the vicinity of the path and the back garden of number 8 cannot be a coincidence. He is up to something there; she knows it, and the Fetterplaces' reports of noises and lights at night support it. He has a shed at his disposal; a wreck of an old building that most people would pass by with hardly a glance. Except, Lily thinks, that it is not what it appears; the warped old planks hide a secret, which is hidden away behind the new timber of the inner walls. And whatever is inside stinks of rotten meat.

Presently she descends from the tram and makes her way down World's End Passage to turn into Hob's Court, at the bottom on the right. She walks slowly. She wants to rush home, seek out Felix and talk it all over with him, but Felix is not Felix just now.

'I am no good at all without him,' she says under her breath. 'I manage to come up with the questions, but without his contribution, I cannot find the answers.'

She is almost at her own front door. She takes out her key and lets herself in.

Mrs Clapper comes scuttling through from the kitchen as Lily removes her boots. 'He's been up and out of bed!' she says joyfully. Her eyes are bright with excitement. 'Mr Smithers has been here this morning and Mr Felix said he stank – him, not Mr Smithers – and needed a wash, so Miss Adderley said we could borrow her Chinese screen and me, her and Mr Smithers took it up to your room and put it round the wash stand, and I fetched hot water and towels and that, and Mr Smithers stayed there with Mr Felix to make sure he didn't fall over while he had a full body wash and . . . er, and the rest, and meanwhile I stripped the bed and laid out a clean, freshly ironed nightshirt, then once Mr Felix was in bed again, he and Mr Smithers ate a *very* good meal!'

As Mrs Clapper finally takes a breath, Lily studies her flushed face. 'Dear Mrs Clapper, you have worked so hard!' she exclaims.

'Well, it wasn't just me,' she replies modestly, but Lily can see she is very pleased with the compliment. 'Miss Sutherland helped too, and at one time when we were all bustling about up there, Mr Felix looked at us and he grinned, Miss Lily, truly, he *grinned*, and he said, "I have no idea who you all are, but you seem to be helping me, for which I thank you most sincerely, but if you wouldn't mind, I would now like a little privacy while I . . ."' She stops abruptly, blushing. 'Well, he wanted a few moments to himself.'

In her time, Lily has nursed many people in the early stages of recovering their independence after illness or injury, and she fully understands.

'That is very good news!' she says warmly. 'To have got out of bed, and stood up, and eaten a proper meal, is *most* encouraging.' She pauses. 'Did he know where he was, or what happened?'

And silently, no longer looking joyful, Mrs Clapper shakes her head.

'He's asleep now, but he's had a wash and he's eaten a proper meal,' Marm greets Lily as she walks into Felix's sickroom. Marm looks up at her. 'Oh. You already know.'

'Yes. Mrs Clapper met me in the hall.' She draws up the second chair and sits down beside Marm. 'She said he didn't recognise any of you.'

Marm takes her hand briefly and gives it an encouraging squeeze. 'No, dear Lily, he didn't. But he understands that we are his friends,' he goes on. 'I helped him with washing, and he leaned on me with utter trust. He *knew* he knows me!' he adds fervently. 'It's a start,' he says gently when she doesn't respond.

'He's been talking, I gather?' she says after a moment.

'Yes, although I have to admit he hasn't been making much sense,' Marm replies. 'It's almost as if the words just spring into his mind and spill out of him without any sort of filtering to see if they have any meaning.'

Lily studies Felix. She is just wondering if he has any idea that they are talking about him when, as if he feels her attention, he opens his eyes. 'Tiger Lily,' he mutters. He smiles, and his eyes close again.

Lily spins round to look at Marm. 'Tiger Lily?' she whispers, trying to hide her excitement.

'From the book.' Marm points to *Alice Through the Looking-Glass*, over on the desk. 'Alice visits the garden of live flowers, and there's a Tiger Lily, a Rose, Larkspur and a lot of daisies. I don't think it means anything, Lily my dear,' he adds, compassion in his eyes.

Lily doesn't reply. But she reflects that Felix might have looked at her and said *Rose*, or *Larkspur*, but he said *Lily*. Admittedly it was preceded by *Tiger*, but she can't help but feel hopeful.

She offers to relieve Marm. She hopes he'll say he'd rather stay for a while, because she would very much like to share today's disturbing discoveries with him. But he accepts with alacrity, explaining that he has been neglecting a couple of useful sources of information and, if he makes haste, he might just catch at least one of them.

Lily smiles as he hurries away. Marm often meets people in a large and lively pub up on the King's Road called The Cow Jumped Over the Moon, and she suspects he is as keen to have a couple of pints and a pie as he is to seek out his neglected sources.

Not that she blames him.

The afternoon wears on. Bunty relieves Lily, picking up *Alice* to read a further chapter, and on her way down to write up her notes in the Inner Sanctum, Lily meets Mrs Clapper, on her way up with a tray of food and drink for Felix.

Mrs Clapper gives her a hopeful smile.

Lily shuts herself away in the quiet of her office. Alone, behind two closed doors, she puts her head down on her arms folded on her desk and gives way to her distress, her anxiety and her anguish.

It is night.

Felix has just woken up in the still, silent, dark house, and he realises straight away that he is far more alert. Images are flashing rapidly and violently through his head, although they seem random and totally without meaning, and he doesn't know if they are fragments of dreams or a sign that he is beginning to remember.

He lies in the darkness, eyes open, trying to make sense of what his mind is presenting to him.

Fear.

The dark figure of a man on a path. A face glimpsed for the space of a heartbeat before the light went out.

Lilies.

Tiger Lily.

A sheep in a dark little shop knitting with fourteen pairs of needles. No – that was surely part of a dream. It was a *woman* who was knitting, and she only had three needles. Her brown hair was in a bun and she had small dark eyes that crinkled when she smiled.

Nurse.

A handcart with odd red shapes stacked in it . . . Could they have been chess pieces? He's sure he heard someone mention a Red King.

The scent of lilies and roses.

The iron stench of blood.

An egg that fell off a wall, and all the king's horses and all the king's men trying to put him together.

Did the Red King have the horses and the men?

He is becoming very muddled, and his head aches with the frustration of trying to sort what is in his memory and what is in a dream. And, as he tries to go deeper into his memory, suddenly he is back at school.

There was a boy, two years older than himself . . . An odd boy, secretive, who liked to walk on the strand with a walrus and a carpenter and eat oysters . . .

Fatigue is catching up and rapidly overwhelming him.

He lets it take him and slides back down into a brief, profound sleep.

Lily senses the presence of someone very close by.

Struggling up out of a dream, her first thought is that it must be Dorothea or Bunty, hurrying to wake her up because there has been an emergency with Felix. 'What is it? Has something happened to him?' she stammers, dazed with sleep.

She can see someone kneeling beside her bed. But it isn't Bunty or Dorothea.

It's Felix.

'Is it you?' she asks stupidly. It is, of course it is, and she can see him quite clearly in the soft light of the lamp burning in the next room.

'It's me,' he confirms. She can't see his face clearly, but she can tell he is smiling.

'Do you know who you are?' she whispers. Her heart is bursting with hope, but she hardly dares ask the question.

'I . . . Not really. I know I know *you*, if you see what I mean, because without any idea why, I feel that I'm totally safe with you.' *Oh*, she thinks. 'Also, I appear to have just got out of your bed. A bed in a woman's room, anyway, and I am guessing it's yours.'

'It is,' she confirms very softly. And yes, you are totally safe, she adds silently.

There is so much she wants to say, so many questions that hurtle into her mind demanding instant answers.

She shoves them all aside, for he is staring at her rather blankly and she senses it is far too soon for a barrage of questions that he won't be able to answer.

And, anyway, the hunger for answers is a very long way from being uppermost in her mind.

She wonders if she should say what she's longing to say. Whether it will distress him; whether she will regret such naked emotion in the morning.

But neither reservation seems to be capable of holding her back.

'I thought I'd lost you,' she says very quietly. 'I thought you weren't coming back to—' She very nearly says 'me', and just in time changes it – 'us.'

He reaches out and touches her cheek. 'I have been wandering,' he says. 'I still don't know what happened, but I'm guessing from the pain in my head and the constant ache in my ribs and all the big bandages that I was attacked.'

'You were,' she says shortly. It surely wouldn't be wise to tell him the details right now.

He nods slowly. 'When did it happen?'

She hesitates. Then, thinking that he'll have to know sooner or later, she tells him. He whistles. 'Four *days* ago!'

'Five now, if it's after midnight,' she tells him.

He is looking down at her, eyes intent on hers, and there is an expression she hasn't seen before on his pale face. 'You've been taking care of me,' he says, so quietly that she can barely hear. 'You, and an older woman in an apron who brings the food, and a man with a thin, kind face, and two spinsters who have a look of intelligence. I *will* remember their names and who they all are,' he adds, quite fiercely, 'but I haven't remembered *yet*.'

His hand is still on her cheek, and now she puts her own hand over it. 'I know,' she says simply.

They stay like that for some moments. She feels that she is in a different reality, and suddenly she has the awful fear that this is only a dream . . .

In this unreal world it seems perfectly possible for him to pick up her thoughts.

He does.

With his free hand he reaches down to her bare forearm and very gently gives her a pinch. 'It's not a dream,' he says.

Presently he stands up, and she leaps out of bed in case the sudden movement makes him dizzy.

'I'm all right, Tiger Lily,' he says. 'That's what I call you in my head,' he adds. 'I'm not going to faint. But I think, don't you, that I should leave you to your prim little bed and go back into the bedroom.'

They are, she realises, in their nightclothes and standing very close to each other. She takes a hurried step back, and she thinks she hears him chuckle. 'I'll come with you,' she offers, which is not at all what she ought to have said, not in those words at least, and through the rush of confusion and embarrassment she hears him laugh aloud.

'Would you like to take my arm, Nurse?' he asks.

Nurse? It is a shock that he should call her that, but instantly she tells herself it doesn't mean he's remembered that she used to be a nurse, only that he assumes she's been nursing him. Which, of course, she's doing right now.

And, her hand supporting him, together they walk back into the bedroom and he gets into bed. She tucks him up. He is so close, and he's looking at her in such a way . . .

She steps back and says, 'Goodnight. Sleep well, and I shall see you in the morning.'

She can still hear him chuckling as she pulls up the covers in the little bed next door.

ELEVEN

The Barrow Man can't stop thinking about the dead man he left under the churchyard wall. He still finds it difficult to control his fury with whoever crossed the invisible border into his secret place and took away the corpse.

The Barrow Man has a profound sense of the sheer *injustice* of that.

The other reason for his persistent, obsessive thoughts is that there was something familiar about the man's features, or perhaps it was the bearing . . .

He tries to recall the face.

He cannot rid himself of the suspicion that he has seen the man somewhere before; even, perhaps, that he knew him somewhere in an earlier episode of his life.

But where? And when? In which phase of his long and widespread past did the encounter take place?

It is difficult, because there have been so many phases.

Deliberately, methodically, he thinks back over his life.

He dismisses his childhood and early boyhood, for the face of the man lodged in his memory is that of a boy fast approaching maturity. The man, whoever he was, did not belong to the life of the child and the boy who was called Tobias Fountain. Perhaps it was at the college. However, his initial thought is that this is unlikely since he made no friends there, certainly nothing approaching a close friend – he has never had a close friend – and so why should a face from those two endless years stay with him?

He travels further into the past.

When he was spirited away from the college after the incident with the cat, he went to London, reasoning that in the unlikely event that anyone from the school, or some agent of his wealthy benefactor, should have a fit of conscience and decide to come looking for him after all, it was surely prudent to lose himself in a huge metropolis. So vast had been the seething masses, so endless the teeming, stinking, overcrowded streets and the dark, dank lanes and alleyways, that he didn't even bother to give himself a new name. He discovered in a very short time that in big cities people were largely anonymous.

Quite quickly, however, he understood that he needed to be elsewhere. Although he carried inside himself the quiet conviction that one day London would be *exactly* the place where he must be, that day had not yet come. So he left, as quietly and unobtrusively as he had arrived, and went north.

In the wild places into which he ventured, he soon became feral.

He stole a well-filled wallet from a drunk outside York Minster and had a bath, a shave and a haircut, purchased some good clothes and caught a train to Scotland. Adopting the plummy, affected accent of some of his more annoying schoolfellows, he became Harry MacFarlane. If anyone asked – they rarely did – he told them that he was a Scot by birth but had been removed south of the border when still a child and was only now returning home. He found work as a clerk in an office. He went out by night to busy places and relieved the careless of their valuables. The company of others rapidly becoming irksome, he left the mainland behind and headed out to the islands.

In a very remote part of Shetland, he conducted an interesting and informative series of experiments on the anatomy of sheep and the difference in the buoyancy of their dead flesh when placed in salt as opposed to fresh water.

He was always learning. From necessity, because he always travelled light, he developed the tiniest handwriting that was consistent with legibility and wrote up all his extensive notes in one large notebook.

Soon he discovered that even on a thinly populated island – particularly on such an island – there was always somebody who wanted to know who you were and what you were about. He realised that the sparse number of inhabitants always liked to know their neighbours' business. It was a good lesson learned, and as he said farewell to Harry MacFarlane and stole a rowing boat to see him on the first leg of his journey back to the mainland, he knew not to venture to such a lonely spot again.

The year 1874 was significant, for it was in the November that he made his first human kill.

He is deep in the past now, eyes closed, moaning softly as he remembers the warm blood pouring out over his chilly hands. He has forgotten all about trying to work out where he had encountered the dead man under the churchyard wall.

Drawn always to water in all its forms, the next place where he spent any time was Liverpool. In the guise of Walter Blackmore, he took on work in the docks and found lodgings with an elderly widow, and for more than three years allowed himself the luxury of being cared for devotedly by a lonely soul who sometimes treated him like a son, sometimes like a potential lover. He had to smother his bone-deep disgust when she tried to flirt with him. She was a woman, a living woman, with a woman's smells; he could not have tolerated living in such close proximity to her had she been younger, and still under the mysterious power of the moon that made the blood of her sex leach out with such regularity. Nevertheless, despite her age, once or twice the temptation to put a permanent end to her pathetic advances almost overcame him. But it was too dangerous to kill in a place where he was known to reside, so he would thrust her roughly aside and go out into the night.

The wide, accommodating Mersey opened her generous arms, and the detritus from his next round of experiments disappeared under the surface. Two human bodies followed, in pieces. For the remains of the third he put his heavy sack over his shoulder and went by night to the wide, sandy strand where the Mersey flowed into the Irish Sea, where he consigned the contents to the outgoing tide.

He grew confident. Over-confident, perhaps. Although he could not bring to mind an occasion where confidence had led to carelessness, somehow there were rumours. Mere whispers, muttered in the dark in the secret places, but dangerous all the same. And then the name Walter Blackmore started to be attached to the rumours.

He left his lodgings and his old landlady in the early hours. His rent was paid until the end of the week and he left some coins on the kitchen table, for she had cared for him more tenderly than any woman and he was glad he had resisted the temptation to harm her.

Other than the coins, he left not a single trace of himself behind.

He arrived in London at the conclusion of four days of criss-crossing England (and a small portion of Wales) on a roundabout journey that only the most determined and ruthless pursuer with a bloodhound could have followed. It was early September, and the year was 1878.

He found cheap and not very clean lodgings in Poplar. The room was several levels below his usual sort of accommodation, but he knew he must lie low, for there were headlines even in the London newspapers about the brutal murders in Liverpool, and the name Walter Blackmore was repeated with worrying frequency.

Nevertheless, he ventured out. Following his usual custom, he found one or two places to sit and listen, in order to absorb the mood of the city and discover the preoccupations of the day. On this occasion it couldn't have been easier, for the matter in every Londoner's thoughts, and the talk on everyone's tongue, was a frightful disaster that had happened on the Thames only days ago.

On the preceding Tuesday, a paddle steamer called the *Princess Alice*, carrying a full load of passengers, had set out on a run known as the 'Moonlight Trip' to take passengers down the river from Swan Pier, close to London Bridge, to Sheerness and back. It was essentially a pleasure trip, and most of the passengers enjoyed some carefree hours among the delights of the Rosherville Gardens. The *Princess Alice* was on her homeward journey and the sun had set when she arrived at Gallions Reach, near Woolwich. It seemed that her captain had become confused somehow, and taken the wrong course. All might have been well, and perhaps he could have rectified the mistake, but another, much larger ocean-going vessel, the *Bywell Castle* – more than three times the weight of the *Princess Alice* – was coming the other way and she too had taken the wrong course. The hefty bulk of the *Bywell Castle* struck the flimsier *Princess Alice* at some speed immediately in front of the paddle box on the starboard side, the Alice was cut in two, and her broken remains sank in under four minutes.

Ropes were immediately thrown from the *Bywell Castle* and she lowered her lifeboat. Fourteen people were gathered up, and a few more were saved through the efforts of witnesses on the shore, who launched small rescue vessels.

There were probably more than eight hundred people on board the *Princess Alice*, although in the absence of a passenger manifest, nobody knew for sure. Most of those who were hurled into the water died quickly. Nobody could swim, and women faced the additional handicap of long, heavy dresses worn over layers of calico petticoats. Many people had been below, in the saloon; divers subsequently found their bodies crushed together in the doorways as they fought each other to get out. When the first rescue ship arrived ten minutes after the collision, it was already too late to save anyone in the water.

One of the most ghastly aspects of the disaster was that by terribly bad luck it happened at the spot where London's main pumping station poured some seventy-five million gallons of raw sewage into the Thames twice a day; the evening's quota had just been released when the *Princess Alice* went down. Any passenger who managed to keep his or her head above water and flounder towards the shore was soon engulfed in fermenting, decomposing sewage that hissed and bubbled like a glass of pop and stank of the privy and the charnel house. And, of course, was as toxic as the deadliest poison.

The dead were taken to several locations. Nobody knew who anybody was: the absence of a passenger manifest meant that there was no definitive list of names. Relatives and friends searching desperately for the missing were confounded by the stinking brown slime and faecal matter that coated the corpses. If they didn't get there quickly, they found that by the time they were bending over a body that might be the one they were searching for, the filth that covered the corpse would already have hastened putrefaction sufficiently to make the body all but unrecognisable.

The man who had recently been Walter Blackmore listened attentively. He felt no particular compassion; what small emotion he experienced was a mild disgust at the lurid descriptions of the state of the corpses.

And as he listened, he saw the bright sunbeam of opportunity.

There he was, haunted by the spectre of a man called Walter Blackmore, wanted in Liverpool in connection with the death of two prostitutes whose dismembered bodies were found floating in the Mersey (the third corpse, it seemed, had not turned up).

He made his usual thorough and diligent transition from one identity to the next. Then, once he had donned his new clothes and practised his new way of speaking and his altered deportment in front of the small and foxed looking glass in his squalid room, he set out.

He went to the nearest of the temporary mortuaries. Locating a harassed and drawn official who appeared to be in charge, he told his prepared story. 'My name is Phipps, Joseph Phipps,' he said in the accents of the street. 'I'm looking for my cousin, because he's newly arrived in London, he doesn't know his way around, and my aunt's going out of her mind with worry because he was meant to turn up on her doorstep on Tuesday night. And he really likes going on the river . . .'

He did not need to say any more.

With a sigh the official said, 'Age?'

'Twenty-seven? Twenty-eight?'

'Description?'

He gave one that could have fitted himself. It could equally have fitted hundreds of other men.

'Over there,' said the official.

For the next unforgettable forty-five minutes, the man now called Joseph Phipps walked up and down the long rows of filthy, foul corpses. When he decided he had taken long enough not to raise suspicion, he selected the next corpse that looked enough like himself and returned to the official. 'Found him?' the official asked brusquely. Joseph Phipps hesitated. 'I *think* so,' he said cautiously. Best not to seem too sure; how could anybody be sure, under the circumstances?

'Well?' The official now tempered brusqueness with a small amount of compassion.

'Walter had quite a big nose, like mine,' Joseph Phipps said, 'and it had this sort of bump in it, halfway down. That body over there' – he pointed – 'has the same nose.' He managed to put a little tremor into his voice, as if fighting to suppress emotion. 'The build and the height look about right,' he went on hoarsely, 'and what I can make out of the face does look like my cousin Walter, and I—'

The official had heard enough. He led Joseph Phipps over to a long table on which there were luggage labels on lengths of string and, taking one from the stack, dipped a pen in the ink.

'Full name?'

'Walter Blackmore.'

'Address?'

Joseph Phipps hesitated. 'Well, I cannot remember the name of the street, but it's in Anfield. That's in Liverpool,' he added helpfully.

'Any guess at the street name?' the official persisted.

'Could have been Anselm Street?' Joseph Phipps hazarded. 'And I'm sure it was an odd number . . . twenty-seven rings a faint bell . . .'

He watched in quiet satisfaction as the official wrote on the label in a very neat hand: *Walter Blackmore, 27, Anselm Street, Liverpool.* As the official bent over the corpse of an unknown man and tied the label through his top buttonhole, he slipped quietly away.

If anyone went to check, thought Joseph Phipps, then they would discover that a man called Walter Blackmore had indeed lived at 27, Anselm Street. But that man was not the corpse lying in the London mortuary. He had turned into Joseph Phipps, who even now had a spring in his step as he walked away.

Quite soon the forces of law and order would realise that the Liverpool murderer was dead, his noxious corpse lying in a London mortuary, and the suddenly dangerous identity of Walter Blackmore was left safety behind.

He quite liked being Joseph Phipps, and he adopted the role of a mild-mannered man of the East End who tended to whine and cringed like a dog if people became aggressive. Which, of course, was as distant from his true nature as north is from south. He found work with a brewery, loading the beer barrels onto the drays. But for some reason he could not settle in London then, although, just as before, he knew he would return.

One night he sat on the hard and uncomfortable chair in his squalid room and emptied his mind, remaining in his semi-trance until he understood his unease. It was Liverpool that had unnerved him. Not the killings – never that – but the fact that the name Walter Blackmore had been bruited abroad, even to the extent of appearing in the London press. True, Joseph Phipps' identification of Walter Blackmore's corpse had ended the speculation, but nevertheless the spectre of the hard hand of the law descending on his shoulder was a little too real for comfort.

Not without regret, he slipped away from the Poplar lodging house in the small hours. In a narrow and stinking back alley he put on a different coat and jacket, donned a fresh style of hat and, changing his posture from Joseph Phipps' apologetic cringe to a square-shouldered, straight-backed military stride, he became Wilfred Stirling. By various modes of transport, he headed out of London and through Essex and Suffolk into Norfolk, and for the next three years he lived the blameless life of a boatman working and living on the waterways of East Anglia.

Largely blameless.

The Walter Blackmore escapade had troubled him more than he cared to admit, and for eighteen months or more, he was content with the bland routine of work, food, work, food, sleep. He was, he reflected in hindsight, restoring himself.

He sensed he was being called – *summoned* – to one particular part of the Fenlands. It was a wide area crisscrossed by narrow channels and ditches that surrounded a village where there was a small railway station and a lunatic asylum. It had all been water once, or so they told him, those water people whose ancestors had always been there, when back in the far past the Fens stretched to the coast. That was before the skilful Dutchmen came, building the dykes that drained the marshes and turned the water back to the sea.

There were rumours about these dark fens; rumours that spoke of an ancient malignancy, a sinister power – perhaps a natural force – which had transmuted through fear and superstition into an instrument of evil that waited ever alert beneath the thin veneer of modern times. Like always called to like; the ancient darkness knew when an echo of itself was near and it rose to meet it, to reinforce it, to draw it out and urge it into action.

It called to him and, hearing it, he answered. Of course he did.

But this, he reminded himself, was his fallow period: after the one blinding flash of violence, he withdrew from the area and headed south. In a leisurely manner, for he was confident he had left no sign of what he had done.

Like a man addicted to alcohol who can give it up for a spell as long as he knows there is another drink waiting for him, he was able to set aside his experiments for months, even years, at a time, provided there were plans for the future. As he travelled the rivers and the navigations on this boat or that, working diligently at whatever task he was ordered to do, his mind flowed freely as he turned over the possibilities. When once again he was faced with irresistible temptation – in a backwater of a village near Thetford – it occurred to him later that the savagery was merely to keep his hand in.

Slowly his confidence returned. Increased. Nobody knows who I am, he thought. Who I have been. Nobody knows what I have done, what actions these hands have carried out.

I am invincible.

He did not hurry; did not allow his eagerness to proceed to the next phase of his life's work to overwhelm him. He knew he was ready – more than ready – but still he waited.

Then at last he answered the renewed and increasingly powerful siren call and came back to London. On a fine morning in the late May of this year, he made his way south along East Anglia's waterways for the final time. He took his time, pausing here and there for a week, a month, and in this leisurely way reached Bishop's Stortford on the River Stour in high summer. Then he took on work on a canal boat heading south, proceeding at a horse's pace down the Lee Navigation and arriving at journey's end in the last week of August. On walking away from his final job as a boatman, he also walked away from Wilfred Stirling.

This time he did not have a new identity worked out: he did not know why, but he just hadn't bothered.

And now here he is, sitting in one of his favourite spots close to Tower Hill, looking down at the river as dusk darkens the sky.

He has been trying to think where he has seen the face of the graveyard corpse before. He straightens his back, closes his eyes and does his mind-emptying trick. His breathing deepens and slows until he is only taking ten or twelve breaths per minute. He goes back to the beginning of the recent trawl through his memories and, much more swiftly this time, runs through them until he is back here in the present.

A slow smile spreads across his handsome face.

Slowly he brings himself back into the moment and his eyes open.

He believes he now knows where the path of the dead man once crossed his own.

TWELVE

In the morning Lily manages to resist the temptation to hurry through to Felix's bedside as soon as she wakes up. It was one thing to be so close to him when they were both in their nightclothes last night, when she was more than half asleep and it felt as if they were in a dreamworld. This morning, in the bright light of day, she has no such excuse, and so she restrains her impatience while she washes, dresses and carefully arranges her hair. When finally she walks briskly across the room to his bedside, she is confident that not one element of her person could offend the propriety or the morals of even the most rigidly upright spinster. And she is, of course, perfectly calm.

So she tells herself.

He is asleep. It is still early – she glances at her gold half hunter – and so she draws up a chair and sits down to wait. Presently, if he shows signs of stirring, she will go downstairs and prepare a breakfast tray. For now, she is content to watch him sleep and say a silent prayer of profound thanks that he has survived the brutal attack.

Felix is dreaming.

He is at his desk in the office and Lily is next door in the Inner Sanctum. He is dressed in very formal clothing and wears a hat that is too small and that sets up a deep ache in his head. It is a top hat. He is polishing a pair of black shoes. Then Lily is beside him and her pure white gown seems to have yards and yards of skirts and he pushes the folds of costly fabric aside because he is afraid they will be soiled by the shoe polish. But as he handles the soft material it starts to crackle because it has turned into paper, and Lily says, quite sharply, *Do not crush the rocking horse fly!* And the white paper turns to black and all the light has gone and he can see a vast thundercloud overhead which turns into an enormous crow and then a very loud clap of thunder wakes him up.

As he floats up to consciousness, he realises that his head aches.

He is still befuddled by the vividness of his dreams. He is half-afraid to open his eyes, but he knows he must.

By turning his head very slightly, he can see the spot where there is sometimes a chair beside the bed and sometimes not. He opens his eyes, just a little; quite often the early light is too bright and it increases the pain in his head.

It is morning, and pale sunshine fills the room.

The chair is by the bed. The woman – Tiger Lily – is sitting in it.

She is looking at him intently. As he opens his eyes more fully, she gives a soft gasp.

'Tiger Lily,' he murmurs.

She leans closer. 'Felix?' she says softly. 'Are you awake?'

Felix.

Is that who he is?

He puts that aside and considers the question of whether or not he is awake. 'I think so,' he replies. Is he? It's hard to tell. He has had such vivid dreams, and sometimes it has seemed that people have been describing events to him which have translated into violent scenes enacted before his closed eyes. There is a dark strand of fear – terror – underlying whatever else has been going on, and he has a worrying sense that, even if everything else is fantasy, whatever is causing the fear is real.

She is still watching him.

He can't look away, for in a world that is suddenly incomprehensible and frightening, she is the one solid, certain thing. Her hands, he notices, are on the side of the bed as she leans towards him. He puts his left hand on her right one, and she gives that soft gasp again.

For a moment they just look at each other. Then he says, 'What happened to me?'

She doesn't answer immediately. He smiles faintly; he imagines he can hear her thinking.

'Can you remember *anything*?' she asks eventually.

'A railway carriage and a sheep doing complicated knitting,' he says promptly, 'and a king and a queen, and a kitten, and people appearing and disappearing in that looking glass on the wall at the end of the bed.' He nods towards it.

She makes a *tsch!* of impatience. 'That wretched book!' she mutters. 'I *knew* it wasn't a good idea, and I wish I'd said so, only Bunty and Dorothea were so keen to help, and when Marm came up with the suggestion, nobody thought it would do any harm.' She stares at him anxiously, her expression slightly guilty.

'I think you will have to explain,' he says. 'I know who Marm is, or at least I know the name' – he registers the flare of joy in her face as he says this and guesses she is filled with relief that he hasn't entirely lost his memory – 'but I'm mystified by Bunty and Dorothea.'

'The new tenants!' she exclaims. 'My tenants, in this house. Bunty is Miss Adderley, the teacher, and her name's actually Bernice but everyone uses her nickname. Dorothea is Miss Sutherland, the one who works in the library, and' – she drops her voice – 'her friends call her Dotty, she told me so, but even with all of us growing close because of nursing you together, I can't quite bring myself to call her that.'

'Perhaps you'd have reached the necessary degree of intimacy if I'd died?' he suggests helpfully. He'd meant it as a jolly aside, but it doesn't make her smile. Far from it – her face goes very white and she says softly, '*Oh.*'

He knows he ought to say something to comfort her, reassure her, but at the moment such delicate nuances of behaviour are quite beyond him.

She withdraws her hand and, after a brief and awkward pause, says, 'They all wanted to do something, Marm and the tenants, and Doctor March seemed to think it was a good idea, and so when Marm brought the book and began reading, the rest of us just sort of joined in.'

'That's the second time you've mentioned a book,' he remarks.

'Oh – yes, of course, you won't know!' she exclaims.

Then she is reaching down and scooping up a book with worn navy-blue binding, holding it out so that he can read the title: *Alice Through the Looking-Glass.*

And immediately quite a lot of what has been puzzling and worrying him resolves itself.

He closes his eyes, and tries to attack the seemingly mammoth task of separating true memories from the bizarrerie of Lewis Carroll's imagination.

Presently Lily says timidly, 'Would you like some breakfast?'

He nods.

Lily races down the stairs. As she reaches the second flight, she can hear the encouraging everyday sounds that suggest Mrs Clapper is in the scullery and already busy. Running down the hall and into the kitchen, Mrs Clapper comes hurrying to meet her. 'What's wrong?' she asks, her voice high with tension. 'Is it Mr Felix? Is he . . . Has he . . .'

'Mrs Clapper, I'm so sorry!' Lily exclaims. 'Nothing's wrong. Quite the contrary – Felix is awake, he says he recognises the name Marm, and we've been talking to each other.' She doesn't add that Felix hasn't been making a great deal of sense.

Mrs Clapper's tense expression softens, and before Lily can tell her any more, she has turned away and started rummaging through the contents of the pantry. 'He'll be peckish, like as not,' she says, 'and if he's going to start trying to remember everything, he'll need some *proper* nourishment.'

'I'm not sure he's ready for—' Lily begins.

But Mrs Clapper shoos her out of the kitchen. 'You get yourself back up there and look after him, Miss Lily,' she says in the sort of voice that will not be gainsaid, 'and I'll bring up the tray, soon as it's ready.'

As Lily heads back to the stairs, she can hear Mrs Clapper's happy, relieved humming.

'Now,' Lily says, 'let us see what you can remember.'

It is almost an hour later. Felix has eaten almost everything on the tray; Mrs Clapper had prepared two poached eggs on fried bread, two rashers of bacon, several tomatoes and three mushrooms, a rack of toast with butter and her own marmalade. He has also drunk two cups of tea. Lily was ushered firmly out of the room because Mrs Clapper reappeared with a clean nightshirt, a warmed towel, a jug of hot water, soap and a washcloth and, after making use of the chamber pot, Felix has been given a very thorough wash.

Lily, waiting on the landing, is well aware that she could have performed these jobs with swift efficiency, for in her nursing past she did so countless times. But she knows Mrs Clapper is right in taking on the role of intimate nurse, for Lily and Felix work together, and for her to have done such tasks for him would make matters awkward, to say the least, when they are back in the office again.

And, Lily admits to herself, that is not the only reason why she's glad of Mrs Clapper's stolid, capable presence.

Now Lily is in the chair again, notebook on her lap and pencil in her hand, and Felix is sitting up supported by several pillows. 'Well?' she prompts.

He says hesitantly, 'I don't know where to start.' She waits. Then, very slowly, he begins to speak.

'I went out at night,' he murmurs. 'I remember a church, and a field. There was grass, and stones . . . no, it was a graveyard, not a field. I climbed a fence, a wall . . . Why?' He frowns as he stares at her, but she manages not to prompt him.

He is silent for some time. Then his face lightens and he says, 'There was a body! A skeleton. In the graveyard, no doubt . . . But no, it wasn't, it was enclosed in a garden, an overgrown garden, and I got in the hollow beside it and studied it for a long time. I had a lantern!' he adds excitedly. 'I know I had a lantern, and that I had to remember all the details because I was going to write them down later. The skeleton was quite short, and small, and . . . *Oh!*' The sudden cry is loud in the quiet room. 'It had been beheaded. Yes, *yes*, I remember now, the old people came to see us and I – we? – had to help them, and . . . and . . .' He stops. 'Sorry, Lily, I don't know what . . .'

But he stops abruptly as they both register that he has just called her by her name.

'Lily,' he says again, and this time he is smiling with delight. 'Your name really is Lily, but without the Tiger part, and you gave me a job even though you thought I was going to be a woman.' Briefly he screws his eyes tight shut, his brows drawn into a deep frown.

Lily waits. She is holding her breath.

He opens his eyes and looks right at her.

'I'm Felix Parsifal Derek McIvie Wilbraham,' he states, as if he is giving evidence. 'I am employed by the World's End Bureau as a private investigator, I work at number three, Hob's Court, Chelsea, you are my employer, Lily Gertrude Raynor, and we . . .' He stops.

'Oh, well done, Felix!' She hurries to fill the sudden silence in case he is dismayed because he can't go on. 'That's wonderful, and it must be such a relief to know who you are!'

He is looking rather deflated. 'That's all,' he admits.

'But it's not,' she says sharply. 'You just remembered the skeleton in the rose bed, and—'

'It wasn't a rose bed,' he interrupts. 'There weren't any rose bushes, none at all. It was just a hole in the ground, a deep hole, and there were pearls and fragments of cloth with the body, and she had such small, graceful bones, and I covered her up again and left her there and climbed back over the wall, and then I was on the path and I saw limbs, arms and legs, and they were red and it was the Red King and the Red Queen from the chess set and they were jumbled up in the barrow . . .' He must have seen the sudden dismay in her face because he stops, then mutters, 'No, that's wrong, of course it's wrong, and I'm confusing what was real with what was in the story.'

She can both see and sense his distress. She gets up and gently removes two of the pillows propping him up. 'It's time to rest now,' she says kindly. 'You have done so well, Felix, and I'm quite sure that now you've made a start, the memories will soon come flooding back. Now you must sleep.'

He is exhausted, and she berates herself silently but harshly for pressing him for so long. He is already closing his eyes, turning on his side and getting comfortable.

She creeps towards the door and slips out. She thinks he's probably asleep already, but then she hears him say softly, 'Goodbye for now, Tiger Lily.'

Lily is sitting at her desk.

She is in turmoil. She is vastly relieved that Felix at last seems to be improving, and that really ought to be enough for now. If she was any sort of a decent human being, she would turn her mind to some less pressing and dramatic occupation such as catching up with the filing, or carrying out a long-overdue overhaul of her reference shelves. The one thing she should not on any account be doing is sitting there biting her lip with suppressed irritation and fighting the urge to rush back upstairs, shake Felix awake and demand that he fights fatigue, pain and (hopefully) temporary amnesia until he has resurrected every single minute of the night he was attacked and dictated even the tiniest detail to her so that she can record them in case he forgets again and these faint signs of impending recovery turn out to be illusory and—

'*Stop!*' She says the word aloud in a horrified whisper.

What on earth is she thinking of? This is *Felix*, not some unknown witness who holds the clue in a case and who has inconsiderately lost their memory. How can she possibly treat him as nothing more than the possessor of the vital information that she needs to alleviate the Fetterplaces' distress?

She folds her arms on her desk and lays her head on them. I have allowed myself to become divided, she thinks wearily. Half of me is the resolute and efficient investigator of the World's End Bureau, determined to do her best for her poor, worried, fearful clients and remove whatever menace threatens them so powerfully. The other half is the woman who took on an employee two and a half years ago, stopped being irritated by him, learned first to admire him for his courage and his optimistic nature, then discovered that she trusted him as much or more than she has ever trusted anyone because she knows he will never let her down.

She knows there is a great deal more that she could add to that, and if she had enough bravery and honesty, she would have done so.

With a very deliberate effort, she stops that train of thought and draws the Fetterplace file towards her.

She runs through all the notes, Felix's and her own. She reads through her very thorough account of what she found in the rose bed. (*It wasn't a rose bed, there weren't any rose bushes*, says Felix in her head.) Then she looks up, eyes unfocused, and thinks about the path behind the house. The one that runs under the churchyard wall. Where Felix was left for dead.

All this – the reading of the file, the retracing of her hesitant steps as she nerved herself to walk along the path – has been no more than procrastination. She knew when she came downstairs and settled at her desk what she had to do next.

The trouble is, she *really* doesn't want to because she's scared.

She embarks on a second round of telling herself the reasons why she has no choice – she is the proprietor of an investigation bureau; the Fetterplace siblings are paying for her services; their fear is fully justified because they are quite right, there *is* someone who has an interest in what is buried in their garden, and this someone is so full of malice that Lily quakes at the thought of encountering him. He seems to be able to . . .

She is rescued from descending any further into the dark world of the evil presence behind the gardens of Mary Rose Court by the timely arrival of Mrs Clapper. She has the usual tray of morning coffee and plate of biscuits in her hands, but she also brings a message. 'Mr Smithers is here, Miss Lily, he's just hanging up his coat and hat and I said to come on in when he's done. Hope that was all right?'

'Yes, thank you, Mrs Clapper. Quite all right.'

As Mrs Clapper strides away and Lily picks up her cup – there are in fact two cups on the tray, and an extra supply of ginger biscuits – Lily reflects that *quite all right* is very much an understatement.

Marm wants to go up to Felix straight away and, given that Lily has just told him the good news, she doesn't blame him. When she reported how Felix said he knew who Marm was, or knew at least that the name was familiar, there was a sparkle of tears in Marm's eyes. She manages to persuade him that there's no point in hurrying upstairs because Felix has just gone to sleep (as a direct result of her badgering him so relentlessly, but she doesn't tell Marm that).

As they drink their coffee and plough through the biscuits, she tells him what she did yesterday. He listens in attentive silence as she describes her conversation with Alethea, and as she recounts the details of what she found in the grave, his eyes widen in wonder.

'There was always a rumour,' he murmurs, 'that Anne Boleyn had an extra finger on one hand.'

'It wasn't a whole finger,' Lily replies. 'More of a lump of bone sticking out of the side of the lower joint.'

Marm nods. 'A very slight malformation, perhaps. Enough, sadly, to fuel the widespread and malicious rumours that she was a witch. It's said she had a mole on her neck,' he adds, 'and, being the stylish, courageous and resourceful woman she was, she took to wearing a jewelled choker to cover it, and all the sycophants who were privately after her blood couldn't help themselves copying her.'

Marm, Lily reflects, is rather a fan of King Henry's second wife.

Reluctantly she picks up her tale, because now she has to tell him about venturing out onto the path behind the gardens. And the sinister shed with the newly constructed walls inside the disguise of the ancient shell. And the stench. And the sudden flare of terror that sent her running back down the path as if every tortured soul from the Tower's dungeons and every headless corpse from the scaffold on the hill was after her.

Silence descends when she has finished. Lily thinks it is a jagged sort of silence, as if the horrors she has just been describing have not yet dissipated.

Eventually Marm says quietly, 'I very much hope, dear Lily, that you are not planning to return?'

She meets his worried eyes. 'I am, Marm,' she says. 'Of *course* I am!' she adds vehemently. 'The Fetterplace siblings are my clients, and they are paying me to find out if someone' – (some*thing* hovers at the back of her mind) – 'is threatening the precious skeleton hidden in their garden. They may be mistaken in the belief that it is that of Anne Boleyn; in fact undoubtedly they are, but it doesn't matter. They are *so afraid*, and that's not right, and if I can remove that fear and let them live in peace with their old bones, then that is what I must do.'

'This someone who frightens your clients so much attacked Felix,' Marm says quietly. 'According to Dr March, if the dear boy didn't have such a thick skull, he'd be dead.'

'Yes, he told me that too,' Lily says. She recalls being gratified that Dr March had shared the remark with her; that he was treating her like a stout-hearted former nurse rather than a weak and feeble woman who would collapse into a dead faint.

'I would bet a pound note to a pint of cold tea that you haven't mentioned this recklessly perilous plan to Felix,' Marm says.

'No, of course not, he's far too weak to hear such . . .' She stops abruptly.

'Such a foolhardy scheme that would place you right in the path of whoever attacked him?' Marm asks coldly. 'Yes, Lily, he's far too weak to hear *that* piece of news. But then,' he adds, 'he would be just as horrified even in his full strength.'

'If he was fully strong, he'd return himself!' she cries.

'If you think that, you're a fool,' Marm flashes back. 'He would not even *think* about going back there until he had organised someone strong, capable and preferably armed to go with him.'

'But . . .'

Lily subsides. Marm is right.

There is an even longer silence. Then Marm says in quite a different tone, 'If you are determined to go back, I will come with you.'

Lily looks at him.

His handsome but dissipated face is heavily creased, and the lines are deep for a man in his forties. His blue eyes are full of intelligence and compassion, but they are also full of broken veins and the lids are reddened, the skin at times flaky. He is perpetually a little dishevelled, the greying hair untrimmed; he always wears the same small number of garments which all look as if they need a good clean, as do his much-repaired shoes. He is far too thin, his shoulders slope and he has the beginnings of a hunch in his upper back. He really isn't very fit and he wheezes when he climbs the stairs. He wouldn't be much good in the face of the sort of ruthless attacker who almost killed Felix, Lily realises. She is still looking at him, and now she is blinking away tears. I truly appreciate the offer, dear Marm, she thinks, which I know is sincere, but I fear you would be no more protection from the darkness and the evil than a cardboard sword.

She waits until she can speak without the emotion showing. Even as she thanks him politely and says she will give the suggestion long and careful thought, she understands that if – no, *when* – she returns to the path under the graveyard wall, she must avoid giving the slightest hint of her intentions to Marm.

To have *two* men she deeply cares about injured or worse would be more than she could bear.

* * *

Lily moves through the rest of the day acting in what she hopes is her normal manner. After their conversation, Marm goes up to sit with Felix and stays for some time. At midday Lily joins them, helping Mrs Clapper carry up a light lunch on trays for the three of them. Not for the first time, she asks Mrs Clapper to eat with them, but, as always, Mrs Clapper looks faintly horrified at the suggestion and delivers her usual firm refusal.

Marm leaves after lunch. He gives Lily a very intent look, and she knows he is sending her a silent warning: *Do not even think about taking any foolish and dangerous risks.* She wishes him a meek good day, and picks up *Alice Through the Looking-Glass*.

She reads, Felix dozes. She is relieved by Bunty, and later does another shift before Dorothea comes upstairs. Lily sits with him again in the evening, tiptoeing away once he has settled down for the night.

She waits in her Inner Sanctum while night comes on.

The ground floor is deserted. Mrs Clapper went home hours ago, and everyone else is asleep upstairs. Lily thinks she has carried it off: she truly believes none of the people who have been with her during the day know what she is going to do.

She understood even as she was talking to Marm that if she is going to go, she must go straight away because her courage will fail if she delays.

She is going this night.

She has made her preparations. She is dressed warmly in dark clothing, and has put a knitted cap on her head with a black shawl over it to hide her bright hair. She wears her workman's boots and the knife is in its sheath. She has a lantern filled with oil ready beside the door, and while she is in the more populated places, she plans to conceal it among the folds of her heavy skirt. She has a case full of Lucifers in the inside pocket of her jacket.

She is ready. All that remains is to find her courage.

She goes through the house and lets herself out of the garden door. Hob's Court is quiet – it is late now – but it is not unknown for her neighbours to return from evening engagements at any time around midnight, and she does not want to have to explain herself. She goes into her grandfather's shed. Very quietly, she unlocks and unbolts the door onto the dark alley beyond and slips out.

As she creeps away, a big, tall, bulky presence materialises out of the shadows and falls into step beside her. And Tamáz says, 'I guessed you'd emerge the back way.'

THIRTEEN

'What are *you* doing here?' Lily demands in a furious whisper, although she doesn't know why she's whispering because there's nobody about. She doesn't know why she's furious either, come to that, when the only reason for his presence is that he's come to help her.

Tamáz seems to be steering her towards the river. 'You cannot do this on your own,' he says. 'Either this haunted path will be deserted, in which case you will likely uncover little that you don't know already, or this violent man will be there, and, given that we know how he treats those he finds trespassing on his patch, he will probably kill you.'

He is speaking quite calmly, but she can hear something in his quiet voice that she hasn't heard before.

'How did you find . . .' She breaks off, as they are emerging out onto the riverside and someone has just given a low whistle.

Alongside the bank is a wherry; clinker built, with the long, projecting bow which passengers can step onto from dry land without getting their feet wet. Two men sit in it, their oars raised. As Tamáz strides down to the craft, one of the men murmurs a question and Tamáz responds. Turning to Lily, he says, 'Are you able to board or should I lift you?'

'Of course I can!' she replies, stung. Then – for events seem to be running away from her – she grabs his arm and hisses, '*Wait!*'

He stops, staring down at her. 'What is it?'

'Tamáz, this is a secret mission!' she says urgently. 'Nobody's meant to know about it, including you, and certainly not those two men in the wherry!'

'They are family,' he replies simply. 'Many of my kin have always been watermen rather than boatmen.'

'But it's *secret*,' she persists. She's at a loss as to how else to express her dismay.

He studies her face, then puts his hands on her shoulders. 'Cushla, it is the best part of five miles from here to the Tower,' he says. 'You and I are more than capable of walking, but we'll be tired when we get there, we may have to flee for our lives, and it's a long step home. These men know the river, they know the tides, and not only will we save our feet by travelling in their wherry; they will also wait for us and provide a fast escape.'

She knows it's a good plan. She's also very grateful that he has come up with it, and for the silent presence of the two men in the wherry. She shoots a quick glance at them. They are both built like Tamáz, and if anything they are even broader in the shoulder than he is. They are watching her, unsmiling.

'What should I call them?' she mutters.

Tamáz smiles. 'No names are necessary. You are not the only one who prefers to act in secret.'

He is waiting. She wonders why on earth she is still so reluctant to accept help, when anyone with the tiniest amount of sense would offer up a prayer of thanks because this dangerous, risky, frightening mission that she seems to have persuaded herself to embark upon has just become a great deal less perilous.

She reaches up and briefly touches Tamáz's hands, still on her shoulders. 'Thank you,' she says, and climbs onto the wherry.

The wherry seems almost to fly across the brownish water. There is a sense of great power emanating from the river, and Lily finds herself clinging on to the reassuring woodwork of the boat's side. Sooner than she expects, the pale bulk of the Tower looms up ahead on the left, and then the watermen are manoeuvring the wherry over to the side and making it fast by a set of rungs let into the stone of the Embankment.

Just ahead there is the low, dark entrance of what appears to be a channel leading in beneath the Tower. Lily's eyes are drawn to it and, noticing, one of the watermen mutters, 'That's Traitors' Gate.'

Lily shivers. The sinister opening gapes like a huge black mouth silently screaming. It exudes dread and fear.

Tamáz goes up the ladder first and holds out a hand to her. One of the watermen follows, leaving one to guard the wherry. Tamáz exchanges a few muttered words with them. 'Slack water presently,' the one in the wherry says. Tamáz nods. 'Good,' he mutters. Both he and the waterman accompanying them, Lily notices, are carrying cudgels.

She starts to feel apprehensive.

To distract herself as she follows Tamáz towards Great Tower Hill, Lily thinks about the slack water remark. Slack water means the tide isn't doing anything, she seems to remember; neither coming in nor going out. So, since the tide has obviously been going out on their journey downriver – because they were going really fast, and at times the watermen barely seemed to be rowing at all – then on the other side of slack water, the tide will be coming in.

And it will hurry them all the way back to Chelsea.

Tamáz stops. 'Which way?' he asks.

Lily has been thinking about how best to approach. To reach the path, they can either go across the churchyard and climb the gentle slope to the wall that separates it from the houses, or head for Mary Rose Court and take the dark, narrow passage between the two blocks of buildings and emerge onto the path in the way Lily did when she discovered it.

That seems to be the better choice. 'Follow me,' she says.

Mary Rose Court appears to have retired for the night. There is nobody about, and only a couple of cracks of light escape from upper windows whose curtains are not fully drawn. The darkness is alleviated by a solitary gas lamp at the far end of the court.

The weed-choked and litter-filled passage between the two terraces of houses is even more perilous in the dark. Tamáz lights a small bull's-eye lantern, and Lily is about to put a flame to hers, but as her eyes adjust she finds she can see well enough without it. The waterman behind her stumbles once and curses softly. They emerge at the far end and Tamáz extinguishes his lamp, for the moon has risen and the stars are bright in the clear sky.

They step out onto the path. The high wall borders it on the near side, the trees and the tangle of undergrowth on the other. The deserted graveyard of All Hallows can be seen through gaps in the branches, barer now that autumn is creeping on. And there, to the right where the path bends, is the shed.

Tamáz is looking at it. 'That is the place?' he says softly.

If it is indeed Marm who has been talking to him, Lily thinks – and who else can it have been? – then the briefing was thorough.

'Yes,' she murmurs. 'It looks like a ruin that nobody has disturbed for decades. But it has . . .'

He puts a hand on her arm. 'I know,' he says.

The three of them move off as one, without anyone giving a sign. Lily walks behind Tamáz and the waterman follows her. But after only a few paces Lily remembers the sudden, almost silent approach of the man the last time she was here. She reaches out to alert Tamáz, but he has already stopped. He meets her eyes.

'We should leave someone on watch at the end of the passage,' she whispers. He nods – she suspects he has had the same thought – and speaks softly to the waterman, who mutters a response and walks back to the mouth of the passage. He has been carrying his cudgel in his right hand. Now he transfers it to the left and with the right draws a knife out of his belt.

Dear God, Lily thinks briefly, how did I ever imagine I could do this on my own?

She and Tamáz walk on, side by side now.

Definite hints of the stench from the shed snake out as they approach.

Crouching there, huddled down in the darkness under the wall, greenery growing unchecked over the roof, it looks as if the shed is lying in wait for them. With malice on its mind. Lily crushes the fanciful thought.

Tamáz leans forward to peer through a gap between the warped old timbers just as she did. He re-lights the lamp, holding it close to the gap. Lily moves nearer to him. He bends down and says right in her ear, 'I will go round the hut and peer through all the wider gaps, and perhaps somewhere there will be a corresponding space in the inner walls.'

She nods, batting away a persistent fly. He pushes back into the shrubs and bushes to first one side of the hut, then the other. He is almost hidden by the foliage when he calls softly, 'Cushla, come here.'

They are at the corner of the hut's side and rear walls. The ancient outer timbers have warped badly here and created a long, wide gap. Inside, the new planks of the lining ought to have been tightly joined in a right angle. But one of them has warped slightly too: just above waist height, there is a narrow space with darkness beyond.

The stench has been growing stronger since they reached the shed. Now it is like something solid.

Tamáz says, 'Do you want to look?'

No, she cries silently, I want you to look, and if it is unbearable, I won't have to.

But she keeps quiet. This is my case, she tells herself, and I must find my courage.

She nods.

Tamáz angles the lantern so that the beam shines straight through the gap. In contrast to the darkness outside, the interior of the hut suddenly looks as bright as a theatre stage in the limelight.

Lily's hand flies to cover her mouth, and the great cry of horror, pity and disgust is muffled to a soft moan.

Someone is staring back at her.

A deathly white face with the vestiges of paint under braided dark hair. Eyes half-closed, mouth distorted in a rictus, teeth rotted and stumpy apart from two incisors and a single long canine. Beneath the thick hair, some of the flesh is decorated with thin greenish veins.

No, not a someone. It is not a whole person; it is a head. There is no body; the head is on a spike that has been hammered into the top of a sort of plinth.

Lily sees black spots form and dissolve. *Do not faint do not faint donotfaintdonotfaint*, shouts a voice inside her mind. She takes a stumbling step away from the gap and slumps into the rough embrace of the bushes. Tamáz takes her place.

Time passes. She doesn't know if it is minutes or hours.

Then he turns towards her and says, 'How much did you see?'

'The head.' She shuts her eyes. She had thought she had only spotted the head – good God, wasn't that enough? – but now she discovers that her brain has recorded other elements of the gruesome interior. 'A pile of garments neatly folded in the corner. Shoes, in pairs. Limbs, I think.' She pauses, draws a shuddery breath. 'Blood.'

Blood like a carpet. Blood like dark red paint.

Out of nowhere something bursts into her mind, demanding her attention as if somebody had dug her sharply in the ribs. She can hear Felix speaking . . . *I saw limbs, arms and legs, and they were red and it was the Red King and the Red Queen from the chess set and they were jumbled up in the barrow.*

Barrow.

She grabs at Tamáz, clutching at his shirt and waistcoat. He winces slightly. 'Is there a barrow?' she demands, shaking him in her urgency to know, to make him understand.

'A barrow?'

Why is he so slow? 'In the hut!' she says in an almost silent screech.

He turns back to the gap. Looks. Looks for what seems like a long time. Steps away. 'No barrow.'

He is out hunting, she thinks. She knows she is right. He is deep amid the rookeries and the dark, stinking little courts, sure-footed, confident of finding his way, of finding what he is looking for, because there is such an abundance of this particular prey and nobody seems too bothered about the everlasting slaughter.

She says in what she thinks is a remarkably calm voice, 'He is away about his business. He will be back, because this is his place.'

She doesn't have to go on. Tamáz nods, takes her hand, and they pelt back down the path so fast that she knows he is affected just as she is. It is no time for courage, for a steady head, for they have just come face to face with such conscienceless brutality, such depraved evil, that the only thing to do is to flee from it.

The waterman has seen them coming, for he has left the shelter of the passage mouth and is hurrying towards them. 'Someone's coming!' he says, eyes wide with fear so that the whites show up brightly. '*Get under cover!*' The last words are almost a wail.

Tamáz picks Lily up bodily, breaks into a fast run and covers the distance to the passage in a few strides. He drops her, pushes her against the wall of the house on the left and presses his body against hers, shielding her with his greater breadth and height so that she is invisible and can hardly breathe. She can feel his heart beating fast, but not as fast as hers. She hears a rustle and a sudden exhalation of breath and tries to peer round Tamáz: the waterman has followed them into the passage and is slumped down on the filthy ground, curled up in a ball with his arms over his head.

Lily hardly dares breathe. She clutches at Tamáz, her head burrowing into his chest. He whispers something – no more than a breath – and she feels movement. His right arm is no longer around her but reaching behind him . . .

The moonlight flashes briefly on bright metal as he draws his knife out of his belt.

Then they are all still. As still as if they were already dead.

In the silence Lily hears the thud of feet, walking in a steady, measured rhythm. The sounds grow louder as the footsteps approach.

She is blind, her face pressed into Tamáz.

I have to see, she thinks. I cannot stand here simply *waiting*.

In tiny movements that she hopes are imperceptible, she moves her head to the left.

The footsteps are nearer now and much louder. Thud, thud, thud. As if whoever is making them is in no hurry, just walking steadily along, mind reflecting back over the evening, anticipating the comforts of home.

Not home. Of course not. A hut, inside a dilapidated old shed, painstakingly hidden from the curiosity of the world.

A hut filled with the unimaginable.

He is very close now.

She feels the whole of Tamáz's body go tense.

She stares out at the path.

The barrow appears first. It is made of wood, it looks old, and the contents spill out over the sides.

The Red King and the Red Queen. It's probably just the Queen, but red she most certainly is.

Lily can smell the blood.

The body of the barrow is past now. The handles are quite long, and at their further end, the hands holding them are dark with the evidence of what they have recently been doing.

A man walks past.

An ordinary-looking man, shoulders slightly hunched as he propels the loaded barrow. Dressed in dark clothing, scarf over the nose and mouth, hat drawn down so that the brim shades the face. Heavy boots, to make those steady, stomping footsteps. The sound of soft humming.

He is only visible in the brief seconds it takes to pass by the end of the passage. Then almost straight away the sound of his steps begins to fade.

Tamáz holds her tightly, as if to stop her dashing away up the passage. She wants to tell him there is no need, for her legs are shaking so badly that they can barely hold her up. The holding turns into a hug; he murmurs something and she thinks he kisses the top of her head. She leans into him.

Time passes.

She hears the soft sounds of the waterman getting up, beginning to crawl on hands and knees past them and up the passage towards Mary Rose Court. Tamáz turns to watch him. Then he says, so softly that she only just hears, 'We should go now.'

He pushes her in front of him, and as if he knows how near she is to collapse, keeps his hands either side of her waist. Step by slow step, they edge up the passage until they reach the far end. Mary Rose Court seems bright after the darkness.

The waterman is being sick in the gutter on the other side of the road.

Tamáz waits for him to finish. Then they hurry back down to the road and, walking now as if they were homeward bound after some innocent nocturnal excursion, make their way back to the river and the waiting wherry.

As the watermen row the wherry out into mid-stream, it catches the inrushing tide and is swept away like a stick on a millrace.

Lily is gazing back.

She thinks it might have been a dream, or a nightmare, dragged out of her drastically overheated imagination. Mist is coming off the water, billowing softly then twisting up and away. Looking through it, just for the blink of an eye, she thinks she can see a dark figure standing above the river steps they have just left behind them.

His wild fury is palpable.

He raises his arms, throws back his head and lets out a great howl like a wolf robbed of his prey.

It's a haunting, terrible sound.

Lily, covering her head with her arms, tells herself it wasn't real. But she cannot make herself believe it.

Tamáz waits while Lily unlocks the outer door to the shed at the bottom of her garden. She steps inside and turns to face him.

'How many victims do you think there were in the hut?' she asks. Other than brief remarks, it is the first time they have spoken since fleeing from Mary Rose Court.

'At least two,' he says after a short pause. 'And from the big stack of clothes, I'd say there had been others before.'

Lily knows she ought to be reporting the find to the police. Should have done so already. It is her duty as a law-abiding citizen. But she is also a private enquiry agent; she has clients paying her very well for her time and her work, and they are guarding an extremely sensitive secret at the bottom of a garden only fifty yards or so from the hut.

'I *will* go to the police,' she says. 'Only not just yet.'

Tamáz makes a non-committal sound. She is well aware he is no great fan of the law.

She stands, looking up at him. 'Thank you,' she says.

He nods. 'Did you find what you sought?'

Did she? She has no idea. 'Well, I know now what's in the hut.' The answer to why the man with the barrow should be so interested in the contents of the Fetterplaces' rose bed, however, remains elusive.

'Goodnight, Tamáz,' she says. She is about to close and secure the sturdy door, but he calls her back. She looks at him enquiringly.

'I hear he is beginning to recover at last,' he says.

There is no need to ask who he means. 'Yes.'

'And he was attacked in that place? Where we were tonight?'

'Yes.'

He looks grave. 'Be careful, cushla,' he says. 'The attacker intended to kill him. He won't hesitate to deal similarly with anyone else who goes trespassing.'

'Yes, I know,' she says shortly. 'And I have undertaken to help three elderly and very frightened people who have attracted his interest.'

He raises his hands as if in submission. 'Take care,' he says. Then he turns away and melts into the darkness.

FOURTEEN

Lily stumbles into bed, the last of her energy exhausted by the effort of climbing the stairs, undressing and having a very perfunctory wash. A quick glance at Felix has shown him to be fast asleep.

She is relieved. She doesn't think she could talk to anyone right now. Even Felix.

She wakes to the sounds of Mrs Clapper bringing a breakfast tray up to Felix. She opens her eyes and is just wondering whether there will presently be a second tray for her when the events of last night crash into her mind. As the horrible images fill her vision, breakfast doesn't seem such a good idea after all.

Some time earlier, Mrs Clapper must have brought up a jug of hot water for her and, since it is still warm enough not to raise goose bumps, she has a thorough wash and takes her time over dressing. It is, she reflects, as if she is a knight of old, purifying himself and donning clean clothes for the ceremony that raises him above the man he used to be. What lies ahead for Lily may not be of the same order, but nevertheless she feels she is preparing for a challenge that is far graver than anything she has faced before.

She opens the door and goes to greet Felix.

As he looks up and smiles at her, she wishes fervently that she could tell him; that she could describe the awful events of last night and have the immeasurable comfort of his response. Of his reassurance; his support. But she can't. If she tells him where she went last night, he will be angry because she took such a risk, distressed because she might have been hurt (killed, even), resentful that she went back to continue a job that he began and didn't finish, and guilty because he couldn't go with her. Since all of that is far too much for a man recovering from a very serious injury and only just beginning to return to his normal state of mind, she has to keep it to herself. Keep it secret.

And as they talk lightly about the bright day outside, Mrs Clapper's way with a rasher of bacon, how much better it is to have the new tenants in the house than the previous one, and other light topics, she understands just how painful it is to keep a secret from Felix.

Lily leaves him dozing and goes down to her office. She wants to make detailed notes of everything that happened last night while it is all fresh – far too fresh – in her memory.

She has been working for an hour or more, and Mrs Clapper has just brought in a large cup of coffee and a plate of jam tarts, when from the hall she hears a tentative, 'Is anybody there?' and the tattoo of Mrs Clapper's heels on the flagged floor as she hurries from the scullery to see who it is and what they want. There is a murmured exchange – Mrs Clapper and a second female voice – and then Mrs Clapper trots through the outer office and, pausing in the doorway of the Inner Sanctum, hisses, 'It's Miss Adderley, Miss Lily. Says she'd like a word, if you can spare her the time.' Mrs Clapper's wiry grey eyebrows have shot up to her hairline, apparently in a gesture of amazement at this unusual turn of events.

'Of course, Mrs Clapper.' Lily closes her notebook and puts down her pen. 'Please ask her to come in.'

Mrs Clapper hurries back into the hall and returns, ushering Bunty ahead of her as if she was a sheepdog with an unruly ewe. Then, announcing she's in the middle of washing the scullery floor and must get on, she hurries off.

Lily looks up at Bunty. Suddenly aware that she hasn't spoken at any length to either of her tenants since they've all been so preoccupied with Felix, she feels rather guilty. She smiles a welcome. 'Come and sit down,' she says, hurrying round her desk and pulling out a chair.

Bunty lowers herself carefully onto the seat. She has a large brown envelope in her hand. Oh, Lord, Lily thinks, she and Dorothea are upset that they've had to look after Felix and they've decided to leave and find somewhere they can firmly shut their door on the rest of the inhabitants . . .

'I'm so sorry that the household has been disrupted,' Lily blurts out. 'It was so good of you and Miss Sutherland to be so supportive and, honestly, Felix really seems to be getting better now. I'm sure you don't need to go on sitting with him, and I promise we will respect your privacy from now on and not disturb you at all, so there's really no need for you to think of—' She makes herself stop. She is rather breathless.

Bunty's expression has gone from embarrassed to incredulous to amused. 'Dear Miss Raynor – dear Lily,' she says kindly. 'Three things. Firstly, Dotty and I were pleased to help. Poor Mr Wilbraham was so badly hurt, and we are both glad to have done what little we did to help towards his recovery. Secondly, if you were going to say there was no need for us to think of leaving in order to find lodgings where there would be no question of nursing men with bad head wounds' – her mouth quirks in a smile – 'then let me reassure you that we are extremely happy here, we know full well that you would not have involved us except in dire need – and actually I think you will find that we volunteered – and there is no question of our leaving. Thirdly, there is this.' She puts the brown envelope on Lily's desk.

Lily stares at the envelope. It is addressed to Miss B. Adderley, in a clear hand. She has no idea what it is. Mentally shaking herself, she sits up straight and asks brightly, 'What is it?'

'Marm and I have a second cousin,' Bunty begins, 'and the two of us decided he was highly likely to be interested in our little conundrum, since such matters are, you might say, his speciality.'

Conundrum. Such matters. Lily isn't sure what Bunty is talking about. 'When you say conundrum, are you referring to the Fetterplace skeleton?' she hazards. Bunty nods. 'He's a bones expert?' Lily asks eagerly.

Bunty shakes her head. 'No. I imagine that he has but a fraction of your undoubted familiarity with the human body, given your nursing background. I speak of a very different field of expertise. This second cousin is a man of no mean position in the College of Arms. It is correct, I believe, to refer to him as a "herald".'

'College of Arms?' Lily repeats, hoping Bunty will understand it is a request for elucidation.

She does, and promptly provides it. 'It is a very old organisation, founded in the fifteenth century by Richard the Third. They have their headquarters on Queen Victoria Street, although of course it cannot have been so called when the heralds moved there in 1555.'

'And what exactly do they do?'

'The company is responsible for the safekeeping of the country's genealogical records,' Bunty says solemnly. 'Among other services, they grant coats of arms, and such is the value and the importance of this gift that before they can do so, they must ascertain that whoever is applying has the right to arms, and this means finding convincing and authentic proof of the lines of descent.'

'So . . .' Lily's brain is slow this morning, and at first she doesn't understand.

Then she does. 'So this second cousin of yours can trace who someone's ancestors were? Which family they come from?'

'In essence, yes.'

'And he's found out about the Boleyns?' But no, she thinks straight away, that can't be what is making Bunty so voluble, because Anne Boleyn married a king and therefore her family history is probably already on record and available to anyone who takes the trouble to look it up.

Bunty is looking at her encouragingly, smiling happily as if quite sure she will work it out.

'He's been investigating the Fetterplaces,' she says.

'Bravo!' cries Bunty, surprisingly. 'Yes! His name is Cornelius Ely Redvers – he's the grandson of our grandfather's sister, which is why he's called Ely Redvers and not Smithers, incidentally – and he has been doing precisely that.'

'Oh, good,' Lily manages. She is a little overwhelmed by Bunty's enthusiasm.

'Marm told me that Cor owed him a favour,' Bunty goes on, 'because, clever old thing that he is, Marm extracted a very close friend of Cor's from a rather distasteful situation which, had it become common knowledge, would have buried his chances of becoming a Member of Parliament without any hope whatsoever of resurrection.' It sounds typical of Marm, Lily thinks. 'Luckily for us, very old family trees are Cor's speciality.'

And now, with a dramatic gesture worthy of the stage, Bunty opens the envelope. She takes out a large sheet of paper and spreads it across Lily's desk. It is, she sees at once, a family tree.

The Skeleton in the Rose Bed 163

'Let us begin with the origins of the Boleyns,' Bunty says. 'Here is Thomas Hoo, Baron Hoo of Hastings, who married Elizabeth Wychingham in the mid-1420s.' She points. 'Their daughter Anne – not our Anne – married a mercer called Geoffrey Boleyn whose star rose rapidly, and high enough for him to become Lord Mayor of London. Their son William Boleyn married an Irish noblewoman, and they lived in grand style in Blickling, which is in Norfolk. Their son Thomas married into the wealthy and influential Howard family, and he and his wife Elizabeth had three children, Mary, George and Anne.' She looks up at Lily. 'And *she* is our Anne.'

There is a pause. Watching closely, Lily sees that Bunty is stroking her finger across Anne Boleyn's name, as if in a gesture of compassion. As well she might, she thinks.

Bunty straightens her spine – Lily wonders if she is already regretting the brief moment of tenderness – and resumes. 'Now we all know what happened to Anne,' she says briskly, 'and to her brother George, who you will no doubt remember was accused of incest with Anne and executed for high treason. He met his death on the scaffold, two days before Anne was beheaded.'

There is a short silence, as if they are both paying their respects.

'Now we come to Anne's sister,' Bunty continues. 'To Mary. She had occupied the role of Henry's paramour before Anne caught his eye and, unlike Anne, Mary went willingly to the King's bed without the benefit of clergy, as the old phrase has it.'

'They weren't married, you mean,' Lily says.

'They were not. Her little sister Anne might well have been scornful of Mary for having yielded too readily to the king – and it is certain that Mary bore him at least one child out of wedlock – but in hindsight it was Mary who was the shrewd sister, for her compliance and her readiness to slip away quietly once Henry tired of her meant that she retained Henry's favour. Whereas Anne, so very much more demanding, fell so far out of it that it cost her her life.'

'What happened to Mary after Henry abandoned her?' Lily asks.

'She married a man called William Carey, and their daughter Catherine married Francis Knollys. Catherine and Francis had a large family, and it is one of their many daughters to whom we must now devote our attention. But before we do, let us turn to the Fetterplace family.'

'I know about the family's history!' Lily exclaims and, jumping up, she hurries through to Felix's desk in the front office and takes his notebook out of the top drawer of the cabinet tucked underneath. Settling down again, she finds the right page.

'Alethea Fetterplace – she's the eldest sibling – gave us an account of the family's fortunes over the centuries when the three of them first came to see us. They claim to have an ancestor who came over with the Conqueror.'

'Oh, *that* old chestnut,' Bunty murmurs wryly.

Lily glances at her, once again surprised at her reaction. Really, she thinks, I am seeing another side of her this morning.

She finds she rather likes it.

Remembering where she was, she goes on. 'This ancestor was awarded an estate in Norfolk for his loyal service. The family grew in wealth and importance and when Henry the Eighth came to the throne, one of them – Arthur Fettyplace – was a courtier, as his father had been before him and his son would be afterwards, the three of them serving a total of five Tudor monarchs.'

She glances up to see how Bunty is reacting to this information. She is nodding, a faint smile on her face, and Lily would place a fairly generous bet that none of it is news to her.

'As we know, the houses in Mary Rose Court were built in the early days of Henry's marriage to Katharine of Aragon, which was in 1509,' Lily goes on, 'and . . .' She is reading on through Felix's notes, but there appears to be no more mention of the Tudor Fetterplaces. 'Er . . .'

'Might I be allowed to take over?' Bunty asks gently. Lily nods rather curtly, and Bunty bends down over the family tree. 'There is strong evidence to support the story of William Odo Fetterplace, and the estate was indeed in Norfolk, on the River Bure near a place called Coltishall.' She pauses. 'Also near to Blickling.'

'Where the Boleyns lived,' Lily mutters.

'Indeed,' Bunty agrees, 'although the Fetterplaces had been firmly established in the area several centuries before William Boleyn arrived with his shiny new money.'

'So are you saying . . .?' Lily begins.

Bunty pretends she didn't hear; she is into her stride now, and Lily doubts anything could stop her. She hides a smile. She really is warming to Bunty Adderley.

'We were speaking of Anne's sister Mary,' Bunty says, 'and her marriage to William Carey, and their daughter Catherine, who became the wife of Francis Knollys and who produced rather a lot of children. Including a daughter, Margaret, born in the 1550s.' She looks up, her eyes shining. 'And Margaret married a man called Edward Fettyplace.'

A soft '*Oh!*' escapes Lily.

She is remembering something Fanny said, about Anne Boleyn's aunt marrying a man called Fetterplace. Not an aunt, she thinks, but a niece. No, for it was her sister's granddaughter who married Edward Fettyplace. Anne's great-niece, then.

Almost immediately, she sees an objection. 'But they can't have had anything to do with Anne Boleyn and the removal of her body,' she says, 'because if Margaret was born in the 1550s, she can't have married until the late 1560s or early 1570s, and Anne had been dead for thirty years by then.'

'You appear to be assuming that the marriage of Edward Fettyplace and Margaret Knollys was the first time the two families had become close,' Bunty replies. 'Whereas cousin Cor's research shows that they had all had dealings with one another for decades before that. You just said, Lily, that Arthur Fettyplace was a courtier when Henry the Eighth came to the throne, but we must remember that Arthur's father, Edmund, held quite a high position in the court of the young king's father, Henry the Seventh.'

Lily closes her eyes to concentrate. 'Then the Fetterplaces were important before the Boleyns came to prominence?'

'*Exactly.*' Bunty leans forward, excitement glittering in her small dark eyes. 'We might let our imaginations canter free briefly and imagine Edmund Fettyplace, well established in the Tudor court, a wealthy man with estates in Norfolk and a fine new house close to Tower Hill, learning of his neighbour William Boleyn's ambition for his family. Edmund's son Arthur recognises William's son Thomas when he arrives in London, and perhaps he decides to be a good Christian and help him in his desire for advancement. And then look! We have arrived in Henry the

Eighth's reign, he has a wandering eye and a loose grip on the concept of marital fidelity, and here are the two lovely daughters of Thomas Boleyn who, one after the other, snag the lusty king's attention. Why, perhaps Mary and Anne were frequent and welcome visitors to the Fetterplaces' London home! The two families were friends, after all, and—'

'I think we have let our imaginations canter free for long enough,' Lily says firmly. Tempting as it is to imagine Anne Boleyn escaping to the house in Mary Rose Court – for it must have been stressful in the extreme to keep Henry's interest alive while refusing to let him bed her, and a safe refuge away from court would have had its appeal – Lily is not going to let Bunty's enthusiasm sweep her away.

After a moment, Bunty says quietly, 'You are quite right to rein me in, my dear.' Her eyes, crinkling in a smile, meet Lily's. 'Will you concede, though, that it is not impossible for there to have been a connection between the Fetterplaces and the Boleyns?'

'Well, if this cousin of yours is reliable—'

'Oh, he is. He is.'

'Then yes, I concede that it's possible, if only because there is evidence of a later marriage between the families.'

Bunty points at the family tree. 'And here it is,' she says quietly.

There is a moment of stillness. Then abruptly Bunty stands up. 'I shall leave the evidence with you,' she announces. 'And now it is high time I left you to the morning's business, especially since I too must go to work.'

With a smile and a nod, she turns and strides out of the room.

Lily makes a feeble attempt to put the family tree aside but soon gives up. It is utterly fascinating. As well as the wealth of detail that this Cornelius Ely Redvers has provided on the two families, the document itself is a true work of art, inscribed in a beautiful hand and illustrated with coats of arms and a good deal of scarlet and gold paint.

She is still absorbed in it an hour later, when Marm suddenly appears on the other side of her desk.

'Mrs Clapper let me in,' he says apologetically. 'I did call out, but I don't think you heard.' He glances at the family tree spread out on her desk. 'I can't say I'm surprised,' he murmurs.

'Good morning, Marm,' Lily says. 'Sit down.'

He pulls up the chair. He sits in silence for a moment, studying her closely. His fingers dance a small jig on his knee; she senses he is nervous. Then he sighs and says, 'You went last night, then.'

'I went. How did you know?'

'Lily dear, you are as pale as a phantom and you have dark circles under your eyes.' He drops his gaze. 'But you are here,' he murmurs.

There are several things she wants to ask him. She begins with, 'How did you come to know about Tamáz?'

If he is surprised at her choice of starting point, he disguises it. 'Oh . . . I believe Felix told me some time ago that you had a . . . er, a friend who was a boatman. As far as I recall, it was after one of your more disturbing cases, and apparently you had gone to . . . er, gone for a good rest on his boat. The peace and quiet of life on the water, eh!' He attempts a light-hearted little chuckle, but it doesn't really succeed.

She watches him, amused by his discomfiture. 'Marm, Tamáz *is* my friend,' she says gently. 'He's not a lover.' She thinks of Marm as a friend too, and also as a sophisticated and hopefully unshockable man, and as he raises his eyes to hers, she sees that she is right.

He nods. 'There was no need to tell me, Lily my dear,' he says. 'It would not matter to me in the least if your friendship was of a more intimate nature, and in any case it is entirely your own business.'

It is her turn to be discomfited. While it is true that Tamáz is not her lover, all the same there have been moments of intimacy, including physical closeness. All too often she has needed the unique comfort of a warm body next to hers, and strong arms holding her in the night.

Marm clears his throat rather thoroughly and says, 'You are probably asking yourself why I took it upon myself to tell him what you were planning.'

She smiles. 'Oh, yes, I've asked myself that more than once. Now I'm asking you.' She fixes him with a glare, but she is sure he isn't convinced by it. Anyway, she already knows what he will say.

'There was no doubt that you would return to the path under the graveyard wall,' he says quietly. 'I understand why you did not accept my offer to go with you.' He smiles ruefully. 'I don't blame you, Lily, for undoubtedly my weapon is the pen and not the sword.'

'Nobody had a sword last night,' she murmurs.

He ignores her. 'For someone like me it was no great challenge to find out the identity and the likely whereabouts of your boatman, and I went to a couple of places and put out the word that I would be grateful to speak to the master of *The Dawning of the Day*. That was shortly after Felix was attacked, and I admit I was surprised at the speed with which Tamáz responded.' He pauses, smiling gently at her. 'He sought me out late in the evening of the day I'd gone asking after him.' He pauses again, and she senses he's waiting for her to comment. Just now, however, she has nothing to say.

'Tamáz already knew there was something gravely amiss up there under Tower Hill,' Marm resumes. 'Although *how* he knew, I have no idea, because he didn't tell me. He also knew that you, or rather the World's End Bureau, were involved. After Felix was hurt so badly, Tamáz too seems to have known that without a doubt you would head up there sooner or later.' He pauses. 'An unusual man,' he murmurs.

'He is,' Lily says. She doesn't really want to discuss Tamáz with Marm and, sensitive soul that he is, he clearly realises this.

Marm nods. 'I'm very glad you were not up there alone,' he mutters.

For an instant she is back. Images flash through her mind, so quickly that she hardly has time to register them. The stinking darkness, the head, the limbs, the pathetic pile of worn, tired clothing. She huddles with Tamáz in the fragile safety of the passage, so riven with terror that she can hardly stand. First the barrow passes, and then whatever *abomination* of a human being is pushing it.

And she hears again that awful, unimaginable howl.

If I had been alone, she thinks, I truly believe I would have died of fear.

She waits for her heartbeat to slow down.

'It was frightful, Marm,' she says. Her voice doesn't sound

like her own. 'Whoever he is, the man who lurks up there is surely deranged.'

Marm was already leaning towards her, his face full of anxiety. He too must have noticed the change in her tone. Now his entire body jerks to full attention. 'Tell me,' he says.

And she does.

When she has finished, and when they have had a brief and fairly fierce argument about whether or not she should go to the police (which she concludes with a childish but effective: 'Well, I'm *not* going and you can't make me') there is a short and not very comfortable silence.

Lily breaks it by asking why he called round this morning.

'Oh – to enquire after Felix, of course,' he says, and she can hear the residual irritation, 'which I realise I haven't actually done, although I imagine you would have told me straight away if there was anything to tell?'

She nods.

'Good,' he murmurs. He pauses, frowning sightly. 'And also to talk about that.' He indicates the family tree.

Then abruptly he says, 'Lily, Felix was hurt *very* badly.' The words burst out of him as if he has been trying to hold them back and failed. 'And only last night, you went out and faced a horror and a frightful peril that might have been the death of you.'

She is shocked, not least because earlier she was thinking exactly the same thing.

'I do want to discuss cousin Cor's work, which I knew about, of course, because Bunty told me what she was going to do. But *please*, dear Lily, do not assume that by doing so now, I am indicating any degree of acceptance of you putting yourself in such danger. I am *not*, and I never will.' He glares at her.

She waits while the echo of his passionate voice fades. Then she says quietly, 'I won't.'

Presently, tapping the family tree, she says, 'Have you seen it?' He shakes his head, and she turns it round so that it is the right way up for him. He gives a soft sigh of appreciation and bends over it.

Some time later, he straightens up. 'I know Agnes Halligan told you a great deal about the Boleyn family,' he says. 'But this work of dear old Cor's takes us much deeper into their history, and indeed that of the Fetterplaces. We might show it to her, don't you think?'

'Definitely,' Lily agrees.

'I have the impression,' he adds with a smile, 'that we are all unreasonably eager to make a positive identification of the Fetterplace skeleton.'

Lily tries to go back in her mind to that time before last night when she was so desperate to see the skeleton; so eager to find out who it – *she* – had been. 'None of us are as eager as the Fetterplace siblings, surely?' she says.

'Oh, I believe they know who she is already,' he murmurs.

Marm sits back, all at once looking exhausted. Presently he gives a soft chuckle. 'I can't think why I am so keen for what they believe to turn out to be true.' He glances at her. 'For the bones to be the mortal remains of Anne Boleyn. But, despite having tried quite hard to reason myself out of it, I can't quite dispel the fervent hope that they are.'

'But how are . . .' Lily stops. She was about to say: *How are we to find definite proof?* But she holds back the words, because, obviously, they won't. It is, she muses, an act of faith.

Slowly Marm spins the family tree round again. With a sigh he stands up. 'Thank you, Lily dear.'

'What for?'

'Oh – for not dismissing my fancies.' He gives her a very sweet smile. 'Now, I dare say young Felix is awake, so, as I am sure he has had quite enough of Alice, I shall go and engage him in lively conversation.'

FIFTEEN

It is late at night, and Felix lies wide awake. He is not sure he can endure much more of this.

His day began far too many hours ago with the arrival of Mrs Clapper and her breakfast tray. Not that she and her burden weren't welcome, for since he began to come back to himself, Felix has been almost permanently hungry, and Mrs Clapper cooks a plate of bacon, black pudding, sausage, mushrooms, tomatoes and fried bread better than anyone he has ever known.

When he had finished the plateful and was starting on the toast and marmalade, Lily had swept into his room and sat down beside the bed. He'd thought at first she was going to talk to him properly. She'd had the air of someone with something really interesting and possibly startling or even alarming to reveal, and she looked tense, her eyes huge in her pale face. But he must have been mistaken, because she went on to speak of Mrs Clapper's culinary skills and how much better it was to share the house with the new tenants than the Little Ballerina. They had laughed as they tried to outdo each other in recalling the wretched woman's worst habits, and he had expressed the hope that she was now back in St Petersburg, or at least in some far corner of the British Isles a very long way from Chelsea.

Either I was mistaken, he had thought as Lily took her leave and hurried away downstairs to begin the day's work, or there was something and she has decided not to share it with me.

And that was such a dismal, depressing thought that he is still troubled by it as the quiet of night falls around him.

After Lily it had been dear old Bunty, who had insisted on reading another chapter of Alice's adventures in Looking-Glass land. What charm the story had for Felix has worn a little thin, but he doesn't like to upset her by saying so. Instead, he let his eyes slowly close and, after a few more pages, emitted a small pretend snore. He heard Bunty close and put down the book, and the floorboards giving their usual series of creaks as she tiptoed away.

Some time later, he was wondering whether the dense clouds that still seemed to be obscuring the recent past would give way in the face of a really determined effort to remember, when he heard footsteps on the stairs. Then there was a tap on the half-open door and Marm's voice said brightly, 'Anyone at home?'

They engaged in the exchange of light-hearted banter of the sort considered suitable by Marm – and everyone else, come to that – for a man recovering from a life-threatening injury. Once again, Felix experienced sharply contrasting emotions: he was irritated and frustrated because he wanted to be treated like the grown man he used to be before someone attacked him, yet at the same time he was angry with himself for being so ungrateful to these kind and well-meaning people who have dedicated themselves so selflessly and tirelessly to helping him along his stumbling way to recovery.

But oh, dear Lord, how he longed for some topic more adult and challenging than Mrs Clapper's culinary skills, inane little jibes at Lily's departed tenant and *Alice Through the* blasted *Looking-Glass*.

When Marm had gone, it was not long till lunchtime, and after that the fatigue returned briefly and he had a short sleep. An hour with Dorothea, who told him a fairly pointless story about the dappled pony she rode as a child that had a nasty habit of trying (and often succeeding) to bite her, then Mrs Clapper bringing a cup of tea and three buttered scones with plum jam, and the tedium of this apparently endless day proceeded through an all-too-brief early evening visit from Lily, supper (which was delicious) and, in between these highlights, far too many hours on his own.

Felix hears the church clock strike eleven. Then twelve.

He is cheered by the fact that the days – and nights – of sleeping almost all the time are over, which surely indicates that he is recovering. On the other hand, this new wakefulness threatens to be accompanied by excruciating boredom: he has absolutely nothing to do.

He must have been asleep, because it was the chiming of eleven o'clock that had woken him. That, he reflects, is the trouble with recovering rapidly but not yet being fully well; he still sleeps during the day, and although these naps are now brief, they are still long enough to make him wakeful in the night. Especially, the thought runs on, when he has done nothing but lie in bed.

This night his dreams have been brief and frighteningly vivid. Unlike the ones when he had a fever, they seem to follow a rational pattern and feel like real events. They feature people he recognises and places he has been to. He has the disturbing feeling that the content is actually his resurfacing memories and not the totally random offerings of his sleeping mind. There was violence and horror in the dreams, and now that he is awake and able to think, he is sure that he has actually seen and experienced those fearful and dread-inducing scenes: there is a very strong sense of recognition.

His recollection of that night is coming back, and what he remembers is awful.

It is a very worrying thought.

Now he is wide awake, and his mind is working fast and furiously as if desperate to make up for the lost time. He is seeing people, places, and hearing words and fragments of speech, then whole conversations. At first it all comes at him in a frantic rush, but then the pace eases and everything begins to make sense.

One o'clock. Two o'clock.

His mind is slowing down now, and he is full of excitement. An urgent need is growing in him to share what he has been remembering.

'Go on, then,' Felix says softly.

He turns back the bedclothes, puts his feet to the floor and carefully stands up. It is not the first time he has attempted to get out of bed and walk around the room on his own. He is delighted to discover that tonight his steps are firmer and his legs no longer tremble. At least, he admits honestly to himself, they don't tremble quite so violently.

He walks to the window and back several times, and gradually his balance becomes more reliable and his confidence grows. He pauses by the bed, holding on to the bed post, then turns towards the doorway that leads to the room where Lily sleeps in her shakedown bed on the floor. The door is ajar.

He takes a couple of breaths, then walks to the door. Pushes it further open, goes on into the shadowy room. The soft light from the lamp by his bed gives gentle illumination.

He looks down at Lily. She is asleep, curled on her left side and facing out into the room. Her fair hair is in its loose night-time plait, lying like a thick golden rope on the pillow.

He crouches beside her. Then suddenly his legs go weak and he sits down on the floor with a thump and a muttered exclamation, because the wooden floor is hard and the thin nightshirt affords no protection for his buttocks.

Her eyes spring open. That will be the nurses' training, he decides, trying to be rational and sensible in the face of the unexpected emotions that are churning through him. She'll have learned to be instantly and thoroughly awake when a patient is in need, a lesson which will no doubt be drummed into a young nurse right from the start . . .

She is trying to sit up, flinging the plait over her shoulder, focusing on his face. 'Felix, what's wrong?' she asks urgently. 'Are you in pain?'

He makes soothing motions with his hands. 'There's nothing wrong with me and I'm not in pain,' he says brightly.

She frowns, and he can hear the unspoken question: *Then why have you just woken me up?*

'Lily, my memory is coming back,' he says. 'Before, I just had flashes – remember, I told you I'd recalled a skeleton and a graveyard and some old people?' She nods. 'Well, suddenly it's all much clearer.'

She stares at him. He can read the sequence of what she's feeling from her expression: anxiety in case he's mistaken, fear of being overly optimistic in case the memories turn out to be false, apprehension at exactly what he's remembered and, finally, driving all the others out, relief – joy? – because he's started to recover.

She puts none of these reactions into words; she simply says quite sternly, 'I think you had better tell me.'

He tries to settle himself more comfortably and, noticing – of course she notices – she reaches behind her for a pillow and hands it to him. It is a great improvement on the bare floorboards.

'I know now who the old people are,' he begins. 'They are siblings, a brother and two sisters called Dukey, Fanny and Alethea, and their surname's Fetterplace.' She nods again, as if in confirmation, but he doesn't need it. 'They had dug up a skeleton in their garden and they believed it to be the remains of someone important. I visited them at their house . . .' He almost has the name of the street and, after a brief pause, he remembers. 'Mary Rose Court.'

'Yes!' she whispers.

'They wouldn't let me near the rose bed, which was both annoying and irrational since it meant I didn't have a chance to study the skeleton.' He pauses. 'I decided I'd have to return after dark and find my way into the garden while everyone was asleep. I had a lantern!' he exclaims. The memory of opening the little door and allowing the light to spill out is vivid and sharp. Then he remembers saying this before. 'But I've already told you that,' he mutters.

'Yes, you have,' she says calmly.

'I did go. Didn't I?' he asks. 'I stood looking down at her, and I had a sort of vision of what it had been like for her, up on the scaffold with the sword hidden under the straw and still hoping that there would be a reprieve, but there wasn't. I hated leaving her there, but I had to, and then I climbed over the wall and . . .' He stops, doubtful suddenly, the memories jumping and dancing in his mind.

He can tell by her abrupt change of expression that she knows what happened next, and it occurs to him with absolute certainty that he does too. 'That was when I was attacked. Wasn't it?'

And she whispers, 'Yes.'

He waits for her to go on; to tell him. He *really* wants to know. But she doesn't say anything else.

He sighs. 'Lily, I'm sure you think you're doing the right thing by not telling me the details of how I got hurt but, believe me, the opposite is true. Since I've started to recover, the one thing I'm absolutely *desperate* to do is to get my full memory back, which involves you explaining exactly what happened, how I managed to get back here and who hit me, although this may be too optimistic because you probably don't know.'

She shivers suddenly, although he doesn't think it's because she's cold. But her nightgown is quite thin, so perhaps he's wrong. There is a woollen shawl draped across the foot of her bed and he reaches for it, handing it to her. She wraps it round her shoulders.

This is not the first time we've engaged in deep conversation in the small hours dressed only in our nightclothes, he thinks. It doesn't seem to have occurred to Lily that it's far from decorous.

He suppresses the urge to smile.

She is still staring at him, and she still looks very anxious. 'Please tell me?' he says softly.

And after a short pause she begins to speak.

Her account is very hard to hear, and she spares no details. He is not at all surprised that she tried to keep it from him. As she describes his injuries, he tries to match them to the increasingly comprehensive picture in his fast-returning memory. He can't recall the heavy blow to the head that nearly killed him, although he knows he probably heard it . . . Heard, anyway, the sound of some hard and weighty object flying through the air in a descending arc that was aimed at his neck, although of course it wasn't the axe he had briefly envisaged and it wasn't aimed at his neck, because if it had been he would have lost his head like that poor woman in the rose bed and he wouldn't now be sitting beside Lily in the friendly darkness filled with happiness. Because she is Tiger Lily; she whispered to him *come back* and he did . . .

It is with some effort that he manages to bring himself out of the maze of half-dreams and back to the present.

'You have broken ribs as well,' she is saying in a matter-of-fact voice – her nurse's voice – 'and extensive, deep bruising all over your chest and lower back, almost certainly from where your assailant kicked you.'

'I can't remember that,' Felix says quietly. 'It must have happened once I was down.'

He is struck by dismay and revulsion at the thought of a man who could stand over the body of someone he thought he had just killed and kick them, again and again, so hard that he broke ribs and caused profound and widespread contusions. He glances at Lily. It seems from her expression that she is thinking the same thing; she makes a soft sound of distress and, just for an instant, reaches out her hand as if to touch him, only to draw it back.

He waits until the sudden sense of powerful emotions thrumming in the air begins to fade. Then he says, 'I remember being in the flower bed beside the skeleton. It . . . she . . .' He stops, shrugging, for he doesn't think he can put into words the way those small, graceful bones and elegant skull affected him. 'The head was separate from the body, and I put it back where it ought to be.'

She gives a soft gasp. 'It was you who arranged her like that!' she whispers.

He is still not fully himself, and it takes a moment for him to understand what that means. 'You've been there too,' he says. And then the memories of the dark figure on the path and the barrow and the splayed, scarlet-painted, disordered limbs of the Red King and the Red Queen and the stink of blood fill his head and he says again, '*You've been there!*' and this time it is a cry of horror because she put herself in the same danger and she could have been killed.

He can't speak.

But she knows; he can tell. 'I wasn't hurt,' she says. 'I heard him. I *saw* him; I watched him walk past with his barrow, but he didn't see me.'

He barely hears her. He is filled with such anguish, such fear for her, for what might so easily have happened to her, that his head is confounded with the loud noise of it. He reaches for her hand and holds it between his own, tightly, not letting go when she tries to pull away, and he says, 'Lily, promise me you will *never* go there again!'

It seems she can't speak. She just nods, a sharp little movement, repeated several times in quick succession. Then she looks at him, gives him a very sweet smile and gently extracts her hand.

Presently she says, in her businesslike office voice, 'I think it would help if we go through our findings and thoughts on the case together.' She shoots him a sharp glance, looking away again. 'I . . . er, I've found it rather tricky to order my thoughts alone. I—' The swift glance again, and he has the sense she is nerving herself, trying to decide whether or not to say something. Apparently deciding, she sits up straight and says stiffly, 'I find that I have difficulty when I do not have someone else with whom to discuss matters.'

He struggles not to laugh. He is both touched and mildly irritated. He understands instantly: she wants to tell him openly that it's been hard to work out problems and puzzles alone; that she has missed him. But because of who they are – employer and employee, working partners, friends, even – she cannot express this in such emotional terms but must remain cool and formal. He ducks his head, for the urge to laugh has gone and now he very much wants to hug her. Dearest Lily, he thinks, here we sit with you in your bed and me beside you, both of us in our nightgowns, and yet you just spoke to me with such rigid propriety that I'm quite surprised you didn't call me Mr Wilbraham.

'I think that is a good idea,' he says, matching her tone. 'Since I have perforce missed several days, perhaps you should begin?'

He senses relief in her instant agreement. There, Lily, he thinks, we're all right now. We're back on safe ground.

He listens as she summarises everything that has happened since he was brought home by kind strangers who had probably thought he was going to die. The late-night knock at the door from her boatman friend who told her that body parts were turning up in the river and that the boat people sensed a fearful and unnatural darkness spreading through the water. Her visit to Alf Wilson at Wapping, who informed her he'd been on the point of contacting her to tell her much the same thing: that he and his colleagues had been dealing with body parts that their long experience told them did not come from accidental deaths and dismemberment by the violence of the current, but had been subjected to cuts so clean and efficient that they had probably been done with a sharp cleaver. Repeated reports of blood and the stench of putrefaction: from Billy Simpson, the night watchman who had found Felix's inert body and probably saved his life; from Dr March, who had tended his wounds; from Lily, when she crept down the passage between the houses of Mary Rose Court and nerved herself to tiptoe along to the apparently neglected shed crouched half-hidden at the turn in the path; from Lily's second visit, when her boatman went with her to look after her because Felix was laid up in bed and had no knowledge of the risky, foolhardy and very nearly fatal venture until now.

Not him! Not him! It should have been me! The words blast through Felix's head like a music-hall chorus.

Lily goes on talking while Felix battles with his anger and his furious resentment. When he has calmed down a little, he waits until she pauses for breath and says, 'I smelt that stench too, out on the path. I had forgotten until now. And there was the smell of blood as well.'

She nods, frowning in thought. 'The shed is the centre of whatever is going on,' she says. And she describes to him in far too much detail what she and the boatman saw when they peered through the gap in the planking.

Oh God, you were in such peril, he wants to say. Now the jealous anger has gone and he is simply in anguish at how close she came to danger. Hoping the emotion will not be detectable in his voice, he says, 'You had someone on watch, you said?'

She nods. 'Yes. One of Tamáz's watermen. When Tamáz and I were . . . when we saw what was in the shed, I suddenly remembered that the man has a barrow, and that if the barrow wasn't in the shed, then he must be out and about with it. And that he'd probably be coming back.' She pauses, and he can see how unnerved she is. 'The barrow wasn't in the shed,' she goes on. 'And I said we should go, and we were already heading back when Tamáz's waterman hissed that someone was coming, and we ran back up the path and ducked inside the passage. We were perfectly safe!' she protests, although he hasn't spoken. 'Truly we were, and he can have had no idea that anyone was there because he was so . . . so *casual*.' Her expression turns to one of indignation. 'He was *humming!*' she exclaims.

Slowly Felix considers every aspect of the pictures she is making in his mind. He accepts that they were full of horror, and that they put her in the most terrible danger, and then with quite a lot of effort he puts them aside. He says, 'Now, what have you learned concerning the Fetterplaces?'

Her voice is much lighter as she resumes her account, and he assumes she is as relieved as he is to move to less distressing matters. 'You know about Agnes Halligan and all the information she provided about the Tudors and Anne Boleyn? Yes, of course you do,' she adds before he can comment. 'She came to tea on the afternoon of the day you went back to Mary Rose Court.'

'Of course I do,' he echoes, trying to sound nonchalant. There is, he thinks ruefully, no 'of course' about it; it has only come into focus with a considerable effort.

'Well, Bunty – Miss Adderley – found someone else who

provided a different sort of expertise,' she is saying. 'He's a second cousin of hers and Marm's who is a herald in the College of Arms, and he investigates really old family trees. Bunty told him about the Fetterplace siblings and their claims to have forebears who were important in the Tudor court – important enough to have been given the Mary Rose Court house early on in Henry the Eighth's reign – and he looked the family up and it's quite right, they did!'

Her face is alight with excitement, and he drags his mind away from thinking how lovely she looks and manages to say with what passes for delight, 'How very satisfying!'

Her sudden swift glance tells him he might not have convinced her. Then she hurries on: 'His name's Cornelius Ely Redvers, only Bunty and Marm refer to him as Cor, and he's actually found a marriage between a Fetterplace man and a woman who was a granddaughter of Anne Boleyn's sister Mary!'

She looks so happy that he hesitates before stating the obvious flaw in the argument. 'But that would make the woman Anne's great-niece, which is two generations on from her time,' he begins, 'and—'

'Yes, Felix, I *know*!' she interrupts impatiently. 'That's just what *I* said when Bunty told me. But Cor's research indicates strong bonds of friendship between the two families long before Anne's time, because the Boleyns and the Fetterplaces had neighbouring estates in Norfolk, so they knew each other years before they were all at court in London.'

'I see,' he says slowly. He sits silently for a while, thinking it through. 'So are we to conclude that it's not impossible for some of the Fetterplace and Boleyn men to have crept out by night to retrieve the body of someone dear to both families? And to have placed her with respect and due ceremony in the Fetterplace rose bed?'

'The Fetterplaces lived in the house by then,' she says. 'I just told you. It was probably the nearest safe place, because it doesn't appear that the Boleyns had property anywhere near the Tower.'

'I admit it's not impossible,' he says cautiously.

Her expression suggests she has been expecting a rather more confident endorsement than 'it's not impossible'. 'Well, it's what the Fetterplace siblings believe,' she mutters.

He almost says, 'Yes, and at least two of them, the brother and the younger sister, have a tenuous grip on reality at best.' He doesn't. He has already disappointed her once and is reluctant to do so again.

He is thinking hard. Trying to make links; to work out motives.

Presently she says, 'When I last spoke to Alethea Fetterplace – I told you, didn't I, that I managed to talk to her alone, because I knew I'd only start to get at the truth if the others weren't there? So I waited until she'd packed Dukey and Fanny off for a walk.' He nods. 'She told me something very important.' Lily pauses for a breath. 'You remember what they said when they first engaged us? That they'd decided to restore the old rose bed and Dukey had dug down and found the bones, and then they started noticing goings-on and lights flickering at the end of the garden in the middle of the night and they all became frightened that someone was trying to steal the skeleton?'

'I remember,' he confirms.

'Well, Miss Fetterplace confessed to me that wasn't true,' Lily goes on. 'She told me that day that digging up the rose bed was just an excuse. Dukey was looking for the skeleton.' She pauses, her eyes on his. She whispers, 'They always knew she was somewhere in the garden.'

He wonders why he isn't surprised.

After a moment he says quietly, 'Why now?' Her eyebrows go up in enquiry. 'If they'd always known,' he goes on, 'if the secret had been handed down from generation to generation right back to May 1536, then why didn't they try to dig out the rose bed years ago, when Dukey was young and fit? And why did they want to find the skeleton in the first place?'

Lily doesn't answer straight away. Then she says, 'I haven't asked those questions. But, now that you have, I think perhaps I know.'

'Go on,' he says when she hesitates.

'It's what you just said about a secret handed down,' she says. 'From father to son, or daughter, all that long time. The father of our three told them. Perhaps just Alethea because she was the eldest, perhaps Dukey because he was the son, perhaps all three of them, because certainly they all know now. And . . .'

He knows what she is going to say. 'And none of them has a

child,' he interrupts. 'None out of the three of them has even been married. Many generations after the union between the Fetterplaces and Anne Boleyn's great-niece, the line ends in the three old people now living at number eight, Mary Rose Court. And unless old Dukey Fetterplace managed to beget an illegitimate child at some point in his seventy years, which I really don't think is very likely, they are the end of that line. There may be obscure cousins and scattered relations, but there will be no more Fetterplaces at number eight, Mary Rose Court. When the last one out of Alethea, Dukey and Fanny dies, the secret will die with them.'

It is a sad thought. There is a moment's silence, as if they are both recognising the fact.

'Then do you think they were just checking she was all right down there in the ground?' Lily says cautiously. 'Or making sure that she really *was* there, and it wasn't just a family legend without any real foundation?'

He shrugs. 'I don't know. Perhaps there was some idea of moving her. Of having her restored to her rightful place in some royal chapel? She was a queen of England, when all's said and done.'

'She was,' Lily agrees solemnly. There is a pause, then she says, 'But I don't believe the idea of moving her to a location where she can be honoured has even occurred to them.' She stops again, then says tentatively, 'Would you like to know what I think?'

He grins. 'Always, Lily.'

She ducks her head, but he has already seen her answering smile. 'I think it was simple curiosity. They'd lived with the tale since the death of their father, and they just had to find out if it was true.'

They both contemplate that.

After some time she says, 'And now the poor old things must be feeling so guilty, because they have discovered she *is* there, and by the very act of finding her and uncovering her, they have endangered those precious remains that their family has so diligently and carefully kept safe for three and a half centuries.'

Her voice dropping low, as if she can hardly bear to say the words aloud, she adds in a whisper, 'And now other people know, and one of them is a *terrible* man who keeps dead bodies in a shed and hacks at them and cuts their heads off.'

Suddenly horror is present in the room. Just for an instant, Felix thinks he can smell rotting flesh.

Then Lily says, 'But why does the man with the barrow want the skeleton?' Felix's head shoots up and he stares at her. 'What is in the hut indicates that it's the flesh of the recently dead that he wants to use for whatever he does,' she goes on, urgently now, 'so why would he want such old bones?'

After quite a long silence, Felix says, 'Supposing he doesn't.'

SIXTEEN

It is only the second time in almost a month that the Barrow Man has not gone out during the hours of darkness. He does not often kill on these night excursions; usually he is satisfied with a visit to the secret shed, where in the peaceful company of the dead he can suppress the turmoil in his mind.

No amount of severed limbs, heads and even whole corpses would work now, however. In any case, the shed – his precious, private, hidden, *secret* shed – has been spoiled. Violated. People have been there. He found the places round behind it where the broken branches and the trodden grass demonstrated as clear as writing that someone – more than one person – had stood there and peered into his private domain. It is ruined for him now. It will never be the same. And for the moment he too is ruined. Whoever looked into his workroom might as well have been staring into his soul.

He feels as if he has been ravaged.

He knows he will have to kill, and kill soon. There is, however, no certainty that this will work either.

Unless I kill *her*, the Barrow Man thinks.

He wishes he had acted before. When he saw the fair-haired woman in the workman's boots on the Wapping steps. It would not have been easy. He remembers only too well how he felt that jolt of resistance as he bent his thoughts on her, but he appreciates a challenge and he knows that in the end his own great strength and his utter determination will always prevail over even the most powerful defensive amulet.

Now it will be an even greater challenge. For she has trespassed into his territory, and glimpsed into the world within his shed that is forbidden to all but him.

She has begun to *know* him.

The very thought of this terrible intimacy is enough to fill his head and his eyes with blood so that he can see nothing but red.

When he discovered that she and the big boatman had found

his shed, he thought he was going to implode. And the reaction had alarmed him; he could not recall ever having experienced such overwhelming rage. He had wasted valuable minutes comforting himself, wrapping his arms around his own powerful body, crooning to himself and tamping down the furious destructive energy until it stopped its attack on him and changed into a weapon which he could turn against others.

Then he had gone looking for her.

The wherry was far out in the central stream by the time he reached the river. He stood at the top of the steps and watched as the distance steadily increased, and very soon – for the tide was with them – they were far away, rounding the great bend and speeding towards Lambeth, Chelsea and Battersea reaches.

He knows now that he should not have loosed that howl, but he could not stop himself.

He sits in the dark little room for some time, his eyes closed, letting the memory slowly fade. It is not a swift process. As his mood calms and he can think rationally once more, an idea stirs deep in the murk of his mind. He lets it surface, contemplates it, thinks about how to go about it and, finally, smiles.

Then he stands up, stretches and opens the door. It is a fine night, if a cold one, and there are several hours of darkness left.

Perhaps he will go out, after all.

Despite the disturbed night, Lily feels brighter and more optimistic the next morning than she has done for a long time. Felix was fast asleep when she came downstairs, and now she sits in the Inner Sanctum tucking into a second helping of scrambled eggs on toast. Mrs Clapper must have caught her sunny mood – and understood the significance – because Lily can hear her singing out in the scullery, where she is preparing a similarly large breakfast for Felix.

Lily's cheery mood adds an unlikely sparkle even to the challenge of dull, routine jobs such as catching up with the filing and bringing the accounts book up to date. She has completed the first task and is halfway through the second when she hears the boom of the street door knocker and Mrs Clapper goes hurrying across the hall to attend to it.

As Marm comes striding into the Inner Sanctum, she thinks,

I *knew* it would be him. She is glad – more than glad – for here is someone else with whom to share her happiness. Before she can do so, however, he has already started to talk.

'I'm sorry to disturb you, Lily,' he is saying as he settles in the chair on the other side of her desk, dumping his briefcase on the floor, 'but I've been thinking.'

'You as well!' she exclaims, before she can stop herself.

His eyebrows go up. 'As well as whom?'

So now she tells him about Felix, and his returning memory, and their long conversation; how there is an indefinable *something* about Felix that tells her better than any words that he is going to be all right. She might have imagined it, but she thinks she sees Marm's eyes close for an instant and his lips move as if in a prayer of thanks.

She doesn't say anything about this conversation having taken place in the early hours of the morning, with Felix sitting on her pillow beside her bed and both of them in their night wear.

Some things are private, even from dear old Marm.

His moment of intense emotion – if indeed it was really there – has passed, and now he is simply full of delight at the news, and at the depth and detail of the conversation, and the way Felix now seems to have a stronger grasp on what is real and what is not.

When he takes a pause from rather lengthily expressing his relief, Lily says, 'As you sat down you said you'd been thinking, Marm. Would you like to explain?'

He strikes his thighs with his hands and says firmly, '*Yes*. And thank you, dear Lily, for reminding me. Now, you did not allow me to accompany you on your perilous mission to continue Felix's investigations into what was going on behind Mary Rose Court. Quite rightly,' he adds swiftly, 'for I would indeed have been more of a hindrance than a help. But since I was prevented from aiding you in one way, I was determined to come up with something else that I could offer; something for which I believe myself to be uniquely fitted.'

Intrigued, Lily says, 'Please, Marm, tell me.'

He studies her intently, frowning. 'I fear I must speak of deeply disturbing matters,' he warns. He shakes his head. 'But then, of course, you have seen the evidence for yourself, and so really I should stop thinking of you as a delicate young woman and appreciate that you are a professional, and—'

'*Please*, Marm!' Lily exclaims in frustration.

'Sorry, sorry!' He holds up his hands in apology. Then he says without preamble, 'There has been an upsurge in reports of human matter in the river. Corpses and partial corpses are an ever-present occurrence, of course, and more often than not these are the sad aftermath of accidents, and the battering – even the partial breaking apart – of the bodies is what happens when they are swept along by a very powerful current and hurled against solid objects such as bridge piers and heavily laden barges, not to mention the detritus carried on the surface.' He leans forward, lowering his voice. 'What troubles me is the other findings: the limbless torsos, the corpses missing their heads, arms, legs, and in every case the cuts are *clean*; one could say surgical.'

'I know,' Lily says softly. 'My friend Alf Wilson at Wapping told me. He fishes things out of the water.'

Marm nods. 'Then it is likely that my source obtained his information from him, or another river officer like him.' He looks at her expectantly. When she doesn't speak, he says, 'Lily, we know of a place not very far from the river where you have seen bodies and parts of bodies with your own eyes. You *told* me!' he exclaims. 'We were sitting just as we are now, and you described that terrible shed, and the smell, and what you saw, and I wanted to leap up and comfort you, only you sat there so calm and still, and your voice was so steady as you described the horrors, that I did not think you would have welcomed such attention.'

Lily remembers. Of course she does. It had taken all her resolve not to break down, and the sense of Marm's compassion and sympathy had all but undone her, even without the offer of physical comfort.

She wonders briefly what is happening to her, that she can witness and describe such brutal depravity so coolly. But I am *not* cool, she thinks; not inside.

'You are saying there is a link between the man with the barrow and the body parts in the river,' she says. 'That he is responsible for murdering women, dismembering them and disposing of them.'

'I am,' Marm agrees. 'As I just said, bodies in the Thames are no new phenomenon. But what has been happening for the last six weeks is something different altogether. It is not—'

'We do not know how long the man with the barrow has been in London,' she interrupts. 'I agree, it seems too much of a coincidence to say he is *not* responsible, but, since we do not know his identity, how can we claim that he is? He would have to be caught, arrested, taken into custody, questioned, and his account of himself would have to be checked. None of these are actions that are within the orbit of the World's End Bureau.'

'I know, Lily my dear,' Marm says gently. 'Which is why, yet again, I am urging you to turn this matter over to the police. I know what you're going to say,' he ploughs on before she can speak, 'that your duty is to your clients, these Fetterplace people, but I've thought of that. Once the man is in police custody, their precious skeleton is safe from his attentions, and they can . . .' He stops, and she realises he has read her expression. 'What is it?'

'Last night Felix raised a doubt about our assumption that the Barrow Man has an interest in the skeleton,' she says. 'Once he'd done that, we realised we'd only ever believed it because the Fetterplace siblings had seen signs of night-time activity at the end of the garden, and jumped to the conclusion that someone was hunting for their old bones. But—'

'But if it was the man with the barrow, then he wasn't there for that at all!' Marm interjects excitedly. The light of sudden revelation is in his eyes. 'He was about his own dreadful business. He probably has no idea the skeleton even exists!' There is a short silence while they both digest that. Then: 'What will you do?'

She shrugs. 'I don't know yet. Felix is going to think about it today and we'll discuss it later.' She hesitates. 'I took his notebook and pencil up to him this morning.' She feels the smile spreading across her face and can't stop it. From Marm's expression, he too can see the significance.

Then, with a soft exclamation, he reaches down for whatever bulky item is straining the sides of his briefcase. 'Something for you to think about,' he murmurs.

And his Lost Women file thumps down on Lily's desk.

As she reads the neat label on the cover, Lily reflects that the existence of this file is one of the many elements that are the basis of her deep affection and respect for Marmaduke Smithers. For he is a crusader on behalf of women who suffer suspicious deaths – specifically, poor women, unimportant women, prostitutes; any woman whose demise has not, in Marm's opinion, been treated with sufficient seriousness by the investigating authorities. He has, she recalls, been furious about the fate of such women for a very long time.

'I'm not sure you'll know, Lily,' he says as he opens it, 'but it is not only the imperfectly examined deaths of women in London that concern me.'

'I do know,' she says. 'You once told me about a school mistress who fell off a train near Havant.'[3]

He looks up, his eyes bright. 'You remember.'

'Indeed, I do.'

He has dived into the file, turning pages until he comes to one he has marked with a slip of paper. 'I have been searching for accounts of female bodies dissected and thrown into rivers,' he says, 'and I came across two such cases that happened during the summer of 1878, in Liverpool.' He stops, his eyes flicking along several lines of writing. 'Yes. Two dismembered bodies found in the Mersey. Both women were prostitutes, one aged about forty, the other perhaps a decade younger. Both were missing their arms and legs, not all of which were found.' He looks up. 'Another woman was reported missing at about the same time. She was not a prostitute. She was engaged to be married, and she'd had a row with her young man and marched out of the pub where they had been having a drink. She set off for her home by herself. Her body was never found.'

Lily nods. She doesn't comment. What indeed, she thinks, could you say?

'Now it seems there were mutterings about a man who might know something about the two, probably three, murders,' Marm continues. 'I should point out that nobody ever said he was guilty, not as such, although in that infamous police phrase, he was a "person of interest".'

---

[3] See *The Outcast Girls*

'Who was he?' she asks.

'His name was Walter Blackmore, he was a dock hand and his address was twenty-seven, Anselm Street, Anfield, where he lodged with an elderly widow who always referred to herself as Mrs Gledhill, although her first name was Dora. Mrs Gledhill, incidentally, spoke very highly of Walter Blackmore, who had lived under her roof for three years and who she seemed to look upon as both a son to dote on and a prospective lover, although apparently when she was asked if there had been anything improper in her dealings with Mr Blackmore, she leapt up and hit the police sergeant asking the question with a shopping bag stuffed with vegetables from the market.'

Lily rather likes the sound of Mrs Dora Gledhill.

Marm has been reading as he speaks, and now he utters a soft *oh!* of distress.

'What is it?'

'Walter Blackmore left one night, round about the time when the mutterings were growing more insistent,' he says. 'He'd paid his rent to the end of the week, but he left a pile of coins on the kitchen table, presumably as a thank-you. When Mrs Gledhill mentioned that to the police sergeant, she was weeping.'

Lily waits while he reads to the end of the page, turns over and reads some more. Then she asks, 'Is there anything other than the manner of the victims' deaths to connect this man with our barrow man?'

And after a long pause, Marm looks up at her and murmurs, 'Perhaps there is.' He takes a breath, briefly closes his eyes, then says, 'On the third of September that year – 1878 – the *Princess Alice* went down.'

'I remember,' Lily whispers, but she doesn't think Marm registers the comment.

'They estimated that about eight hundred people were on board – there was no definitive list of passengers, not even a total number – and most of them died. The river and police authorities were left with scores of unidentified bodies, which quickly began to rot because the weather was mild and most of them were drenched in human waste because the boat had gone down close to a major sewage outlet.'

Lily tries and fails not to imagine the horror of that.

'Makeshift mortuaries sprang up,' Marm continues, 'and people missing a relative or a friend made their way to them and endured the grim task of inspecting line upon line of befouled and stinking corpses in the hope – or, I suppose, the terrible fear – of coming across one that they recognised. And—'

'And someone recognised Walter Blackmore?' Lily suggests.

Marm looks up at her and manages a quick smile. 'Dear Lily,' he says. 'Paying attention, as always. Yes. It is recorded that some three or four days after the disaster, a man claiming to be Blackmore's cousin picked out the body of a man of about his own age.' He reads on. 'Not much in the way of details, I fear, although the cousin, whose name was Joseph Phipps, claimed that he and Walter had looked quite similar, both having the same large nose with a bump halfway down.'

'And did they?' she demands. 'Did the corpse resemble this Joseph Phipps?'

'I have no idea,' Marm says. 'I assume he did; sufficiently, at least, to satisfy an overworked clerk who was probably only too pleased to have one corpse out of hundreds identified and carted away for burial. I know it sounds harsh, Lily, and of course he should have been more diligent, but the pressure to clear away the bodies must have been intense. And,' he adds, spotting something and tapping the place on the page, 'the cousin provided Walter Blackmore's address, and when the Liverpool authorities checked, someone of that name had indeed lived there.'

'And left some coins in gratitude for his doting landlady,' Lily murmurs.

Something is troubling her, something that snagged her attention and that she promptly forgot again.

She quite hopes it will come back.

Felix has spent a gratifying hour or so going through his notebook. He feels very strongly now that he is returning to himself; so much so that he has got out of bed, performed his ablutions without any assistance and even had a shave. He has put on a dressing gown and installed himself at the little table over by the window, which serves quite well as a desk.

He makes some notes, thinking hard.

All at once he is overcome by utter fatigue. Trying not to let it depress him, reflecting that it is still only a week since he was attacked, he goes back to bed and falls deeply asleep.

As he rises to wakefulness again a short time later, he is struggling to capture a recent memory. Two – or maybe three – days ago, he must have been dreaming just before he woke, because as he returned to consciousness he was in the middle of a vivid vision of his schooldays, and his mind was filled with images of a strange, secretive boy who was older than him. That day, or night, whenever it was, he had still been muddling up memory and what had been happening while he lay feverish in bed, and scenes from *Alice Through the Looking-Glass* wound their way into pictures of his school days. The strange boy had thus become even stranger, walking and dancing on the sands in the company of a walrus and a carpenter. 'I am quite sure,' Felix says aloud now, '*that* never happened.'

Apart from anything else, there is no sandy coastline in Wiltshire . . .

He has just seen the face of that odd boy again.

It is as if his dreaming self is determined to push it forward until he pays attention. So he closes his eyes, makes himself relax and returns to his younger self.

And, slowly, the memories clarify.

The strange boy was not at the college for long. Perhaps a school year plus a term, or at most two terms. He had been in the same house as Felix. Felix has a recollection of a boy who came to the school in the January term of one year and, by the end of the next school year, had gone again. The boy was big for his age, well-built and strong, and he had been considerably more mature and closer to manhood than his contemporaries. He had held himself apart, and somehow contrived to pursue his own interests to a far greater extent than anyone else. He had no time for sports, clubs or societies; he hadn't engaged in a single communal activity outside the classroom and the hours of the school day. He had spent all his spare time in the biology laboratories; Felix has a sudden, violently vivid memory of some disgusting experiments involving blood, guts and bodily fluids, and an image springs up of a great buzzing pile of black flies on a piece of unidentifiable flesh.

Now Felix wonders what on earth the boy was up to, and why

the masters and the school authorities allowed him to get away with it . . .

He muses on that for a while, because there is something on the edge of his memory. After a moment he has it: there had been a drama – a tragedy – in the boy's recent past. He had lost one of his parents . . . yes, his mother. He had lost his mother.

But there was more. Fathers were killed on active service in the Queen's armed services; mothers died in childbirth. It was not uncommon for boys to receive that dreadful summons and to return, hours or sometimes days later, red-eyed, washed out with shock and grief, sporting the black armband that denoted mourning. There had been an extra element to the death of the strange boy's mother: the word *murder* had been whispered.

Not in the boy's hearing. Not, at least, after the first and only time. The older boy who had begun to spread the salacious story had been stopped by the strange boy's fist, which in a single hard and well-aimed blow had broken the other boy's jaw, removed two incisors and laid him out for the rest of the morning. If the strange boy had received a punishment, Felix had no memory of it.

What had happened to him?

Felix has been making notes as the past has returned to him, and now he puts his pencil down and shuts his eyes again as he dives back into his college days.

And the first thing that springs up is a name: Godwin, H. P. He can see it written on a board, an oak board with metal slots where little cards can be inserted, each one inscribed with a name written in black ink in a beautiful italic hand . . . 'Hubert Percy Godwin,' Felix says aloud.

He feels like cheering.

Godwin, then. What happened to Godwin?

'He disappeared,' Felix says, astonished at his sudden certainty. It had been in the middle of term – the summer term, he thinks – and it had happened with no warning at all. One day H. P. Godwin had been there – in the background, admittedly, but definitely there – and the next he wasn't.

Then the rumours had begun, and they hadn't stopped.

The Master had stood in chapel one morning and told the entire school that they must cease all gossip and speculation about their former schoolfellow; that staff, school prefects and house prefects were going to be on full alert for any infringements and any boy found guilty of breaking this direct command from the Master would suffer severe punishment.

The rumours didn't stop; of course they didn't. But the boys all became a great deal more careful. They learned very quickly to keep their horrified and fascinated speculations to themselves in daytime and wait till after dark to share them with a few close friends, all of them sworn to secrecy with blood oaths.

What had Godwin done? What was so dreadful that the whole college had been alive with gossip?

Felix pictures the school buildings. The chapel. The classrooms. The laboratories, the sanatorium, the . . .

The sanatorium.

Matron, holding herself stiffly upright as she strode across a courtyard, disguising her distress and grief in a flurry of harsh remarks and a sudden and uncharacteristic malevolence towards any boy unlucky enough to be unwell or injured just then.

Why?

'Her cat!' Felix exclaims. 'Something happened to her cat.'

It had been a large and overindulged tabby, indolent and aloof. Unmarried, childless Matron had cosseted it, overfed it, talked to it as if it could understand. And it had been found one morning minus its head.

'Did Godwin do that?' Felix murmurs. Was that why he left? Was it the final straw for the college, and did their kindness, tolerance and compassion towards an odd, difficult boy finally run out? It certainly seems likely.

Felix reflects on those strange times for some minutes. He can remember so little about H. P. Godwin, no doubt because the boy guarded his privacy so determinedly and utterly refused to share a single detail of his life away from school. Where did he come from? What became of him after he left?

He reaches for his notebook and pencil and writes a few sentences. He has no doubt that the college records go back for decades, and will include details of Godwin's home address and next of kin. Whether the school officials will be willing to share this information with Felix is another matter.

But he is determined to have it, whatever it takes.

Because he can see that face; the pale, thin face of the young Hubert Percy Godwin, with its hollow cheeks, the cleft under the chin, the deep, dark eyes and the heavy eyebrows that always made a vee shape across his forehead, as if he was perpetually frowning in disapproval or in warning.

Felix has seen that face quite recently, and not only in his dreams. A white oval, the nose and mouth obscured and the top half bisected by the shallow black vee of heavy eyebrows.

It is the face of the man who very nearly killed him.

SEVENTEEN

The Barrow Man sits in his usual spot on the small hump at the rear of the churchyard, his back resting against his barrow, his eyes on the river surging past below. It is pleasant to be out and in the open during the hours of daylight; habitually he keeps to the shadows. But this place is safe; he has checked more than once, propping a bundle of old clothes shaped in the approximation of a human form against the barrow and then creeping out into the churchyard to see if he can spot it. He can't, even though he is actively looking for it. It is all but certain nobody else will espy him.

The afternoon sun is warm on his upper body. He closes his eyes to enjoy it. But it is hard to stay still and silent, for his blood is humming and fizzing in his veins and he wants to cavort with joy. Relax, he tells himself. Be calm. He takes deep breaths, trying to remove the tension from his body. For some time he succeeds. Then, abruptly, he sits up straight, eyes wide open and alight with excitement.

He can no longer suppress his delight. Ah, he could *crow* at his own cleverness! He has employed all the prodigious power of his mind, drawing on his ability to observe without realising he is doing so; to record relevant facts in some secure place within his extraordinary brain. To record them and, much more importantly, retrieve them when he needs them.

He draws his gaze back from the river and does a very thorough survey of the churchyard. No-one is about.

And so he says aloud, 'I have found her.'

Then he throws his head back and gives an inhuman sound like a deep-throated growl.

When the surge of pleasure starts to abate, he revives it by going over *how* he found her.

Once he had struggled free of the wild fury that invaded him as he watched her and the boatman speeding away in the tide-borne wherry, rationality resumed control. As with all problem-solving exercises, he started with what he knew. And out of the paltry facts concerning her age, her appearance and her air of being constantly alert, something occurred to him.

He had seen her twice: fleeing from him that night on the river, and leaving the office of the river police. What, he wondered, was her purpose? What business could she have had in either location? All he could think of was that she was some busybody, some bored product of an overprivileged upbringing, some Christian do-gooder, who felt it her responsibility to venture into the dirty underbelly of the city because she thought she could help.

He had come across such women in the past. They always provoked coruscating scorn and his ever-present, destructive anger.

But when his mind had cleared, he made his plans.

He watched the small room above the river at Wapping for hours, standing unobserved and noting the comings and goings. He identified the man in charge, and recognised five others who regularly came and went. There were also visitors, but none stayed long. The pattern was of a routine of changing shifts occasionally interrupted when a member of the public turned up to report something they thought needed looking into. Then one of the officers, sometimes two, would hurry off, presumably to investigate. Several times all the officers would burst out at once, but that was when something – quite often a carcass, usually an animal – bumped up against the pilings and needed retrieval.

Although the office was sometimes empty, it was never deserted for long and there was no possibility of guessing the length of time it would remain empty.

It wasn't important. It merely meant he would have to adopt another identity.

At the back of his shed, tucked under his workbench, he kept an old wooden sea chest full of items of clothing and accessories. He could turn himself into many people, from a gentleman out late after the theatre to a slaughter man heading off for the night shift. Over the years of wandering, he had encountered people from a variety of backgrounds and places, and he could mimic the accents of a man from Shetland, a Devonian, a Frenchman or a Spaniard. For this mission he decided to be Polish.

He dressed with care in garments that suggested a once prosperous man fallen on hard times: a professional man, who for some reason had to flee his native land and take work in a new and far more lowly occupation. He tied a red spotted neckerchief round his throat. Over the worn-out coat and neatly patched and darned trousers he put on an enveloping apron made of thick brown leather scored with dozens of small and large scratches and cuts. He darkened his upper lip to suggest a moustache, pulled on a soft old felt hat with a wide and face-concealing brim, and headed for Wapping.

There was only one man in the office. He was silver haired, a large pale bib of unkempt beard falling down his chest. He was bent with age, and he looked so settled in the ancient wicker chair beside the desk that it would surely take a major disaster to get him out of it. The Barrow Man paused and let himself slip into the persona of the Polish leather worker.

Then he climbed up to the office and, with feigned nervousness, opened the door. He stepped over the threshold. He moved silently; the old man in the chair was half-deaf and for some moments went on staring aimlessly out of the dirty window. Then the Barrow Man cleared his throat and said tentatively. 'Pliz? Mister, pliz? You 'elp?'

The old man spun round and glared at him. 'What do you want?' he demanded belligerently, instantly adding, 'I weren't asleep! Don't you go saying as how I was!'

The Barrow Man cringed, putting up his hands palm outwards in a gesture of abject surrender. 'No sleep, no, no!' he said with pathetic eagerness.

The old man scowled at him. 'What?' he barked.

The Barrow Man had prepared a story about a suspicious canvas-wrapped bundle left by the tide on a strip of gravelly beach downriver. Even as he talked, he was running his eyes around the small and cluttered room. By the time his rambling tale was told, he had already spotted what he needed.

He had planned to ask about the fair-haired woman. To describe her, to say that she had told him where to go about the bundle. To explain that he wanted to thank her because his wife was making his life unbearable all the time it was there and the sooner the river authorities came and dealt with it, the better.

He had no need of this plan.

There was a large map of the river and its embankments pinned to the wall. Just above the bottom edge and placed right in the middle there was a rectangle of white card. On it was inscribed *World's End Bureau, 3, Hob's Court, Chelsea.* It was the card of a private enquiry agency, and the proprietor was someone called L. G. Raynor.

And with a secret smile the Barrow Man thought: not a do-gooder, then, but someone else who pried and meddled where they had no business to.

She was a private enquiry agent.

The old man was becoming impatient, glaring at his visitor as if he hated him. Forestalling him, the Barrow Man embarked upon a clumsy explanation about a message for someone called O'Reilly, but the old man ran out of his small store of patience and bellowed angrily, 'No O'Reilly here, nor any knowledge of one! Be gone with you, and stop wasting my time!'

The Barrow Man bowed almost double, muttering soft apologies, and backed out of the office, closing the door with exaggerated care. He slipped away as soundlessly as he had arrived.

Halfway back to his shed he turned into a dark and noisome little alley where he removed the apron, rolled it up and tucked it under his arm. He replaced the felt hat with a peaked cap, changed his posture from browbeaten crouch to square-shouldered confidence, brushed the dirt off his coat and buttoned it tidily. He removed the red spotted neckerchief, revealing a starched collar and a purple cravat. When he emerged into the open once more, anyone who had noticed the cringing man in the apron and the soft felt hat hurrying away from the Wapping river depot would not have recognised him in this upright man striding along with his head thrown back and his cap at a jaunty angle, cheerfully humming a ribald music hall ditty.

Yes. He was fairly sure that such caution was not necessary.

But it is his habit to be careful. Which is why he has spent eight years experimenting with a variety of ways of killing and nobody has caught him.

He is waiting for nightfall. The hours slowly pass. Then, at the prompting of some subtle signal only meaningful to him, he gets to his feet. The moon has risen, and its chilly, silvery light makes a dancing black shadow as the Barrow Man lopes across the deserted churchyard. He crosses roads, still busy for it is not yet late, and steps onto a tram. No need to tire himself by walking, and in any case he is impatient to reach his destination.

The King's Road: a pub called The Cow Jumped Over the Moon. He descends from the tram, looking around.

He smiles a private smile: his research has borne fruit, and the pub is indeed at the corner of the main road and a street called World's End Passage. He heads down it; it slopes gently as it descends towards the river. He looks out for first Lacland Place and then Riley Street on his left. Just before he reaches Riley Street – he is almost at the embankment now – there it is, on the right: Hob's Court. He walks on, not stopping or even slowing, and turns right at the end of World's End Passage. He walks past an overshadowed niche set a little back from the road; he stares at it intently for a moment, but he can see nothing but darkness and concludes that it has been blocked off. He strides on. Blantyre Street, Luna Street. On, on, until he has verified what he read from his map and ascertained that it is as he thought: the houses have only one entrance.

He stops, leaning against a lamp post and staring out over the river, casually folding his arms: a man with time on his hands, enjoying a moment to look out at the lights reflecting off the water. Slowly his gaze runs from left to right . . . and he spots something.

The thrilled realisation floods up through him, although his stance is still relaxed and nobody watching him would have noticed that he is now as alert as a gun dog shivering with the excitement of the chase. Then, taking his time, resuming his soft, contented humming, he strolls on upriver. Slowly, unhurriedly, he draws closer to the sheltered basin where the boats tie up.

All is quiet there, because it is evening now. There are three – no, four – canal boats tied up, three along one quay, one on the opposite one. There are the sounds and the smells of horses. A low wooden building that he assumes is a stable block is at the far end of the nearer quay. Most of the boats show lights. There are soft, everyday sounds: the murmur of voices, a swift laugh, the clatter of a knife on a plate. Suddenly a wedge of light spills out as a hatch is opened. There are heavy footsteps, then the sound of a stream of liquid splashing into the water: a boatman is emptying his bladder.

The Barrow Man creeps along in the shadows until he reaches the stables. Then he slips into deeper shade and waits.

After perhaps an hour he has identified the handful of men who live on three of the boats. The fourth boat is in darkness. Eventually he hears footsteps approaching along the further quay.

And, finally, vindication, for he was quite sure the man he sought must lurk nearby.

Now he is staring at the man who was on the wherry with the fair-haired woman. The one who violated the Barrow Man's privacy; tramped all over his secret domain. The boatman reaches the darkened boat, goes aboard, fastens the hatch and presently light glows through the windows before curtains block it.

Slowly the Barrow Man comes out of his hiding place and moves soft-footed along the quay until he is opposite the boat. He can just make out the name: *The Dawning of the Day*.

Ten minutes later he is standing in the shadows once more. Now he is gazing out along Hob's Court. He has calculated which house is number 3, and his eyes are fixed on the steps leading up to the front door. He stands there for a long time; he does not count the hours. Nobody goes in, nobody comes out.

But his patience is endless when he is on a mission.

And so he is still there the next morning, to see a wiry, brisk-stepping, middle-aged woman with steel-grey hair pinned up in a thin bun under a shapeless hat hurry along Hob's Court, extracting a key as she walks. As she reaches the door, it opens, and the woman at the top of the steps says something, her voice excited, her face alive with delight, and the woman with the bun exclaims, 'Oh, Miss Lily, that is *such* good news!'

The two women go inside and the door is closed.

But the Barrow Man is already walking away.

He is congratulating himself, for he was right. Unlike almost everyone else who reads one of the World's End Bureau cards before they have met the personnel, he did not automatically assume that L. G. Raynor was a man. Of course, this proprietor might also have a first name that begins with L. But the Barrow

Man is all but certain the Bureau is run by the fair-haired woman, and her name is Lily Raynor.

He is almost on the King's Road now, and there is a tram approaching that will take him where he wants to go. His luck, he reflects with a smile, really is in this morning. As he takes a seat on the outside deck, he reflects that there is no obvious way to work out what the G stands for that is Lily's second name. But he hardly thinks it is going to matter.

Felix wakes up in the morning feeling better than on any day since he was attacked. His head does not hurt, he can draw quite a deep breath without that stab of pain in his ribs – or, at least, it is less agonising – and his mind is clear. When he gets cautiously out of bed and does his usual few laps of the room, he feels no dizziness. He glances through the half-opened door and, seeing Lily still fast asleep, he decides to act before she can advise against it. It is early and the house is quiet, and he is careful not to make any noise as, slowly and very carefully, holding tight to the banister, he descends to the middle landing and then to the ground floor. He heads down the passage to the kitchen, and on into the scullery. It is dark back here: it is too early for Mrs Clapper, and nobody has yet unfastened the shutters on the kitchen window. But it doesn't matter; he knows his way. He walks past the larder, hand against the wall for balance, and then he has reached his goal.

He opens the door to the lavatory and closes it, pushing the bolt across. With a sigh of pleasure, he raises the lid on the wash-down closet and sits down.

Some time later, standing in the scullery and pumping up water for washing, he smiles, and the smile develops into a chuckle. This has been his first experience of an injury or illness so severe that he had to be bed-bound for days on end, and so he had no idea what to expect. He would never have predicted, however, that the greatest satisfaction for someone at last on the mend is to be able to attend to the body's private needs *all by yourself*.

He returns through the kitchen, wondering briefly whether to light the range and wait for a kettle of water to heat, so that he can take up a jug for shaving. No, he decides; it will take too long.

And, if he is honest, he *really* needs to go back upstairs and sit down.

Some time later, Mrs Clapper appears with the jug of hot water. Felix shaves and then dresses in his usual clothes, which were laid out on top of the ottoman in the corner, his linen carefully laundered. It feels strange to wear day clothes again, but he has made up his mind that he will return to his rooms in Marm's apartment today.

Slowly he descends to the ground floor. Lily and Mrs Clapper must have heard his careful progress; they are waiting for him in the hall. Now he stands up before them straight-backed, square-shouldered, chin up. They both look dismayed to see him. Lily opens her mouth to speak but then apparently changes her mind. Mrs Clapper shakes her head and mutters something about people who think they know best when they don't, but then, glancing at Felix's set expression, she turns and heads back towards the kitchen.

And Lily says gently, 'It must have taken quite an effort to wash and dress without assistance. I dare say you would like to sit down now, so let's go through to my office, shall we? I'm sure Mrs Clapper will bring us something suitably restorative. Once she's forgiven you,' she adds, and he's not at all sure whether or not he was meant to hear.

As he follows her through to the Inner Sanctum, he is relieved that she didn't berate him for his impetuosity. He wonders slightly guiltily if there was a section in whatever *Learning to be a Nurse* handbook she had studied that emphasised the importance of not taking the dignity away from a recently bed-bound and helpless patient who has just reclaimed it.

Mrs Clapper does indeed bring refreshments – Felix notices with quiet amusement that his tea has been slopped in the saucer – and now he and Lily sit either side of her desk, together again and back where they belong. Felix feels like cheering.

There is something he must say before their professional selves take over and it becomes impossible. Putting down his cup, he says, 'Dear Lily, thank you for looking after me. You gave up your room and your bed for me. You, Mrs Clapper, the tenants and dear old Marm have cared for me with kindness and dedication, and I don't think I'd be sitting here now had it not been for you.'

'Nonsense!' she mutters. Her head is down, but he can see she is blushing.

He gives her a moment to collect herself, then goes on, 'I shall return to Kinver Street this evening. Marm is coming here later, and we'll go together. You will be able to reclaim your room!' he adds, trying to sound cheerful although all of a sudden feeling anything but.

She keeps her head lowered for what seems a long time. Then she looks up. 'I do not entirely approve,' she says carefully, 'for you are far from fully recovered, but I understand why it is important. Provided Marm is happy to look after you, I will not stand in your way. Of course,' she adds, flustered again, 'it is entirely up to you, and I . . .' She stops.

For a long moment they look at each other.

He wonders if she is thinking what he is thinking. He is sure she is, then equally sure she isn't.

Shall I say it? Silently he asks the question. Shall I be the brave one who puts it into words? But supposing she really isn't thinking it, what then?

The decision seems to have been taken out of his hands: he hears himself say softly, 'I'll miss you.'

The red flush of embarrassment has faded and now her creamy skin is rosy pink. Her eyes are brilliant. He thinks she looks beautiful.

'I'll miss you too,' she whispers.

There is utter silence in the room.

He senses she is as relieved as he is when they hear Mrs Clapper's footsteps crossing the hall and she strides into the office to collect the tea tray.

The brief interruption, Felix reflects as Mrs Clapper departs, has served them well. He takes out his notebook and puts it on the desk.

Lily, observing him, nods briskly. 'Yes, let's take this chance to discuss what—' she begins.

He doesn't let her finish. 'Sorry, Lily, but there's something I must tell you,' he says. She looks up, alarm in her face at his tone. 'My memories of the night I was attacked have continued to clarify, and although there are still quite large gaps, I now have a much clearer picture.' He pauses, for this is still hard. 'Lily, I have remembered what my assailant looked like.'

'*Oh!*' Her sound of distress is so quiet that it is almost inaudible.

'And,' he continues, 'I've seen him before.'

Her face is now chalk white. 'Where?' she asks.

'Years ago. At school. He was two years older than me.'

'Tell me about him,' she commands.

'His name was Hubert Godwin. He was a solitary boy, and he was a mystery, which made the rest of us all the more determined to find out about him. We never did, and after less than two years he left.'

'He left?' she repeats.

'He vanished,' he says. 'One day there, next day gone.'

'Expelled?' she suggests.

'I don't know,' he admits. 'I suppose so. There had been some worrying incidents, then Matron's cat was killed, and rumour had it that it was done with particular brutality.'

'But . . .' Lily stops. She spreads her hands. 'What are we to make of this?'

'I have written to the college,' he says. 'I wrote in my professional capacity – I got Mrs Clapper to bring me some of our WEB writing paper. I said I was investigating a man who had been at the college in the 1860s and gave the name, although respect for my client's privacy prevented me from saying why we were asking about him. I asked if they could supply any details.' He perceives her unasked question. 'I gave the letter to Marm to post on his way home.'

She glances at her little gold watch. 'The mid-morning post should be here soon,' she says.

He is reaching in his pocket. Holding up an envelope, he says, 'This must have come by an early delivery. It was on my desk when I came down.' He opens up the single sheet of paper and glances at it. 'The school records are confidential.'

'That's . . . that's *it*?' She sounds cross.

'Apparently. But there was this as well.' Now he is removing the contents of a second envelope, and this reply runs to three pages. 'It's from someone called Claudina Whitwell, the wife of the school chaplain. She'll be quite old now, because I remember the name Whitwell from my days there.'

'Why is she writing to you?' Lily asks.

He clears his throat, looking down at the letter. 'She says that her husband was summoned by the Master yesterday because someone was asking about Hubert Godwin. That was me, of course. She explains that her husband – the chaplain – believed it was time for honesty, but the Master maintained that the policy of keeping the matter within the college had served well for fifteen years and he saw no purpose in revealing what was best forgotten. Arnold – that's her husband – was quite cross, she says, and she seems to have taken this as an excuse to write to me.' He pauses, looking up at Lily.

'Don't stop now!' she exclaims.

And so he picks up the letter again and reads:

> *Hubert Godwin was a troubled boy from the start. He was enrolled in the college not by his parents, who were of humble stock, but by a wealthy benefactor, a marquess, whose name I feel I should not reveal. The bare facts were that his mother was dead and his father was in an asylum for the criminally insane. Given the deeply distressing circumstances, such as we were advised of them, one cannot but conclude that the father murdered the mother. Mr Whitwell and I speculated as to the wealthy benefactor's motive, and although my charitably minded husband preferred to believe the marquess acted from pure altruism, I cannot but wonder if it was guilt that prompted his generosity. According to the lurid reports in the papers at the time of the husband's trial, the boy's mother had been a rather pretty and delicate woman. She was employed in the marquess's household, which would have provided plenty of opportunity for dalliance.*

'Goodness!' Lily exclaims. 'Mrs Whitwell sounds as if she's been longing to share the tale for some time.'

'She does indeed,' Felix agrees. 'But, Lily, listen to this: "The boy was not known as Hubert Godwin until he arrived at the college. It was felt to be better for him to put the past firmly behind him, and—'"

'Better for the wealthy marquess too!' Lily interrupts indignantly. 'If the gossip was right and it was his dalliance that led to the poor woman being murdered by her furiously jealous husband, then he most certainly would wish to keep *that* secret.'

'He would,' Felix agrees, and reads on:

> *If memory serves, the family name was Fountain, the father was Ezekiel Walter Fountain and the boy was called Tobias. They lived in Bradford on Avon, if I remember aright, and the young Tobias was fascinated with the natural world from an early age, ever eager, according to reports, to find out about what he called the workings of things. What makes something be in the living state, and how that differs from being dead.*

He reads on for a few lines, nodding as if to verify something. 'It's consistent with what all the rumours said about Hubert Godwin,' he says. 'He particularly liked dissection, and it was whispered that the cat—' Abruptly he stops.

'Please, Felix, tell me,' Lily says. 'I promise not to faint.'

'*I* might,' he mutters. 'Very well. When the remains of the cat were found, its lungs had been removed and replaced with two little bags made of fine leather. Whoever did it – and there were no suspects other than Hubert Godwin – had apparently tried to see if the poor animal could be kept alive by having these false lungs pumped up and emptied.'

Lily has paled again. 'But its heart would surely have stopped,' she whispers. 'The shock of such a procedure would . . .' But she stops. She presses a hand to her mouth.

'I'm sorry,' Felix says.

She shakes her head. 'No need to apologise. I made you tell me.'

After quite some time she says, 'What else does Mrs Whitwell say?'

He returns to the letter. 'Not much. Hubert Godwin left, and when the college contacted the marquess to ask if he had settled down somewhere else, the marquess said the boy had vanished. She doesn't say for certain, but I think she's hinting that Hubert extracted quite a lot of money out of the marquess, presumably in exchange for not revealing precisely why Ezekiel Walter Fountain lost his mind and killed his wife.'

'So . . .' Lily pauses, frowning. 'So, nobody knew where Hubert went, and where he has been for the last fifteen years.'

'No,' Felix agrees. 'But I think we know what he's been up to.' He meets her eyes. 'And where he is now.'

EIGHTEEN

Marm arrives in the middle of the afternoon. Lily can tell he has come straight from The Cow Jumped Over the Moon; his face is flushed and he is even more garrulous than usual.

As he settles himself in the Inner Sanctum, Lily slips out to the kitchen and asks Mrs Clapper to bring in a large pot of coffee.

When Lily resumes her seat behind her desk, Felix is in the middle of telling Marm about having recognised his assailant, and what they have found out about how the boy who he then was came to be at Felix's school.

Even as he is speaking, Marm has his notebook out and is flipping back through the pages, muttering. 'To sum up, then,' he says as Felix concludes his narrative, 'we have a boy called Tobias Fountain whose father killed his mother and was declared insane, and this marquess, this man of wealth and position, salved his guilt over his involvement in the murder by paying for Tobias's education, only by the time he arrived at your prestigious college, Felix' – he looks up with a grin – 'he had been given a new name and was now Hubert Godwin.' He is writing as he talks. 'What year did he disappear?'

'1866,' Felix supplies.

'Hmm.' Marm bounces his pencil on his notebook. 'We must presume, I think, that, having had his name changed once by other people in order to separate him from his own past, Hubert Godwin did the same thing again. I can see no obvious way to find out who he became in 1866, but I think we may say that in Liverpool in 1878 he went by the name of Walter Blackmore, and when he arrived in London in the September of that year, he had become Joseph Phipps and he found work in the docks.' He looks up at Felix. 'I know you're very eager to find out how we know, young Felix and, if Lily will indulge me, I will explain.'

Lily nods her agreement, and listens as Marm succinctly describes what he discovered in his Lost Women file, and gives his account of a man who killed and dismembered two women and disposed of their body parts in the Mersey. How, in order to evade police interest when his name was mentioned in connection with the murders, he shed the identity of Walter Blackmore like a snake abandoning its skin and became someone else; someone, moreover, who had the nerve to attach the name he had just left behind to the body of a stranger.

Hearing Marm's tale again, Lily can scarcely believe it. Glancing at Felix's expression, she suspects he feels the same.

'Where has Joseph Phipps been between 1878 and now?' Marm asks. 'If we are right to connect this man of many names and many brutal crimes with your attacker, Felix, then it is difficult to envisage that he has spent those four years as a diligent and blameless member of the community.' He pauses, gazing towards the high window. 'Now, last night and this morning I spent some time going through my files and, as you would expect, any number of women died here in London in that time, and many of their deaths were violent and, as always, inadequately investigated by the authorities.' He makes a fist of his hand and gently thumps it down on Lily's desk. 'But it is only in the past few weeks – months at most – that these reports of female body parts in the Thames have started to come in, and—'

'That's what Alf Wilson said!' Lily exclaims. 'When I went to see him, he told me he'd been planning to seek me out, because there had been limbs and pieces of bodies turning up regularly. Animal bodies at first, then human – female – bodies, and the damage was deliberate, not the result of the violence of the water. And then there was what Tamáz told me, about how the boatmen kept finding body parts, first in the Limehouse basin and later in other places, and how they all felt there was some very dark and malignant intelligence behind it.'

She hopes she hasn't sounded melodramatic. But it is important, she is sure, to make Felix and Marm understand just how evil an influence is being spread on the water by these crimes.

'Thank you, Lily,' Marm says gravely. 'Then if we are to assume that our killer's presence in a place is revealed because, sooner or later, he *always* kills, then perhaps we must assume that he was somewhere other than in London between 1878 and the summer just passed.'

Lily watches him. There is a new, brighter excitement about him. Felix must have seen it too: 'You've found out something,' he says to Marm. 'Haven't you?'

'Possibly, possibly,' Marm admits. He is turning more pages in his file. 'As your Alf Wilson pointed out, Lily, it is not difficult to distinguish accidental damage to a body that has been in the water from deliberate dismemberment. Which brings me to the mystery of an arm, a leg and a scalp without a skull inside it that turned up in the Little Ouse near Thetford in March of this year. Very unusually, these body parts were identified, and once the poor young woman's name was known, there was a great deal of anger in the area. Many people besides her family and her friends were crying out for vengeance.' He stops, looking down at his file, the fingers of one hand delicately touching a newspaper cutting. 'Her name was Millicent Garvey and she trimmed hats for a living,' he says softly. 'She was stepping out with a young man and they were saving up to be married.' He looks up at Lily and Felix in turn. 'As you both know, the lost women in my files are most often prostitutes – not that it should make any difference, for everyone who dies a brutal death deserves justice. But poor little Millie Garvey was ruthlessly dismissed as a woman of low morals purely because she had been returning home late at night!' His voice has risen as anger overcomes him.

'Millie had been seen in the company of a man who several witnesses said was not her fiancé,' he continues after a moment. 'Three of the witnesses provided a name: Wilfred Stirling. And when they went looking for him, he wasn't there.'

'And that was last March,' Felix says quietly.

'And, according to Alf Wilson,' Lily adds, 'the animal parts started to turn up in the Thames round about June.'

Marm is frowning. 'We may well be making connections where none exist,' he says, 'but, assuming this former schoolfellow of Felix's has continued his experiments into dissection and dismemberment, and is indeed doing so here in London right now, two questions occur to me. Did he recognise you, Felix, and why did he try to kill you?'

Lily feels a shiver of cold fear as Marm speaks. In her joy at Felix's steady recovery, she has all but forgotten the cause of his grave injury. But Felix is speaking: she makes herself listen.

'... and he was two years above me,' he is saying, 'and, in my experience, you remember boys older than yourself whereas you don't usually recall the younger ones.'

'So are you saying he didn't recognise you?' Lily asks hopefully, although she doesn't really know why it is important.

He looks at her with a gentle smile. 'I have no idea.' Turning back to Marm, he says, 'As to why he tried to kill me, I've been assuming it was because I was getting too close to his shed and the area he treats as his own. Ironically,' he adds, 'I had no idea he was there. My sole aim was to get into and out of the Fetterplaces' back garden without anyone seeing me. If he hadn't made his presence known by attacking me, there would be nothing to connect the bodies in the river to the man with the shed and the barrow.' He shakes his head, a look of faint surprise on his face. 'More than that – we wouldn't even know he existed.'

It is late, and twilight has become full darkness. Lily sits in the Inner Sanctum listening to the silence.

She has been trying to be sensible. To act like the proprietor of a thriving business that she is and catch up with the accounts while she has the chance. She has done quite well; the ledger in which she maintains the running tally of income and outgoings is now almost up to date, and she has four cheques sitting ready on her desk that she will pay into the bank tomorrow. She has answered three requests for the Bureau's assistance, turning down two and penning a list of further enquiries to the rather manic-sounding woman who sent the third.

For the last hour she has been fighting the vivid memories of this afternoon. Now, her mind temporarily free, they come racing back like an incoming storm.

Felix has gone.

She knows perfectly well he will return tomorrow; that, at precisely his usual time, he will come striding into her office with a smile on his face and some anecdote about a witty remark of Marm's, or a person he's noticed on the way from Kinver Street whose appearance or behaviour has caught his eye. But it won't be the same, because tomorrow night, and every other night stretching away into the future, he will leave again, to spend the evening in Marm's cheery company and the night in his own bed.

For a bitter moment, Lily drops her head on her folded arms and gives herself up to her distress.

Presently she straightens up, dries her eyes and says firmly out loud, 'Stop it.'

She makes herself think of happier things: of the heartwarming way that Bunty and Dorothea, knowing that this day was important for Felix, appeared at the foot of the stairs just as he and Marm were leaving. How Felix, smitten with sudden guilt in case his earlier stumbling thanks had been inadequate, thanked them all over again. Holding one of each of their hands, he said with a smile that he would never see an edition of *Alice Through the Looking-Glass* without thinking of them.

The ladies made their escape as quickly as they could – embarrassed, Lily reflects now, by Felix's obvious emotion, and keen to return to the privacy and seclusion of the private haven they had made for themselves in the rooms on the first floor. But they came when they were needed, she muses. They are good, decent women, and I am lucky to have them here.

Mrs Clapper had stayed behind to give Lily's bedroom and sitting room a final check. The bed has been made up with fresh sheets, the little shakedown bed on the floor of the other room is tidied away and every single surface has been wiped, polished and buffed. There is an earthenware jug of chrysanthemums on the desk.

'I shall be very glad to have my own room to myself again,' Lily says aloud.

Now she simply has to make herself believe it.

Time passes. It is late now; Mrs Clapper has left and Lily knows she should go to bed. But she doubts if she will sleep; too much is going on in her mind. She gets up and walks softly through to the scullery, putting the kettle onto the still-hot stove for a last cup of tea. As she is carrying the cup and saucer back to the Inner Sanctum, she hears the rattle of the letter box. Going on to put her tea down on her desk, she hurries back to the street door. She opens it, for it is too late for even the last postal delivery of the day, and she is curious to know who has left the scrappy piece of paper now lying on the mat. But Hob's Court is quiet and empty of life.

She returns to her desk, holding the piece of paper close to the lamp. And dread courses through her.

The words are written in pencil, in a hand that is sometimes so light as to be barely legible, sometimes heavy enough to tear the thin, cheap paper. The writing is haphazard, the spelling so poor that the meaning is not immediately apparent.

> *Yur nedeed in BoatBAsion a mane is badely-hrt and bledin com to DAWNIN to HELLP*

There is no punctuation. The spacing is chaotic; some words are run together, some far apart.

Then, jumping into life as if she has been stabbed, she throws down the note. Briefly she wonders why on earth she is wasting time looking for non-existent punctuation when the only three words that matter are blaring through her awareness like the clanging of a fire alarm. *Bleeding. Dawning. HELP.*

She races out to the hall, drags on her workman's boots, takes her warm coat off the hook and drapes her thick shawl over her head, tying it across her chest. She picks up her medical bag, her heart thumping in anxiety. It may not be Tamáz who is badly hurt and bleeding, she keeps telling herself. The note doesn't *say* it is.

But then if it's not, if Tamáz needs her help so desperately for one of his crew, then why isn't the note in his hand?

Why didn't he come to fetch her himself?

The Barrow Man shifts his position minutely, careful not to make a sound or a movement big enough to attract attention. Not that there is anyone around. The river end of World's End Passage has been deserted for the best part of an hour.

He stands deep inside the recess of an abandoned doorway in the narrow lane that opens out almost opposite the end of Hob's Court. He is cold, and now and again he lifts his hands and blows softly on them. He is clad in workman's breeches of heavy canvas, worn and filthy, and there is little warmth in the fabric. His coat is too thin for the swiftly falling temperature. His feet are warm, for now, for he has his good boots on and two pairs of hose underneath them. Nobody looks at a man's feet, so there is no need to increase his discomfort by wearing cheap old boots with holes in the soles.

There are more clothes in the Gladstone bag at his feet – a waistcoat and topcoat, a collapsible top hat, a thick, warm muffler made of soft wool – but he will not touch them. They are for afterwards, when the night's work has been completed and he emerges into a different identity. He glances down at the bag, pleased by the very sight of it. It is a costly item, made of fine, expensive leather that is still shiny with newness, and the brass catches gleam in the faint lamplight. It is empty of the knives, scalpels, suture kits and small medical instruments that it formerly contained, for he required the space for his change of clothes. Besides, he won't be needing them tonight.

A smile creases his lean face. The man on whose lap it had rested was fast asleep on the upper deck of the tram. A young doctor, perhaps, newly qualified, exhausted by a long, hard day, and the expensive bag a present from proud parents. Proud *rich* parents, he amends, who, once they have overcome their irritation at their son's carelessness, will no doubt supply a replacement.

The contents – those blades and instruments – are of the finest quality too. They will not go to waste, for the Barrow Man has a use for them. They are wrapped and packed away in the larger bag of personal belongings that awaits him in the left-luggage room at Euston station. Trains to Birmingham and Manchester run late into the night, and he is going to be on one. Yesterday he plotted a route on foot through the back streets from the King's Road to the station. Today he rehearsed it, and now it is clear in his mind.

He knows his time in London is over. For now, although he certainly plans to return. He has been deeply unsettled by the invasion of his territory by interlopers. *Three* of them! He has to fight to control the wild anger each time he thinks of it. One he has already dealt with. The face of the man he recognised from his school days briefly appears in his mind's eye, but then it is gone. No need to remember it now, for the man is dead.

The other two – the fair-haired woman and the tall, well-built boatman – he will dispose of very soon.

The smile is replaced by a savage scowl. Fury burns in him, deep down inside. He has been busy tonight: fully absorbed in a delicate task that had to be *just right*. It was a task that he did with great reluctance, and that he would not have had to perform had it not been for the infernal curiosity and unforgivable nosiness of those three people. In particular, the fair-haired woman and her boatman. They found his shed. He knows that without a doubt. They stood outside it, peered through into its secret, hidden inner shell, laid their eyes on his precious work.

And now he has set its destruction in motion.

One of the many jobs he has done in the course of his itinerant life was in a slate quarry. They spotted that he was intelligent and good with his hands, for he was tired, then, of presenting himself as slow, dull and not very capable. They had taught him how to set off an explosion. How to run a fuse from the charge so that it could be detonated from a safe distance. Tonight he used a very long fuse, for it was imperative to be far away when the charge ignited and the blast went off. But it will have worked just as he intended. He is quite sure, for he has practised the whole process.

Before he ran out the fuse, he made one last check of his careful arrangements and then doused the secret heart of his shed with the entire contents of a large can of kerosene. He did not linger after that. The thought of his experiments, his current clutch of bones and skulls, the carefully collected items so valuable when he wanted to assume another identity, spread out and waiting for their imminent destruction was just too awful.

He was on the far side of the churchyard, emerging onto the path beside the river, when he saw the flash and, seconds later, heard the muffled bang. He paused to glance up to his right, as any man hearing a sudden and unexpected sound might do, then, with a shrug, carried on walking.

The blaze was intense, but localised and short-lived. The tangle of undergrowth that had largely concealed the shed was soaking wet, for luck was on the Barrow Man's side and it had just been raining hard. Once the accelerant had burned off, taking with it almost all of the shed's mostly flammable contents, the flames died down.

By then he was well on his way to Chelsea.

He hears a church clock strike the hour. He has no need to count the chimes; he already knows it is eleven o'clock.

He picks up the bag and, quick and silent as a hunting panther, runs across World's End Passage and into Hob's Court. Up the steps to number 3, the tattered and dirty piece of paper slipped through the letter box's flap, and he is off again. He is back in his dark recess when the sudden spill of yellow light reveals that the door has just opened. He leans forward, just far enough to see her look out.

I am here, he says to her silently. *I am waiting for you.*

He is smiling again.

He had not expected her to take so long.

Was the note's tone insufficiently urgent? Had she failed to make out the words? Did he try too hard to make it read as if it had been written by a semi-illiterate, so that she didn't understand it?

He stands tense, biting at his lower lip. Should he return? Knock on her door, perhaps, beg her to hurry for there is no time to lose and a man's lifeblood is ebbing away.

But he hesitates, for it is not his way to approach his victims face to face.

What is she *doing*?

He knows he is allowing his usual tight self-control to slacken. That will not do. He edges right back into his recess, closes his eyes, slows his breathing and gradually regains dominance over his treacherous emotions.

And then he hears quick footsteps.

He leans forward and peers out.

A woman is hurrying down the last few yards of World's End Passage, just before it opens out onto the embankment. She is dressed in dark clothes, carrying a bundle, or perhaps a bag. He did not see her leave her house, but he knows it is her. The fair hair is not visible – her head is covered by a thick scarf or shawl – but he can hear the thump of those heavy boots as she strides along, sometimes breaking into a run. She is in a hurry now. Whatever was delaying her – fear of the dark, or a sudden, worrying flash of unreasoned apprehension – has been overcome. She is hastening as fast as she can to save the life of her boatman.

He picks up his Gladstone bag, steps out of his dark recess and goes after her.

She is on the embankment now. He can make out the pallor

of the face under the enfolding shawl. She stands quite still, turning to look back up World's End Passage as if checking to see if anyone is observing her. Following her.

He is doing both. But he makes quite sure she doesn't know.

He stands in deep shadow, utterly still. His hands are empty, for he has hidden the Gladstone bag under a tangle of greenery. He is calm. His breathing is gentle and steady. This will change, of course, and quite soon. Not that he is aware of this; not in his conscious mind, for the frenzied devil that takes possession of him when the killing rage comes upon him drives his everyday self – one could hardly call it his *normal* self, for nothing about him is ever normal – so deep underground that neither element of him truly knows the other.

She is still standing there, clutching the bag.

Go on, he says to her silently. You have been summoned; you know you are desperately needed.

And then he understands: she is afraid.

Out there alone in the night, the silent force of the river running just behind her like a dark, ancient god summoning his full reserves of power to hurl them at the cowering world, she senses the threat. Oh, but it is not a danger out of the myths and legends of the far past that she should be fleeing from!

Suddenly she stands up straight, squaring her shoulders, and very faintly he hears her muttering to herself. He can't make out the words, but he suspects she is trying to summon her courage and nerving herself to move.

Before she can take even a step, he is out of the shadows and racing across the narrow gap between them. He is *so fast*. It feels to him as if he is flying over the ground, and he spreads out his arms so that the wide hem of his black coat opens out like a bat's wings.

He is upon her.

The shawl over her head is thick and of generous size. It is as if serendipity has provided the very item he needs. He pulls the front edge right down to her chin, covering her face. He grasps the shawl's ends and wraps them round her throat, tying them firmly, and all her bright hair is concealed. The devil within has him firmly in its power now and just for a heartbeat he watches as his strong hands delve beneath the shawl and find her throat. His thumbs press deep. His grasp is as tight as a jackal's jaws closing on its helpless prey as he twists, jerks and hears the crack.

The devil inside him roars up like a huge firework and a vast explosion of deep sexual pleasure erupts through his whole body, peaking to ecstasy that all but blows him apart.

Slowly it ebbs. It passes, leaving him sweating and shaking.

And as the devil departs from him – until the next time – he returns to himself.

She lies huddled at his feet. The shawl is still secured over her head. He picks up the lifeless body and puts it over his shoulder, arm clasped around the hips to hold it in place. Then he collects his bag and sets off for the boat basin.

As he strides along, he is thinking what he should do with the corpse. How best to arrange the evidence he will provide for those who will discover it. He is without his usual equipment, for he left the barrow inside the shed and now it will be no more than a black, charred ruin. The pack with the belongings that always stay with him wherever he goes is safely hidden, awaiting his collection. All he has with him tonight is the leather roll containing three knives: one a cleaver, one with a serrated edge and one like a scalpel. The two straight-bladed knives have been recently sharpened and both have a lethal edge.

These three will have to suffice.

He looks over to the river. The tide has turned. Good. Whatever he deposits in the water will flow the right way. But not all of the body must be borne away . . .

Thinking hard, he trudges on.

Presently the boat basin comes into view. Lights still show on some of the river craft. He hears the soft murmur of low male voices and, getting nearer, makes out a trio of bulky forms huddled around a brazier. The smell of tobacco mingles with the wood smoke.

In a nightmare flash he is reminded of his father. Ezekiel Fountain smoked an ancient churchwarden pipe with a particularly long stem, for he disliked having the heat and smoke of the burning tobacco in the bowl too near his face. Once when his small son had carelessly knocked it off the hearth he had—

Just for an instant the devil threatens to return.

He holds down his rage.

'No,' he murmurs. He must not think of that, for now he needs his cold, practical self.

He walks on.

He is approaching the basin now. There are three boats tied up along the right-hand quay. These all show a soft light, and there are signs of life from within each one. From the nearest boat he can smell a savoury stew, and the aroma of warm bread drifts out to him. He hears a woman's quiet voice, a child's quick reply, the sound of gentle laughter. One of the three men round the brazier glances towards the sounds, his teeth showing amid the thick beard as he smiles.

Not that way, the Barrow Man thinks.

For he has already studied the three boats, and none is the one he seeks. He retraces his steps and, still with barely a sound, leaves the embankment and sets off along a narrow path bordered on one side by shrubbery and stunted trees and on the other by a shoulder-high fence. It continues for several hundred yards, at which point a footbridge branches off to the left, spanning the creek and giving access to the far bank.

He pauses, listening, watching. When he is as sure as he can be that he is not observed, he pads swiftly across the bridge and into the shadows at the other end. Then he turns left again and slowly, carefully, makes his way back to the quay on the south side of the boat basin.

And there, in the profound shadow of a trio of alders, he gazes out at *The Dawning of the Day*.

It is the only boat on this side.

Once again, his luck is in.

He lets his load slide off his shoulder and carefully places it on the ground among the undergrowth. He takes a couple of paces away and looks back. It is all but invisible.

Cat-like, soft footfall by soft footfall, he covers the ground soundlessly until he is level with the bow of *The Dawning of the Day*. He stands still, listening. There is no quiet conversation, although he knows someone is within. Apart from the gentle glow of a lantern that he can see through the small windows, he can sense the boatman's presence. The lack of voices suggests either he is alone or else whoever is below with him is asleep.

The Barrow Man studies the boat. Then he looks down at the water. The neck of the inlet is narrow, so that boats would have to go in and out one at a time. Good; that implies that the water flow in and out – in particular, out – is not likely to be very powerful. Little water actually flows down the creek, for it is partially silted up at the landward end, and some years since it was in regular use. The only water moving out of the basin is what has lapped in from the river.

He has already verified this, but it is a relief that the same conditions that pertained when he came to study the creek also apply tonight. All is as it should be; a strong current flowing out into the river would sweep away what he is about to put into the water of the basin.

Right beside *The Dawning of the Day*.

He pads back to where he left the corpse. As he walks, he takes the leather roll out from where he tucked it into his waistband. The first knife – the cleaver – is already in his hand as he crouches down over the body. Its freshly honed edge catches the faint light from the boat.

He loosens her jacket, unfastens the skirt and draws these heavy garments and the underclothes away from the cooling flesh.

Then he begins.

NINETEEN

Felix cannot settle.

He and Marm have been back in the Kinver Street apartment for an hour or more and, although Felix was pleasantly surprised to discover that the walk home from Hob's Court did not prove arduous and that in fact he'd have happily sat up with Marm over a brandy and a chat, Marm told him very firmly that 'the invalid' must go straight to bed.

'You need your sleep, young Felix!' Marm declared with a cheery smile. 'Yes, I know you tell me you feel fine, that you're not in the least weary, but I must insist.'

'But . . .' Felix began.

Marm did not let him continue. His face suddenly serious, he said quietly, 'You are now my responsibility. Lily has cared for you devotedly – with Bunty and Dorothea's help, of course, not to mention the excellent food and the intimate ministrations provided by Mrs Clapper – but all the good work will very swiftly be undone if you now begin to be profligate with your returning energy and vitality. Go to bed, Felix,' he went on firmly, overriding Felix's further attempts to protest. Heading for his bedroom door, he adds, 'That is where I am bound, so why not follow my sensible example?'

There was no point in staying up by himself, Felix thought, and so, very reluctantly, he did as he was told.

He has been lying wide awake ever since.

To begin with, irritation at Marm's insistence was the dominant emotion. But gradually this has been replaced by a sense of unease. This has grown steadily until finally, unable to stay in bed, he is sitting up, staring at the night sky through the bedroom window.

He wonders why he can't settle. He is not in pain, not worrying in case he should have a relapse; his memory has returned, as much as it is likely to, anyway, and he is looking forward eagerly to tomorrow, when he and Lily will get back to work, and—

Lily.

He knows in a flash that he is worried about Lily.

He left her in the Inner Sanctum. She said she was going to bring the accounts book up to date. Mrs Clapper will have gone home some time ago, but Bunty and Dorothea will be upstairs in their rooms. Lily is perfectly safe, for her house is sturdy and secure, the doors solid and the locks and bolts strong.

How can she be in danger?

And yet he knows she is. There is no reason behind it; it is pure instinct. Some animals, he reflects, are said to be aware when their mate is in danger. Is this also true of human beings?

'She is not my mate,' he says softly aloud. 'But I love her.'

He sits very still, acknowledging the truth of this. He is faintly surprised that the realisation has come to him just at this moment. Smiling briefly, he shakes his head.

Then he stands up, puts his clothes on again, picks up his boots and tiptoes softly out of the apartment.

The night is clear and cold. He is glad of his topcoat, and wishes he had thought to put on a scarf. He walks through the maze of small streets and emerges onto the embankment, turns right and, increasing his pace, sets off upriver.

He makes the return journey considerably more quickly than the outward one, when Marm kept insisting they must walk slowly so as not to tire Felix out. Now he is alone, he is burning with impatience, and Marm is no longer nagging him. Presently he breaks into a trot, and then he is running.

Reaching the river end of World's End Passage, he pauses to catch his breath. He delves into his inner pocket for his keys, and hurries on into Hob's Court. Even as he opens the door and slips inside, he knows she isn't there. He checks quickly, and the absence of her medical bag and her workman's boots confirm her absence. But he can see that there is a light, coming from the Inner Sanctum, he thinks. He goes through the outer office and even as he approaches her desk he can see the scrap of cheap paper.

With growing horror, he reads it.

He knows where she has gone.

As he returns to the hall and searches among the sticks and the umbrellas in the cupboard for Lily's grandfather's old cudgel, he cannot suppress the thought: Why did she believe this when I am so totally convinced it is nothing but a cruel and dangerous ruse to get her out of the house on her own?

He finds the cudgel.

He hurries down the hall, through the kitchen and the scullery and out of the back door, which is unlocked. Through the old shed, to the rear door that opens onto the dark little passage. This door is locked. She must have secured it from the outside and taken the key. But the spare hangs on its hook; his hand groping in the darkness finds it, just where it should be. He lets himself out, locks up again and runs off down to the embankment.

He is tiring now, much more quickly than he had anticipated. He tries to ignore his jelly-like legs and the increasingly impossible battle to draw air into his heaving lungs, but finally he has no choice and has to stop. His partially healed ribs feel as if they are being stabbed repeatedly with a long, sharp blade. He stands bent double, cudgel under one arm, hands on his thighs. He thinks he is going to be sick, but the moment passes.

Then from up ahead he hears a shout, then another, and then a man's loud, deep cry of abject, agonised despair.

He straightens up and runs on.

Tamáz stands on the quay beside his boat, sick with horror.

There is a body draped over the stern rail, and it has not got a head. There is a head, however; it has been left on the quay, not a yard from where he stands, and the thick wool shawl that was wrapped around it has slipped, revealing the bright hair.

Blood is soaking into the wood of the deck. A slick of it flows over the rail and into the water. He can hear the drips.

He had been alone on his boat, sitting in the soft lamplight. Not doing anything; just thinking, for he has much to think about. Someone must have come aboard, must have stood there by the tiller arranging the headless corpse in that callous, brutal way. But Tamáz had heard nothing. *Nothing.*

He glances down into the water. There is little movement, but some gentle undercurrent must be flowing slowly out from the basin and into the river, and it carries a couple of fragments from a broken pallet, a branch, several clumps of dead leaves and two – no, three – pale white objects.

The Skeleton in the Rose Bed

It is when he sees what they are that he cries out.

Then two things happen at once. He hears the sound of thumping footsteps racing along the embankment from the eastern side of the basin. And he sees – thinks he sees – the outline of someone else hurrying across the bridge that crosses the creek as it narrows from a basin to a cut.

He stares out as the man running along the embankment comes into view. He thinks he knows who it is . . . he does. He checks that his knife is in its sheath on his belt. Then, accelerating fast, he runs off along the path on the western side of the creek.

His terrible anguish threatens to overwhelm him at every stride. For he knows whose head it is, whose body lies across the stern rail of *The Dawning of the Day*. But he must not think of her now; must not let the howling grief punch him to his knees. For someone is fleeing the scene and, even now, as Tamáz fixes his eyes on the figure on the footbridge, he can see the man is almost halfway across. It isn't the time for excesses of despair and sorrow, for another emotion must take dominance.

When Tamáz catches up with Lily's murderer – and he will – he is going to kill him.

Felix runs down the eastern side of the inlet. He can see the footbridge ahead, and the silhouette of someone – a man, he's sure – standing at the apex of its upward curve. He can hear someone approaching along the path on the opposite side. It sounds from the howls of fury as if it is a man. Felix has spotted *The Dawning of the Day* moored along the far quay, so it's not a wild guess to assume it is Tamáz Edey.

Why is he howling?

Felix has the weird sensation that a chilly hand is gripped around his heart. Don't think, he commands himself, don't even begin to wonder what this means.

If he did – if he let the terrible fear grow into certainty – he does not know if he will be able to go on moving forward.

He is almost at the footbridge now. He pauses, just for a few breaths, and the mist clears from in front of his eyes. He knows he is nearly spent, but there is no choice now. He grasps the cudgel and runs on.

The man on the footbridge is standing right in the middle, at the highest point. He has a cleaver in his right hand. There is light enough to see by; a lamp illuminates the boat basin and the bridge is not shadowed by overhanging branches. The sky is clear and the moon rides high.

Felix would have recognised that face in far less light. He has seen it in his dreams, and in the ravings of fever. It is the face of the man who left him for dead.

'I knew you first as Hubert Godwin,' he says, trying desperately to control his gasping, panting breaths. 'But if I am not mistaken, you began your life as Tobias Fountain. Since you left school you have also been known as Walter Blackmore and Joseph Phipps, and I am sure there are other names.' He stops suddenly as a sharp pain stabs into his ribs. He tries not to groan.

'You have been busy.'

The words issue from the middle of the bridge, and the voice is a cold monotone. Felix feels a shiver of dread.

'You believed you had killed me,' Felix says. 'You were wrong.'

Under the black vee of the brows, the deep-set eyes are no more than dark holes, shadowed by the brim of the hat. What can be seen of the face between the hat and the heavy beard is dead white. For an instant Felix has the dread thought that this is not a man but some horror from the dark outer reaches far beyond the world. Fighting his fear, he steps forward onto the bridge.

The figure before him laughs: a sound like no laughter Felix has ever heard.

'You think to apprehend me?' the voice of ice asks derisively. '*You*, with your damaged head and your broken ribs? Yes, you see, I remember well what hurts I did to you.'

'I do,' Felix replies.

He takes another step onto the bridge.

Then he sees movement at the far end of the bridge. Tamáz Edey is advancing soft-footed and stealthily, and he too has a knife.

Felix moves on. He darts repeated glances at Tamáz and back at the man coming down from the middle of the bridge. He thinks he sees Tamáz give a nod.

And he raises the cudgel and races towards the oncoming figure.

The next few seconds are a blur of violent movement, curses and shouts of fury. He lands a hard blow on the top of that deep-brimmed hat and hears the dark figure let out a howl of pain. The cleaver rises up in a wide arc, but as it descends Tamáz's long-bladed knife is there to parry it and it jerks out of the dark figure's hand. Then Tamáz is on him, and Felix catches a glint of light on a smaller blade he carries in his other hand. Felix swings the cudgel low and hard and it catches the dark figure behind the knees, and as his legs abruptly collapse he falls below the stabbing blade. Then as fast as a flash the dark man is up again, swinging a punch at Felix that catches him right on his damaged ribs and temporarily takes away his breath. As he bends over, choking and gasping and quite incapable of drawing in air, he hears a shout of pain from Tamáz and a hard thud as a body falls against the parapet of the bridge.

Felix tries to get up but he finds he can't.

He thinks he might very well be about to die.

The Barrow Man is badly hurt.

The pain in his head from the cudgel blow is making him sick and dizzy, and his vision is obscured by a field of dense black interspersed with brilliant stars. His legs throb with agony from where the cudgel smashed into them, and he fears they will not hold him up for much longer. There is a deep cut on his right forearm. The boatman had a knife as sharp as his own.

He knows he must go over the bridge, back the way he has just come. As he reaches the path on the far side he can move more easily. Along under the concealing trees, and then the brief and welcome darkness is behind him as he reaches the quay and emerges into the lamplight. But soon he will be safe. He has located an escape route of secret ways, and the first of them branches off from the riverside only a hundred yards or so west of the boat basin. He *must* reach it. He has to. If he cannot find the turning, or if he stumbles, the boatman and the man whose face he recognises from school will catch him. They will kill him. He knows that.

He is attempting to run along the quay now, but he keeps staggering. He is almost level with *The Dawning of the Day*. He can smell the blood of the fair-haired woman. He can just make out the dismembered body draped over the boat's rail. He wonders if the cold white amputated limbs have reached the river yet. He looks out across the water and thinks he sees a pale shape that could be—

There is a sharp cry from the thicket of undergrowth just to his right, and he feels an agonising pain as something slices deeply across his face, between the corner of his eye and his right ear. He feels his flesh open up. He feels his own warm blood start to pour down his cheek. The pain is indescribable.

Then there is a blow across his shoulders and he feels the knife slice through the layers of his clothing, just touching against his skin. With a snarl of rage, he spins round to face his assailant.

Green eyes blaze up at him from a face tight with rage, and then the knife is stabbing towards his chest, repeatedly, relentlessly, making him step back so that he stumbles on his damaged legs. He falls, and this snarling enemy is on him, and although he tries to grab the thin wrist that wields the knife – it's a *boning* knife, he realises in amazement – the Fury is too fast for him and he cannot see properly and the blade is stabbing, stabbing at him and with a huge effort he thrusts up at it and forces it away, not very far, for he is weakening fast now, but just long enough to give him the space to get up and try to run off along the quay towards the river.

Something launches itself at him and springs onto his back, legs wrapping round his waist, arms round his throat and the hand holding the boning knife is trying to twist its point to thrust it into his eye. He tries to run on, but he no longer has the strength, for as well as the head wound he is losing a lot of blood from the deep cuts to his arm and his face.

He has reached the water. The dark power of the Thames flows past almost at his feet. He draws back his arms and with a great cry uses the last of his strength to drive his elbows into whatever entity is riding on his back. The right elbow makes contact, hard enough to wind – he hears a sharp *ooof* of escaping breath and the grip eases. He repeats the jabbing thrust and the weight falls off him. The sudden cessation of the effort makes him stagger and he almost falls, and even as he tries to right himself, he feels a boot kick very hard into his backside.

He topples into the river and the full force of the current picks him up.

The Barrow Man's assailant is slumped on the ground, gasping, groaning, trying to clutch at ribs that seem to be on fire.

And presently someone comes to crouch on the path.

A hand is placed under the chin, and the head is turned towards the man who has just arrived. Hazel eyes meet green eyes. There is a choked sob, and he says, 'Oh, Lily, I thought you were dead.'

Then strong arms go round her and Felix clutches her to his chest in a grip so tight that it stops her breathing again.

TWENTY

All traces of the fair-haired woman have vanished when a detective and two police constables arrive in the boat basin early the next morning. The detective tasks the brighter of the two constables with checking both quays and the surrounding undergrowth. When he returns, he reports the discovery of a brazier that might have been used recently, only it's been doused with a few bucketfuls of river water, so it's impossible to say. The shelter where the horses are stabled is, he suggests, 'cleaner than what you'd expect,' and, he adds, 'looks as how someone's tidied it up deliberate-like.'

The detective frowns. Such speculations really are not what he wants to hear. He wouldn't be here at all except for the fact that the letter that came by today's first post was – unlike the untidy and mis-spelt note on cheap paper pushed through Lily's letter box the previous evening – on very good-quality writing paper, written in a sophisticated, elegant hand and, in the words of the desk sergeant who was the first to inspect it, 'read like one of them novels'. The detective, grabbing the letter, had to agree that it was the work of somebody well educated.

Which, of course, the man who had once been the schoolboy known as Tobias Fountain and Hubert Godwin undoubtedly was.

> *Go to the creek at Chelsea where the river boats tie up, for there yet another young woman has been most violently and brutally murdered, and her sad and pitiful remains are to be discovered draped across the stern of the boat that is named* The Dawning of the Day. *There you will also discover that her body has suffered beheading and dismemberment. It is the boatmen who will not be blamed for nothing.*

Not only do the three police officers find no body, no body parts, no clothing and no effects; they also find the creek empty of boats. It is with some degree of disgruntlement that they stomp back to the police station to record yet another hoax.

Lily and Felix are in the Inner Sanctum an hour earlier than usual. Last night has etched frantic anxiety and the traces of horror deep into both their faces, and Lily is enormously comforted to have him there with her.

It was very hard to watch him walk away last night. He had stuck to her side while they crept up the dark passage to the entrance through the shed, and then he insisted on checking and double-checking that she had locked and bolted the door, and he did the same with the doors from the shed into the garden and from the garden into the scullery. Neither of them had said much. The events of the evening were too dreadful to speak of while they were so fresh in the memory. They stood together in the hall and eventually he said, 'I must go. Marm will worry if I'm not there in the morning.'

And all she could think of to say in reply was, 'Very well.'

Now, in the bright light of day, the very first question Felix asks is, 'Why were you there, Lily? Whatever *possessed* you to go out alone at night when you knew he—' He stops abruptly. As if he is thinking what might have been, his face has gone pale.

'There was a note.' She picks it up, noticing that her hand is trembling. *He* wrote this, she thinks. That terrible man touched this dirty scrap of paper, inscribed those words with a blunt pencil.

Felix brushes it away. 'I read it,' he says curtly. Then, in a rush, he leans forward and says urgently, 'Lily I *knew* there was something wrong, that's why I came looking for you. You weren't here, your heavy boots and your bag had gone, and I came in here and found the note. Great God, Lily, are you *mad*?' His voice has risen to a shout, and now he flushes with the blood of anger.

She waits for a moment. She realises that it's the thought of what could so easily have happened to her that is making him so emotional, but all the same it is awful to have him shouting at her. Apparently reading her expression, he mutters, 'Sorry.'

She nods an acknowledgement. 'I truly believed Tamáz had been badly hurt,' she says. 'The fear of finding him with some mortal injury – dying, even – made me act without really thinking about it.'

'But you . . .' he starts to say.

She speaks over the interruption. 'But luckily the time it took to walk to the boat basin allowed me to reflect a little. Even as I approached, I was keeping over to the right-hand side of the path, under the shadow of the trees and the greenery. As I crept round the bend and could see into the basin, there were three boats on the near quay and *The Dawning of the Day* was over on the far side. And, Felix, I so wanted to hurry down to the footbridge, cross over and race to find out what had happened and what I had to do, but I forced myself to wait.'

His eyes are steady on hers. He smiles very faintly, and says, 'Very wise.'

'The scene looked exactly as it usually does,' she says very softly. 'People on the nearside boats were preparing food, talking softly, calling out to children that it was bedtime. There was a light in Tamáz's boat – the curtains were drawn, but I could see through the little gap – and smoke was rising from the stove chimney. I must have stood there for half an hour or more, and in that time there wasn't a single sound that anyone had been badly injured, or was even in distress.'

'Why didn't you go over to *The Dawning of the Day* and check?' he demands.

She sighs. 'I should have thought that was obvious.'

'Not to me.' His voice has a note of asperity.

'I realised I had been lured there,' she says. 'I suspected it was because of our investigation, and therefore that it was the man with the barrow who had sent the note. I did think about going over to Tamáz's boat and telling him what I feared, but it could have been exactly what the man with the barrow wanted. So I went very cautiously and slowly along the path beside the three boats, over the footbridge and onto the path on the far side. I pushed my way into a gap in the undergrowth and waited.' She pauses, for it is very hard to think about what happened next, and even harder, she discovers, to put it into words.

Felix watches her closely but does not speak. He seems to know that any comment from him will only make it worse.

'At last he came,' she says, her voice not much more than a whisper. 'He was such a big man, and all dressed in black, the folds of his coat voluminous and full. And he had . . . he had a body over his shoulder. A woman's body' – the words are pouring out now – 'and I knew she was a woman by her skirt and petticoats and her little buttoned boots. She had . . . her head and face were bound up in a woolly shawl, but it had slipped up at the back of her head and I could see her fair hair.'

'Just like yours,' Felix murmurs.

She nods quickly. 'He put her down on the grass under some trees, about ten or twelve paces back down the path,' she says. 'Then he . . . well, you know what he did, you saw the . . . you saw afterwards.'

'Yes,' he says. 'Lily, there's no need to put it into words.' His voice is kind. He hesitates, then says carefully, 'It will be small consolation, but the victim was undoubtedly already dead.'

'How do you *know*?' she hisses. She wants so desperately for it to be true, but how can Felix be sure?

He pauses again, then says, 'Because for one thing, for someone to treat a body in that way would be very difficult while there was still life in the victim, whereas once life is extinct' – she senses he is choosing his words with great care – 'the killer can take his time. For another thing, if she had still been alive, you would have heard that poor woman screaming for help. And you didn't.'

Slowly she says, 'I didn't.'

It is a relief. But, as he said, it is a small consolation.

Then and on subsequent days, Lily, Felix and most of all Marm do their utmost to discover who the dead woman was. Both Lily and Felix saw the head, but trying to describe the face proves so deeply distressing that they both have to admit defeat. All they can say is that she was probably between the ages of twenty-five and forty, pale skinned and with light-coloured eyes and long blonde hair. Felix manages to recall an impression of what the decapitated body was wearing, but he can do no better than to say it was a dark jacket, fitted closely into the waist, and a full skirt. Lily adds the detail of the little buttoned boots. But it describes the apparel of half of the women in London and probably more.

Marm tries drawing an image, but, perhaps influenced by the fact that the killer mistook the victim for Lily, he makes the face rather too like hers for comfort. Wordlessly the three of them abandon that idea. Instead Marm does the rounds of all the pubs in a half-mile radius of World's End Passage, and he, Lily and Felix knock on every door and ask all those prepared to open up and speak to them if they know of a woman who has gone missing in the area. There are too many answers, and yet too few. As Marm says, so many women disappear, and in the majority of cases, nobody cares enough to find out why.

Word spreads, of course. Very soon the speculation begins. Why was she out by herself late at night down by the river? Out to meet some man in secret and planning to get up to no good with him, public opinion decides. Either that or off to seek one out.

And when Marm hears this, naturally he redoubles his efforts.

The Barrow Man's attempt to leave incontrovertible evidence that Tamáz Edey, master of *The Dawning of the Day*, killed and mutilated the woman he pounced on in place of Lily has failed. The evidence has also vanished.

Tamáz took it.

On the night of the killing, while Felix hurried Lily back to number 3, Hob's Court, Tamáz carefully washed the blood from the dismembered, headless corpse, dried the cold flesh, cleaned the worn garments as best he could and then placed the body on a blanket. He stripped off his clothes, waded into the water and swam out to where the limbs were still floating at the mouth of the creek, and he retrieved the head from the quay. These detached parts of the woman he returned to her, putting them back in place and then securing the folds of the blanket securely around her. He took the wrapped corpse below, placing her on the spare bunk. Then, still naked, he spent a long time washing his boat clean of every last vestige of the terrible brutality that had been done that night.

Finally, he washed himself, performed a small and private ceremony under the clear pre-dawn sky, then fetched the one companion he truly and totally trusted and, with his help, took his boat and its sad cargo out of the basin and off into the night.

He knows exactly where he will bury the woman. It is a beautiful spot, out in the quiet countryside. She will, he thinks, have peace there.

The Dawning of the Day has not been seen in Chelsea, or anywhere else in London, since that night. The boat is now far away.

The master, however, has returned.

Lily has said hotly and emphatically to Tamáz that she and Felix will speak up for him; that they'll provide absolute proof that he is no killer and that the woman was the latest victim of the man with the barrow, and they will back this up by supplying the various names that the Barrow Man has used over the years. But Tamáz has remained resolute. He explains to Lily that however much proof she and Felix supply will never be enough, because the police are always suspicious of boatmen and take very little convincing to arrest, accuse and convict men from the water community.

Lily can't bear the thought of the free spirit that is Tamáz in a prison, or, even worse, being led out to his execution in some sordid gaol.

She goes out to meet him late one evening by the river. It is still so strange to see him away from his boat. But she realises he can hide far more easily and efficiently when he does not have *The Dawning of the Day* to conceal.

'What will you do?' she asks him.

'I will be safe, cushla,' he replies. 'Best if I do not tell you, but please be assured that there is somewhere to go. Somewhere we have always gone,' he adds, 'when the world decides it doesn't like us because we're too different and we won't be what they want us to be. When they accuse us of foul crimes and try to rid themselves of a few more of us.'

'Will we ever meet again?' She can hardly speak for weeping.

He bends to kiss her. For the first time it is a true, deep kiss, and it goes on for some time.

Then he says, 'Who can tell? Ever is a long time.' He kisses her again. 'Goodbye, my love.'

As he turns to go, she catches the glimmer of tears in his eyes.

* * *

It is an afternoon of the following week. Lily and Felix are on Tower Hill.

Felix leads the way across the graveyard, and they climb the gentle slope to the path under the wall. He had wanted to do this alone, but Lily has insisted and, in truth, he can't blame her. He has to keep stopping himself from asking if she's all right, and from reaching out to take her hand and give it a comforting squeeze. Lily is back in professional mode: as the proprietor of an investigation bureau, she does not welcome questions about her state of mind and she certainly doesn't want her hand squeezed.

They walk along to the bend in the path.

The shed has gone.

The outer shell that looked ruined and abandoned and the inner walls of new timber are no longer there. All there is to see is a rectangle of fire-blackened earth. The bones, the skull, the rotting flesh, the worn old garments, have disappeared. The blood that painted the floor has vanished.

It is full autumn now, and the trees are almost bare. The tangle of vegetation is dying or dead. But it will grow back, Felix thinks, as he and Lily stand and stare. In the spring, when the natural world wakes from its winter sleep, the trees and the rampant wild plants will fill this space, and perhaps the imprint of the terrible things that happened here will fade away.

Beside him Lily says softly, 'They'll be forgotten, those poor women he brought here and who ended up in the river. *We* know what was once here, but nobody else will. It will all be covered up.'

It is so close an echo of his own thoughts that he is profoundly moved. Still he doesn't reach for her hand, but it's all right because she reaches for his.

They go through the narrow passage, brush themselves down and mount the steps to number 8, Mary Rose Court. They are expected: Lily has written to the siblings to ask if they may call because there is news.

Alethea Fetterplace admits them and shows them into the drawing room, where a small table has been brought in and set out with a tea tray and a plate of biscuits. Dukey and Fanny sit on a small and uncomfortable-looking sofa. Alethea fusses over cups of tea, side plates and napkins. Lily and Felix settle into the chairs put out for them.

Miss Fetterplace seems to be taking rather a long time. Finally, Dukey says, 'Alethea, *do* sit down!' And she does.

Felix and Lily have agreed that Lily will give their report. But before she does so, she spreads out the beautifully written and artistically decorated family tree prepared by Cornelius Ely Redvers. The siblings gasp in delight, and Fanny whispers, 'I *knew*! I *always* knew!'

Now Felix sits back, picks up his tea and listens as Lily explains with admirable brevity that in all likelihood, there will be no more nocturnal disturbances at the end of the garden because the premises that were being used by the would-be intruder have been burned down and all traces of him – 'and whatever he was up to in there,' Lily adds – have vanished, and . . .

'We *saw* the fire!' Fanny interrupts, eyes wild and wide, face flushed. 'Down beyond the gardens, along to the right as you look out!' She stares rather frantically at her sister and then her brother, as if demanding their verification. 'We *did*!' she insists. 'I said it was him, didn't I? Dukey, Alethea, *didn't* I?'

'Repeatedly,' her sister says resignedly. She catches Felix's eye, and he smiles.

'It *might* have been our night stalker having a bonfire,' Dukey states pedantically. 'But a fire is a fire, after all, and it did not burn for long.' He turns to Felix. 'Local hearsay maintains that there used to be an old shed up there at the corner of the path, perhaps once used by those who tend the graveyard,' he explains. 'For myself, I cannot say, having never ventured out to search for it.' He seems, Felix observes, to be trying to convey a message; something he does not want his sisters to know. As Felix returns his steady gaze, he gives a minute shake of the head.

Aha, thinks Felix, and resolves to tell Lily when they leave that old Dukey seems to know rather more than he admitted.

'And so I believe we can safely say,' Lily concludes, 'that whoever lies in your rose bed is perfectly safe. It appears that her presence is only known to the five of us in this room' – she tells the lie straight-faced, Felix observes, silently counting the number of their friends and colleagues who are in on the secret and making it at least half a dozen – 'and you have the solemn word of Mr Wilbraham and myself that we will never speak of her to anyone else.'

'We . . . should we bury her again?' Fanny whispers. She glances at Dukey. 'Are we allowed to?'

'*Hmmph!*' he snorts. 'Our garden, our ancestor, our decision.'

Fanny claps her hands in delight. Alethea closes her eyes and appears to be muttering a prayer of thanks.

They have finished tea. Felix glances at Lily, who nods, and then addresses the Fetterplace siblings. 'Shall we perform the re-interment now?' he asks gently.

The three old faces look puzzled, then doubtful, then, tentatively, relieved and happy. 'We were planning to make a proper ceremony of it,' Alethea says, her voice trembling with emotion. 'Call her by her name, and Dukey has prepared a few words.'

'We could do that now,' Lily says.

Alethea moves closer to her siblings on the sofa, and there is a muttered conversation. Then she straightens up, gives Lily and Felix a quaint little bow, and says, 'Fanny wishes to put on a special outfit she has prepared, and I should like to tidy my hair and put on my hat. Are you content to wait?'

'We are,' Lily and Felix say together. Felix, who has been thinking of the practicalities, says, 'There will be quite a lot of earth to move. Perhaps Mr Fetterplace and I might make a start?'

'But we . . .' Fanny looks at Alethea. 'We were going to make sure she was *arranged* properly – you know, her poor head, and . . .' She looks flustered, and her eyes are bright with tears.

'She is already very correctly arranged,' Lily says gently. 'I have seen her,' she adds, as Fanny still seems doubtful, 'and I promise you, she is lying comfortably, everything as it should be, and her precious possessions are right beside her.'

'Promise?' Fanny whispers.

'Promise,' Lily replies.

In the end, and as Felix expected, it is he who does the majority of the earth shifting. Dukey does his best, but he is an old man. Whereas I, Felix thinks wearily, am a *young* man who is recovering from a hard blow to the head and broken ribs from a violent kicking. But he does not let the increasing pain show, or he hopes he doesn't, because if he slackens his pace, Dukey will try to make up for it, and already the poor old boy is more than a little out of breath.

Presently Alethea and Fanny come out to join them.

Felix senses someone beside him. Turning to look, he sees Lily. She has picked up Dukey's shovel and is heaping earth into what is left of the hollow in the rose bed. He smiles. She swings a loaded shovel as well as many men Felix has encountered.

They have finished. The earth is smooth and flat. It looks like a freshly turned bed awaiting the planting of healthy new rose bushes. Which, Felix thinks, is what it is.

He stands still, head bowed, as Dukey speaks his prepared words. He has put his topcoat back on and huddles into it for he is getting chilly now, the sweat of effort drying on him and making him shiver.

Dukey's voice is quiet, for what he is saying is for no ears other than those of the four people out there by the rose bed with him.

Nobody would ever suspect, Felix muses, that a queen of England lies down there.

He is still not sure if he really believes it. But now really isn't the time to say so.

Marm has had no success in discovering the identity of the woman who died that night.

Lily and Felix do not reveal to the police that Felix was attacked by the man with the barrow, and they do not mention the shed, although Lily is still haunted by what she saw inside it. It is doubtful that anyone would believe them: Felix suffered a severe head wound that laid him out for days, and for some time kept speaking of barrows full of red-painted chess pieces and sheep with knitting needles; and Lily is, of course, a woman, and women are known for their hysterical fancies.

But the Barrow Man fell in the river, there's been no sign of him, and he is undoubtedly dead. The other reason for not speaking up is that Lily and Felix have become very fond of the Fetterplace siblings. Any major police investigation into what went on along the path under the graveyard wall would surely bring the old people great distress. If the police decided they really ought to investigate the recently replanted rose bed, it might even lead to the discovery of the bones.

And that would never do.

Lily and Felix often speak of that graceful skeleton. It is probably not Anne Boleyn's, they conclude, allowing sense and rationality to hold sway. Many women lost their heads within the Tower and on Tower Hill's scaffold; the bones could belong to any of them.

But often, when one or other of them changes the subject and speaks of something less emotional, they catch each other's glance and smile. They know full well they are sharing the same thought: If it *is* Anne, then it's best to leave her where she is, for she is with people who treasure her and love her.

Lily and Felix quite often share the same thought nowadays.

It makes both of them very happy.

Some power must have been looking out for the Barrow Man after all, the night he tried to kill Lily and slaughtered another woman instead.

Yes, he was caught between two furious and violent adversaries, both of whom inflicted serious wounds. Yes, Lily herself had burst out of the undergrowth, cut him, leapt on his back and, when he finally managed to dislodge her, booted him into the Thames. And yes, the current swept him away, and for a desperate time he was under the water, turned over and over, driven into floating and submerged objects until his whole body was bruised, battered and lacerated and he thought his lungs were going to burst.

But apparently the devil really does look after his own.

Not far beyond Battersea Bridge, one of the new steam-driven boats was setting off into mid-channel, and its master wanted to see how well it accelerated. The churning wake caught the half-drowned man, and his inert, insensate body was washed back to the shore, where the waves left him above the water line on a narrow strip of shingle.

He came back to himself to find a skinny dog licking his face and whining. Before its owner came looking for it – if it had an owner – the Barrow Man kicked it away and struggled to his feet. Minutes afterwards he had climbed up onto the embankment and was already losing himself in the maze of ill-lit streets behind it.

Back in the damp and unsavoury little room that has been his London hiding place this time, slowly he recovers. His bodily hurts heal quickly; he has always been a strong, healthy and resilient man. But in his mind he is still profoundly troubled.

Because, despite the near miracle of not having drowned, he has the alarming notion that his luck has turned.

It is not only that he was very nearly caught this time. The same thing happened four years ago in Liverpool. Admittedly there were few moments in the intervening years when he had felt even remotely threatened, but then he had been out in the country and, besides, the urge had not come upon him often.

He knows he would be safe if he lost himself once more out in some quiet corner of England's vast rural landscape. But he also knows that he could never be content with that.

Sooner or later the city always draws him back. Inevitably, he will end up in London again.

And it is in London – here – that he is now feeling so threatened. So vulnerable.

These are alien words to use in the context of himself.

He lies back on his narrow and uncomfortable bed, closes his eyes and lets his mind run free.

After a day and a half of this silent meditation, he knows what he will do. He gets up, washes with the remains of a bowl of cold water, dresses in his least shabby shirt and trousers and puts on his topcoat. Cramming his hat on his head, he sets off for the library and is soon installed in the reference room. He consults several heavy tomes, then very politely asks the librarian if he may please study the back numbers of a selection of daily newspapers. In particular those which cover trials and the sentencing of felons.

Returning home, he treats himself to a fish supper.

His plan is workable.

It is late January, in the year 1883, and the plan has worked.

He sits alone on the hard bench, jolted against his fellow passengers as the unsprung vehicle with the bars on the windows jerks through pot holes and swerves to avoid wandering pedestrians and erratic traffic. He feels like smiling, but to show any sort of pleasure might arouse suspicion. He makes his face droop into what has become its habitual expression. But he is still smiling inside.

He had quit his sordid room very early in the morning after his visit to the library. He made his way through the near-deserted streets and was waiting at Euston station when the left-luggage office opened. He collected his bag and boarded a slow train to Stoke-on-Trent, for no other reason than that he'd never been there before. Nobody knew him. Nobody was likely to recognise him. When he stepped off the train he became Ted Hench.

He implemented the next stage of his plan about a fortnight later. He had found work, of a sort, carrying wares from a pottery manufactory to the canal. He was lodging in a room that was even smaller, dingier and grubbier than his London accommodation. But he would not have to endure it for long.

On a bright winter morning he made a clumsy attempt to steal a pocket watch and a coin purse from a fat, wealthy and very well-dressed man waiting outside the station. He was very swiftly apprehended, charged and sent for trial.

He was sentenced to eight years' imprisonment. He had expected more. For his trial he adopted the persona of a genial dimwit who tried very hard to be honest but, through his fecklessness and total lack of any ability to appreciate the consequences of an action, never quite managed it. His kindly smile and willing obedience were already earning him a certain amount of indulgence even before he got to Stafford Gaol.

The transport has reached the gaol, and he goes through the humiliating but painless process of becoming a prisoner. His cell is tiny, and also damp. The overcrowding appals him; he is not used to the company of others. The work routine as set out to him on arrival sounds pretty dreadful. The flax dressing and the weaving of rough cloth for prison garb will be numbingly boring, and he has never had to do such work before. But he tells himself it won't kill him.

He has done a great deal of research. Lying on his shelf of a bed this first night, he runs through what he has learned.

He has reached the conclusion that even serious criminals serving more than four years in prison will in general have their sentence reduced. This, he adds to himself, is presuming that their behaviour while incarcerated is good. And his will be exemplary. He is quite capable of obeying each and every rule, even the most petty, when it is in his own interests to do so. He will use what free time he has in thinking about the future, for he has a great deal of planning to do. The ceaseless work will be of a manual nature, and so his mind will be free to think. And, even in prison, the nights will be his own.

He knows there is a very long way to go before he even begins to approach the summation of his life's work. But, this first night, the prospect of that summation is too stimulating when just now it is so distant.

He muses on how he will deal with incarceration – or, to be exact, with months and years when he will have little or no opportunity to indulge his taste for killing and dismemberment. But there will be vermin, no doubt, and he is cheered by the thought. He will just have to become an expert in the internal organs of *rattus norvegicus* and perhaps, if he is lucky, also *rattus rattus*.

He smiles wryly.

No. Overall, he is not at all dismayed by the recent turn of events. He has managed to remove himself from the fairly rudimentary investigations that followed in the wake of the bodies in the river. There may have been rumours and speculation, but none of his names has been linked to the crimes by the authorities, and now he does not believe they ever will.

But then, that last time in London, he did not in fact take on a new name. He was, at last, truly the anonymous man.

The unknown killer.

He calculates that he has five or at most six years to prepare for the next phase. He settles on a likely date of summer 1888 for his release. Now he will turn all his prodigious intelligence and powers of subtle persuasion to making events turn out as he wishes them to.

His thoughts revert, as they so often do, to the ever-present problems of disposal. He is turning over in his mind various alternatives to the ejection of limbs, heads and part-torsos into bodies of water. Interment? Fire? Acid bath?

Suddenly, like a starburst in his brain, he thinks, why not leave them where they lie?

His mouth drops open, for it is a revolutionary idea. Always, since the first clumsy experiments with insects, birds and frogs, he has been obsessed with clearing away the evidence. It has become a fixed routine, so that the very notion of *not* doing it is astounding.

But why not leave my work for others to find?

The thought gives him an almost sexual surge of pleasure.

Presently he picks up where he left off.

All the while he has been consigning bodies to the water, the fine details of what was done to them have been blurred.

Perhaps it is time to display his skills to a wider audience . . .

He lets the image of a vast crowd of people gaping in amazement and awe fill his mind. It stays there for some time.

Returning to reality, he reflects that he is very, very good at anonymity. At slipping away once his work is done and not leaving a trace. At concealing himself behind yet another identity, stringing the new bead onto the string of all those that have gone before.

Sometimes, now, even he has forgotten who he is . . .

He lies in silent contemplation, eyes half closed in the dim light.

Yes, he thinks as he comes out of his light trance.

He knows now exactly what he is going to do when he is free. He also knows where he is going to do it. Now that he will not be constrained by the need to be close to water, the choice is endless, but he has made his selection. Before he left London, he made a thorough exploration of Whitechapel and he knows it will be perfect.

He closes his eyes, smiling to himself. As he drifts into sleep, he enjoys a last waking thought.

Some time around the late summer of 1888 – August, say – the sinks and the rookeries of the East End of London will have to prepare for what he is going to do next.